The Reapers MC, Ravenswood Series

Reaper Razed

Book Three

Harley Raige

Copyright © 2023 Harley Raige
All rights reserved.

No part of this book may be reproduced or transmitted in any form, or by any electronic or mechanical means, including photocopying, recording, or by any information storage and retrieval systems, without written permission from the author, except for the use of brief quotations in a book review.
For permissions, contact: harleyraige@gmail.com

This is a work of fiction. Names, characters, organisations, and incidents are either products of the author's slightly deranged, mildly twisted imagination or used fictitiously. Any resemblance to actual persons, living or dead, is purely coincidental.
Edited by www.fiverr.com/immygrace

For updates on my upcoming releases please follow me
www.tiktok.com/@harleyraige

www.instagram.com/harleyraige

www.facebook.com/harleyraige
Join our group
www.facebook.com/groups/the.rebels.of.raige
Become a Rebel of Raige and join the Rebellion!

Authors Note

The author is British. This story does contain British spellings and phrases. This book also contains possible triggers, including but not limited to murder, torture, kidnapping, mentions of rape of a minor. It also contains explicit sexual situations, strong violence, taboo subjects, a shit tonne of offensive language and mature topics, some dark content,
plus, M/M and F/M.
18+

Dedication

To all my Smutty Bookish friends new and old,
I couldn't have done this without your support.
This ones for you!

Contents:

Reaper Razed
Authors Note
Dedication
Contents:

Steel	1
Dice	7
Ray	10
Pa Cade	21
Joseph	23
Steel	29
Pa Cade	37
Steel	48
Ray	55
Dozer	71
Black Rook	73
Black Queen	75
Dane	81
Gerald	85
Liam	91
Black Queen	94
Dice	101
Steel	105
Dozer	108
Ray	113
Dice	119
Ray	127
Demi	136
Dane	141
Steel	148
Skye	154

Tank	165
Skye	171
Steel	179
Black Queen	184
Dice	186
Dane	196
Skye	201
Ray	208
Skye	221
Ray	230
Bran	239
White Knight	246
Bran	255
Dane	260
Steel	266
Skye	269
Ray	282
Tank	285
Dane	290
Dice	297
Dane	309
Skye	314
Ares	319
Ray	337
Pa Cade	348
Ray	352
Steel	360
Acknowledgements	365
Books by Harley Raige	366

Steel

There's a screech of tyres outside. I jump up and run to the door, flinging myself down the stairs as the van pulls to a stop at the bottom. Dice is hanging half out of the window.

"Visitor for the barn!" He nods as he speeds off along the track.

I message Ares to let him know they're back and heading to the barn. As I jog around the side of the clubhouse, he comes out the back door, followed by Priest and Roach.

Priest had been driving the town car, which had taken them to the event, then he had returned the car and headed back here to give us the lowdown on what had happened so far.

Pushing into the barn, Dice is getting some ropes and a chair sorted. I fling the back of the van open and freeze.

Bernie pushes me back and raises his finger to his lips. The judge is bound, gagged and blindfolded.

"Outside, now!" I snarl. I start pacing as soon as the barn doors shut. "Where the fuck is she?"

"We ran into a little... trouble. She stayed to cause a distraction so we could get the judge away, let's get him strapped up, and we can head down to the club house, and I will fill you all in."

"Make it quick, Bernie. I'm about to lose my fucking shit if I don't get eyes on my wife in the next ten fucking minutes!" I turn on my heels and stomp back to the clubhouse.

I'm sitting at the bar when Bernie, Ares, Dice and Priest arrive. Obviously, they must have left Roach holding the fort, watching the judge. Without looking in their direction, I spit, "Someone better start talking and get me eyes on my wife before I lose it."

"Tech room, we'll sort through it all in there," Ares says as Dice rushes off ahead to power everything up. The screens flutter to life as we enter the room.

"Just gimme a sec. I'm gonna pull up all the footage we've been recording, and we can rewind it back from live. "Where were you at, Bernie?"

"Escape route three, fifth-floor balcony. We jumped onto the balcony of the next building as we got cornered by a... minor issue. Ray stayed to hold them off."

There isn't much space in the room, but I'm still managing to pace the fuck out of it. "What the fuck do you call a minor issue, Bernie?"

"There were eight guys, full tactical, who stormed the building, but Dice saw them first and informed us, and we made a clean getaway. Ray held them off, and she's gonna circle back and meet us at Rendezvous Two, which is here."

"You left her to fucking fend for herself with eight guys? Are you fucking kidding me, Bernie?"

"Woah! Woah!" Ares tries to calm the room, and by the room, I mean fucking me! It's at this point I realise I've got Bernie round the throat against the door, taking a breath and relaxing my hand.

He reaches up and puts his hands on my shoulders. "Don't worry, son, she's got this."

"Bernie, if anything happens to her, I'll never forgive myself for letting her go."

"Erm, guys… we may have a problem. I've searched all the surrounding cams, and they've all had the feeds cut. I'm rewinding the alley cam now…"

We all stop and just stare at the monitors, but there's nothing. "Keep going. You've been back, what? An hour? Speed it up!" I spit at Dice, and he just nods.

The screen fuzzes and buzzes as he speeds it up. I'm really starting to panic now.

"That's us all on the balcony," Bernie points out. "There was a guy shouting from the hallway. I jumped, and she sent the judge after me, then went back after the guy… look."

We all stare at the screen. We have just seen the two of them leap across. Well, the judge was thrown across unceremoniously and dragged back onto the balcony by Bernie, but Ray clearly went back inside after throwing him her shoes. A few frames later, we see her run, jump up onto the railing and leap…

We are surrounded by gasps at what we see. Ray leaps from the railing as a guy grabs for her, missing her, but manages to grab the bottom of the dress, causing her to swing around upside down and slam into the railings…

"Shit!"

"Motherfucker!"

"Hades!"

"Bastard!"

I'm not sure who curses what, but all I know is that I don't say anything. I freeze. I can't speak. I can't breathe. My heart's pounding in my chest, my vision's blurring, my mind's racing, and still, I can't speak.

The next moments cause what can only be described as some kind of breakdown. I witness my wife, the love of my life, my soulmate, my other fucking half, my everything, rear up against the railings and launch herself into the air, five fucking stories up, dragging what can only be described as about a 250 lb man over the railing and plummeting to the ground. He goes directly head first into the pavement, and she breaks her fall on the railings of the balcony on the other side before dropping to the concrete, then dead.

That's the only possible outcome. There's no movement from either of them, nothing, just nothing.

"Hey, son, you need to breathe, okay?" I feel his hands on my shoulders. Looking up at him, I now realise I'm sitting on the floor. I must have slid down the door. The reason my vision's blurry is that I'm crying, literally tears streaming down my face. I'm gasping as if something is gripping my throat or my heart and stopping the air from getting to my lungs and the blood from circulating.

"Steel!" Bernie says again, trying to get my attention. "She's gonna be okay. It's Ray, don't write her off just yet, okay?"

Dice cuts in, "They cut the feed right there. The last we see is of the two of them on the concrete, then nothing. I've checked all the feeds, and they cut them at the same time. I can't find her… I can't fucking find her."

Clearly, the panic attack I'm having has now decided it isn't the time and has fucked off as I rear up, rip the door open, and storm through the clubhouse. No one questions me. They know where I'm going, and they're right behind me. We mount up and ride out without a word.

As the hotel comes into view, there are a few people milling around, but nothing suspicious, no armoured vehicles or men in full tactical gear, just civilians coming in and out of the hotel.

Pulling up around the corner, I head to the alleyway. When I get there, there's nothing, well, nothing apart from two "cleaned" patches on the concrete. I drop to my knees and just stare into the alleyway.

"Steel, we need to go. We need to regroup and recheck the footage second by second. We will find her!"

"She's gone…" I let out a shaky breath. "She's really fucking gone!"

"Steel," Bernie barks, "we need to go." He grabs me under one arm as Ares grabs the other and drags me back to the bikes …

…I'm back at the clubhouse. I don't know how I got here. I'm numb. I've got tequila in my hand. I don't know how long I've had it, but I can't taste it. I can hear chatter around me, and I can't bring myself to care what anyone's saying.

I can hear Ares barking orders, but I don't care at who. I stand and push the stool back. It skitters across the floor, and I turn and walk across the room. It feels like I'm in a trance. People are talking to me, touching my shoulders, but I just keep walking. I push through the door and head home. *Home*. That doesn't even sound right now. At least it's all dark in the apartment. At least I don't have to face the girls.

I walk into our room. It smells like her. I lay face down on the bed, and it smells like her. I cry myself to sleep, and all the time, it smells like her.

Dice

Ares is barking orders at everyone, trying to come up with a plan to find Ray. Steel is sitting at the bar, but he's not here since he found those two "clean" patches of concrete in the alleyway. It doesn't look good. Someone's cleaning up a mess, removing traces, erasing answers.

I'm mourning for my best friend, my ride-or-die, my reason for breathing these days. She's given me so much life and fun I didn't realise I was missing till she bulldozed in and crashed into us all.

I look over at Steel again. He's just sitting there. He's had that same glass of tequila for an hour. I know because I have my own glass of tequila. It's Ray's favourite, but I can't bring myself to drink it. I'm sitting at our table, nearly as spaced as Steel, nearly as broken as Steel, nearly as lost as Steel, he shoves up off his stool and strides out of the place, not hearing or seeing a single person, and I decide to do the same, I head to the only place I can be useful… the tech room.

I painstakingly make my way through every frame of the alley cam. I watch, rewatch and watch it again. I keep checking, and the cameras are back live again. I've checked everything I can find. I've checked the footage from inside the hotel.

I have stills printed of all eight guys' faces who stormed the place pinned to the wall. I've crossed the one off who clearly nosedived into the concrete while running searches on the others in the background. I've cleaned up the footage of Ray in the alleyway, and I'm sitting watching it over and over again to see if I can see her blink, or breathe, or anything, but… *wait, is that a finger twitch?* Rewind again, rewatch, rewind, rewatch. It fucking is!

Her finger twitches. It fucking twitches! I take a deep breath, and that's when the tears of relief come. I sit and sob. It's stupid, really, as it could be an involuntary muscle spasm. She could be injured, seriously injured, or even dead, but that single twitch, that motherfucking, goddamned, minute twitch, has given me hope, and fuck, if I didn't need it right about now.

I set off again, trawling the screens. I find a store over the road whose camera looks into the alleyway. Fucking jackpot. I see Ray drop. I see her hit the floor, and then she's there for a while not moving, then there's a bus that pulls across in front of the camera, one of those open-top tour bus things, and when it moves… she's fucking gone.

Wait, what? Back up and rewatch. Vanished! The mess of a guy is still in the alleyway, and… she's gone. I can't see where she went. I can't see if she walks off or if someone takes her, but the next thing I see is the armoured car coming. The men pour out and clean up, checking the hotel footage. It must have been them that cut the feeds. The feeds nearby stop as Ray lays on the floor. They must have missed this store's footage and thank fuck!

They clean the two patches after gathering up their guy or what's left of him and leave. I rewind it and watch it all again before running into the bar. Bernie and Ares are asleep, propped up in the booths. Priest and Tank are at our table, asleep on it. "She's alive… I think?" I scream as I run into the bar.

They all startle. "Get Steel!" Bernie barks.

"No, watch it first. I don't want to be wrong. I can't be wrong. Watch it first. Come on."

We all run back to the tech room and watch and rewatch it. "Fuck, did she walk away from that? If she did, where the fuck is she?" Ares is pacing. "I can't tell Steel till I know for definite. You saw him last night… fuck… he's broken. I've never seen him even remotely that low, ever."

We watch it again and again. It's coming up for 9 a.m. "We've watched it enough to get Steel," I say to Ares. "He's least likely to punch you."

He nods and heads out the door.

When they walk back in, we are all on edge. Steel watches the tape and then again and again. "Fuck, I need a minute!" He stalks to the bar. We follow close behind him, pacing back and forth. "Where the fuck is she? What if they've got her? What if she's dead? What if—"

The warning siren starts blaring…

Ray

...They say that your life flashes before your eyes in an instant when death is upon you, but for me, it's the endless possibilities I will miss out on. The main one is Steel. Will he grieve for me if I'm gone? Will he move on with another if I'm gone? Will he go on to have children with someone else if I'm gone? Will he forget me? Will he be better off without me?

And as all these thoughts roll through my head, I have an epiphany. *Would he fuck! He's mine!* The sheer thought of him ending up with anyone other than me, having kids with anyone other than me, has me determined that I will come back from the Underworld to reap my revenge on the slut who dares try to replace me. I will drag his arse down there with me. He's it for me.

As I shove off the balcony, I'm hanging upside down. I rear up and launch myself across the alleyway. The brute gripping onto my dress is not expecting the sudden lunge as I pull him off balance.

I'm heading to land on the balcony on the third floor. Bernie and Joseph had jumped to the fourth-floor balcony. I'm falling rather than jumping, so this is gonna be a rough landing. I reach out to hang my elbow over the balcony edge to catch myself on the railings with my left arm, but I'm falling too fast, with too much speed. As I try to lock over it and grab on, there's an almighty twang as my whole body slams into the metalwork of the railings while my shins smash into the ledge of the balcony, and fuck, it feels like my shoulder is dislocated. It has been ripped out of its socket. Still, I have succeeded in slowing myself down drastically. As I drop toward the second floor, I reach out with my right hand and grab at one of the bars. There's a shooting pain through my hand, and I grip tighter.

I slide down the metal bar, and my wrist jolts as I hit the bottom. "Fuck!" I bellow as pain radiates through my fingers, hands, shins and wrist as I hang there from the bottom of the second floor, swinging slightly. Well, I think I do, but in fairness, I think my hand goes, *nah, fuck it*, and drops me! Looking below me, there's a clear drop into the piss-smelling alley, so I drop and roll. I roll my left ankle. "Shit!" As I drop, I smash my shoulder into the floor and roll onto my back, wheezing from the impact. "Motherfucker." I stare up at the sky for a few minutes while I try to draw breath.

Between the buildings, there's a shout from the fifth-floor Juliet balcony. "MARCO!" Glancing over to the side nearest the hotel, I grin as I see what's left of Marco. He plummeted head first, but as I had dragged him over, his face smashed into the balcony and the wall and then he landed head first, all eighteen stone-ish of the fucker, slamming into his own head and exploding it like a watermelon.

Cursing as I get to my feet, stumbling up the alley to the back, there's a dumpster. I scramble up the pile of rubbish the best I can, with the pain radiating from my left shoulder and my right hand, scrambling to the top and jumping over the fence into the neighbouring property. There's a getaway car parked a few blocks away in case of emergencies.

I just need to get there. I drag myself behind a row of shops. I hear shouting coming from the alley. Fuck, I need to get out of here. I stumble through a gap in the fence, pushing a crate behind me to cover the gap a little. There's a dumpster. Maybe I can hide in there. As I move towards it, there's a growl from behind me. Turning slowly, there's a huge Rottweiler, heckles up, teeth bared, snarling at me. He's fucking huge, at least ten stone, but he looks underweight for his size. There's drool flying from his jowls going everywhere.

He snaps at me. He's littered with scars, looking like he has had a hard life. I huff out a breath, point straight at him, and growl, "I swear to fucking Hades. Do. Not. Test. Me. Today. Dog!"

The dog stops growling, straightens up and cocks his head to the side.

"Don't you dare give away my location. I will make your life hell!" I turn and scramble very ungracefully to get in the dumpster, dropping the lid and submerging myself in all the rubbish. It fucking stinks, but I'm completely hidden unless that stupid mutt gives away my position. I get comfy-ish, cradling my injuries as the dog whines, then jumps on top of the dumpster with a huff. He lays down, and I let out a breath.

I can hear muffled yells and shouts, and as time passes, I slip in and out of either sleep or consciousness. It's hard to tell. I have no clue how long I've been here, but it was late evening when I climbed in. It was darkish; I must have fallen asleep or passed out. I'm woken with a start by the whining and scratching at the lid of the dumpster, slowly trying to lift the lid with my back but unable to shift it.

"Move off the twatting lid, you fucking idiot!" I whisper-yell at the dog. There's a yap as he moves off, standing and forcing the lid open with my shoulder. It's daylight. "Fuck!" I manage to ungracefully scramble up the rubbish and roll out of the dumpster, glancing around. I'm alone, well, me and the bloody dog looking at me like I'm the weirdo. "Shut ya face, you!" I shake my head at him, assessing my injuries. I wiggle my ankle fuck that's sore, black and blue but a bad sprain, nothing more. My right hand possibly has two broken fingers, the skin is missing from my palm, and my wrist is likely to have some kind of sprain, at least.

It's sore as fuck, but again, it could be worse. My right shoulder is definitely dislocated. Grabbing my knife in my left hand and standing on the bottom of my dress, I struggle to slice a chunk from it. My hand is thrashing, but I manage, with plenty of cursing, to make a sling and strap up my loose hanging left arm.

I slide my knife back into the holster, grateful that I still have that. My gun is long gone. "Fuck, I loved that gun." Pa Bernie had got me one after I had borrowed Carmen's. Anyway, tough shit. He can just get me another. I drag my arse away from the dumpster and the dog barks at me.

"Shut the fuck up, dickhead." I snarl back, knee the crate away, and push through the hole. The dog appears beside me. "Where the fuck do you think you're going?"

He just cocks his head to the side and sits beside me. "Nope! No!" I stride off into the shadow of the building as I skulk around the side of the shop I have been hiding behind. My ankle is swollen and hurts to stand, but I can suck it up. Looking across the front of the shops, there's no one around, and the shops aren't open, so it must still be early.

I hustle to where I know the car is. Swinging the door open, I knock my broken fingers. "Motherfucker." As I go to get in the car, I grit my teeth. "Stupid fucking arseholes putting the steering wheel on the wrong side of the fucking car!" I growl out as I step back to slam the door with my hip.

The stupid fucking dog shoots into the passenger seat. "Are you fucking with me, Hades?" I yell to the ground."

The dog barks.

"I swear to fucking Hades…"

He barks again.

"If you don't get out of this car, I'm gonna lose my shit!" I sigh. "Why the fuck are you barking at me?" nothing. "Get out!" Nothing. "Don't play fucking deaf, you stupid animal. I'm so not in the mood!" Nothing. "Fuck. You. Hades!"

Bark.

"Hades!"

Bark.

"Fine, stay in there then! You'll be sorry coming home with me!" I climb into the driver seat, and the dog, "Hades," by the sound of it, looks out the window to ignore my eye contact. "Stubborn, stupid animal!"

He whines at me and nudges my elbow. I scruff my unbroken fingers around his head. "Fine, Hades, you can come home with me, but we both need a bath. You fucking stink." With that, he barks at me and lays across the seat, resting his head on my lap. "Dickhead!" I mumble at him as I fumble to start the car and move with all my injuries.

We head off, keeping to the back streets and keeping a low profile. Driving at the speed limit and using my signals is fucking challenging, to say the least. As we get nearer to Ravenswood, it's getting busier. Looking at the clock on the dash, it says 9 a.m.

I have to take the long way around to avoid getting noticed. As I get nearer the MC, I hear the warning siren sound. There's no way I'm sneaking up on my husband or my brothers. As I pull into the parking lot, it's nearing 10 a.m. There's shouting and guys running around.

Steel storms out of the clubhouse, his gaze catching mine as he storms towards the car and grabs the handle. Hades shoots out of my lap, growling and snarling at the door. "Whoa there, dickhead, he's mine!" I snap at the dog. He looks at me, then back at Steel. "Hades, no!" I snarl, and he whimpers.

Steel slowly opens my door and pulls me out, crushing me in his arms. "Fuck... baby, you're never leaving my side again. We thought you were dead. I thought you were dead. I've been worried sick."

I wince as he crushes me to him, and Hades growls beside me as he stalks out of the car.

"So you stopped to pick up a stray?" Steel cocks a brow at me, looking at him… really looking at him, his face is puffy, his eyes rimmed in red, and he looks like he hasn't slept for a week.

"Steel, this is Hades, Hades, this is Steel!" Hades cocks his head at me again and just stands there.

"Well, okay then. Let's get you in to see Doc. I love you, but you fucking stink and need a bath!"

Turning to Hades, he says, "That means you, too, dickhead." He whines, which makes us both laugh as I look over towards the club house. The guys are gathered there, and Dice and Bernie both look a mess. "I'm fine, just a few bumps."

Bernie walks over to me, and Hades growls. Bernie shoots him a look, and he stops. He hugs me. "Fuck, Squirt. Thought I'd lost you. I'm sorry."

"Don't be. I'm good. Where's Joseph?"

"We secured him in one of the rooms for now. The barn was too secluded to keep a close enough eye on him." He laughs.

"Brill, I will get patched up, then I'm gonna put the fear of me in that bastard!"

Bernie laughs again. "You did that when you threw him off a fifth-floor balcony!"

"Hey, he survived, didn't he?"

Dice steps in to give me a hug. "Fuck, Ray, we lost signal, we couldn't find you… I couldn't find you." He shakes his head and steps back. I give him a tight smile.

Steel shoves me towards the MC. "Come on, let's go see Doc." As we walk off, Hades follows right at my side, Steel swinging the door open for me, and I push in past him.

Ares is right there. "Fuck, Ray!" He grabs me for a hug. There's a low growl that radiates from Hades. "Fuck, Hades, give over. These are my brothers, okay."

"You just decided in the middle of a job to pick yourself up a dog, like that's normal?" He cocks his head at me.

"He kind of found me, then hid me while they were looking for me. I probably would have been caught by those bastards if he hadn't, then he just followed me, and here we are."

"Perfect." Ares smiles at me, then fusses at the dog's head. "Fuck, you two stink!"

"No shit, Sherlock. I'm gonna see Doc, and then I'm heading home for a bath." He nods as I stride down to the medical room.

As we enter, he says, "Fuck's sake, Reaper!"

"It looks worse than it is."

"I'm the doctor. I will tell you that. Sit!" He points to the bed. As I climb up, Hades nudges Steel to get in, then pushes into the room and sits beside the bed.

"Friend of yours?" Doc cocks a brow.

"Yup." Doc checks me over a sprained ankle and wrist, feet cut to ribbons, three broken fingers and a dislocated shoulder, no skin on the palm of my hand, smashed in shins, bruises everywhere, and a swollen cheek with a cut that will be fine with wound closure strips. It's split, but not too deep.

I must have hit my face as I tried to stop on the first balcony. After I'm patched up, we head around the back of the garage for Hades to do his business before heading back home.

The girls, Carmen, and Viking, are waiting for me when I get back. The girls rush at me, clinging onto me like I will disappear if they don't. "I'm okay." I breathe into their hair, smiling down at them.

I smile at Carmen and Viking. "We saw the footage. We thought you were dead!" Viking tells me.

"Footage?"

"When Dice and Bernie came back without you, Dice scanned the area for cameras he could hack. Fuck, Ray, you're a badass motherfucker. No one should have survived that. I mean, the fucker you took with you was mush!" He pulls me into his chest. "Seeing it, seeing you like that, fuck, Ray... I love you, ya know!"

"I love you too, Vike." He kisses my head and holds me like that till Steel clears his throat.

"Bath's ready."

I kiss Carmen on the cheek as I pass, and she looks at me with glossy eyes. "I'm okay." I nod at her, and she swallows and nods back. Before I step away, I rest my head on her shoulder, the nearest to a hug I can manage. A solitary sob spills from her. I turn and walk away straight into the bathroom.

Steel goes to shut the door behind me, and Hades barges in.

"Can you throw him in once I'm out?"

I look at Steel, and he eyes Hades. "I'll give it a go." After my bath and a lot of help from Steel, I start to feel more like myself. I climb out to snuggle into my fluffy dressing gown and sit on the vanity.

"Your turn, big lad." I nod at Hades. He takes a step back, then another, followed by another with a small growl for good measure.

Steel laughs. "Come you, ya big baby." He walks over and picks Hades up, he whimpers in Steel's arms, and Steel plops him into the bath. He splashes around a bit, and then Steel grabs my shampoo and starts scrubbing him. This overgrown puppy's look of sheer joy is adorable as Steel scrubs behind his ears. He licks his face.

"Ah, he likes me." Steel coos.

"I fucking missed you, baby!" I rush out, leaning against the mirror. I just need a second to process it all.

As we all walk back out into the kitchen, I ask Steel to put some water out. Next to our bedroom doors, next to the patio doors, Steel throws down a blanket on the floor.

Hades walks straight over and has a drink. As I wander into the kitchen, he follows. "You hungry, boy?"

"I am." Viking shouts over from the sofa.

"When aren't you, fucker?" I laugh out.

Steel pushes me out of the way. "Go and sit down, baby, I will make us all some pasta, and if Hades is staying, we can go to the store and get him some shit tomorrow, okay?"

I smile up at him and kiss his cheek. I drop onto the sofa and listen to the chattering around me.

I wake up with a dead leg and a 10-stone Rottie lying across my lap. "Fuck, didn't anyone tell you you're not a lap dog? My fucking leg's dead." Hades huffs as I stretch and nudge behind his ears anyway. Steel must have put a blanket over me, and Hades has laid down on top of it. Steel brings us all dinner to the sofa, and he places a bowl for Hades to cool.

After eating, there's a knock at the door, and Pa walks in. "You up to see Joseph? We need to find out what's going on."

I head into the bedroom to change, well, to try and change, but fuck, this is impossible. "Fucking hell, Steel, can you give me a hand?"

After the embarrassment of having to get my husband to dress me, I head out of the living room to where Bernie's waiting.

"Babe, you need your splints and sling on at all times. Let me strap you up before you go!"

"Baby, I promise you can strap me up when I get back, but I need to look un-injured for this bit." I kiss him on the cheek and head out of the door.

Pa Cade

The phone rings. It's the call we've been dreading. We've been sitting at the kitchen table just waiting. "Bernie, is she okay?"

"Yeah," he breathes out. "We've got her, she's banged up, but she's okay!"

We collectively let out a breath.

"I'm too old for this shit!" Steven shakes his head.

"My fucking heart has been in my throat since we knew she was missing. I can't stop shaking." JJ looks paler than normal as he scrubs his hand down his face.

"I've booked a flight. I'm coming," I inform Bernie.

"It's okay, Brother, she's okay."

"She's my daughter, Bernie. I'm not being away from her for a moment longer. I thought I could do this, but I can't." I scrub a hand down my face and exhale sharply. "I can't do it anymore. I can't wake up every day knowing she's on the other side of the world. Steven and JJ are gonna run the Adventure Centre. I'm moving back to the States."

"She's all of our daughter, Cade!" he spits. "You're overreacting. She's got a dislocated shoulder and a couple of broken fingers. She's fine."

"You know what I mean! And no. I'm not being this far away. We've sorted it this end. I'm wrapping up. I'll be there within the week. I'll let you know when my flight's landing."

"Cade, be reasonable."

"Reasonable? Bernie… I can't be here without her."

Letting out a deep breath, he says, "I understand, Brother, I do. Let me know when you're arriving, and I will come to get you. You can stay with us as long as you need, okay."

"Thanks, Bernie."

"I'll talk to you guys soon."

"Well, that went better than expected." Steven smiles.

"You sure you guys can run this place?"

"Please! This place runs itself, and you know it." JJ laughs.

"I think I need a minute," is all I can say as these emotions are threatening to spill over, and I refuse to cry in front of my brothers, not because I think it will make me less of a man, but more because if I start, I'm not sure I will stop till she's in my arms.

Joseph

I wake up, and my head is ringing. I've had the weirdest dream. I'm blaming the whiskey or scotch or both. My arm's above my head at a weird angle, so it has gone to sleep. I try to move it, but there's a clunk. As I try to sit, I can't. Looking up at my arm, it's handcuffed to my bed. Rapidly blinking and trying to focus, I look around the room for Celeste, but I don't recognise the room. This isn't my room. This isn't my bed.

My mind's foggy, and my eyes are stinging and blurry, and looking down at myself, I'm still in my suit. Taking a few deep breaths, I start trying to piece bits together. I remember Celeste wanting to have sex in the bathroom at the event. I remember… damn it, did she throw me off a balcony? My mind is fuzzy. I vaguely remember being tossed off a balcony and maybe a van. Why can't I remember?

I yank at the cuffs and shout out, "Celeste?" Nothing. "Celeste, you can undo me now." Still nothing, and now I'm starting to panic, remembering men in black outfits and shouting. Rubbing at my eyes, they fly to the door as it unlocks.

"Marcus?" I gasp out. "Where's Celeste?" He smiles as he walks in, locking the door behind him.

"Celeste is a little… busy at the moment. She'll be along as soon as she's available." He looks at me sternly. "I think we need to have a little chat, Judge. We need to figure out who's after you and what they want and arrange you some security. Till then, unfortunately, you'll have to stay here."

"I don't remember anything. Why don't I remember anything?"

"That'll be the… drugs we gave you. They'll wear off shortly, and things will become a little clearer. I'll be back later. There are some clothes in the bathroom, so shower and change. Someone will be along shortly with food for you. We'll keep you here till we can sort out your security, and once you've talked to Black Widow, we will release you."

He uncuffs my wrist. I immediately grab it and rub at it. "Black Widow?" *Why does that name sound familiar? Ah that's what Celeste called herself!*

"Shower! Don't leave this room, don't be stupid, Judge. We're the only things keeping you safe at the minute."

He leaves, locking the door behind him. I head into the bathroom. There are joggers and a t-shirt on the counter. How crass. I wouldn't be caught dead in these, but it doesn't look like I have much choice.

After showering and heading back to the room, there is a jug of water and a sandwich on the bedside table. I look out the window, and all I can see are trees and the windows screwed shut. Who are these people, and are they good or bad? I have no idea. I hope they haven't hurt Celeste.

I've been in the room all day. They've bought me three meals and drinks, but no one's spoken to me. The same young lad has delivered my food but has not said a word. He's dressed in jeans and a t-shirt with no distinguishing tattoos, marks or logos that I can see.

It must have been late. It's already dark when the door swings open, and Marcus and Celeste walk in. They are both wearing jeans and long-sleeve T-shirts. Celeste has her hands tucked into her pockets as Marcus opens the door for her.

"Celeste?" I gasp. She looks different, tired, maybe? "What's happening?"

"My name isn't Celeste, Joseph. I need you to sit and listen very carefully, do you understand?"

Her voice is different, tight, clipped, not angry as such but firm, commanding attention. Gone is that flirty girl who hung off my arm at the hotel last night. *Was it last night? Or the night before? How long have I been here? Where is here?*

"Joseph!" she snaps.

My eyes snap to hers. I realise I've been lost in my thoughts.

"What do you remember about last night?" she asks, leaning against the wall before letting out a deep breath.

I shake my head. "I'm not sure. It's all a blur."

"Okay, listen up, you booked security and an escort for the event last night. We were informed of a potential threat against you, so we intercepted—"

"We? Who's we? Threat? What threat?"

Huffing at me, she says, "Joseph, this is going to take far longer to get through if you keep interrupting. Just keep the questions till the end, yeah!"

"Understood."

"We intercepted the detail and cancelled your order with the security firm. We were chased by eight men in full tactical gear in armoured trucks. They clearly wanted you. Who are they, Joseph? And what do they want?"

Letting out a shaky breath, I ask, "How do I know I can trust you, Celeste?"

She shakes her head at me as if I'm a stupid man and screws her eyes closed before taking a deep breath. Marcus casts her a glance with a worried look before schooling his features.

"Joseph, if it weren't for us, you would already be dead or worse!"

I open my mouth to ask what could be worse than dead, but the look she gives me could have frozen the fires of hell, so I change my mind and close my mouth.

"Joseph, who are these people, and what do they want?"

"Will you help me? If you help me, I'll tell you."

"Joseph, I'm losing my patience. It's been a long, long *fucking* day," she says through gritted teeth.

"They got in touch a month or so ago and wanted me in their pocket. When I refused, they threatened my life. I still wouldn't budge. They wanted information but didn't tell me what it was about. They called themselves 'The Armoury'."

Celeste and Marcus shoot a grim look at each other before staring back at me. "You're sure they said 'The Armoury'?" Marcus asks.

I nod. "That's all I know. They wouldn't say what they wanted till I'd signed some paperwork for them to blackmail me with later down the line."

"Okay, so you're gonna stay here tonight, then tomorrow you're gonna call the security firm who were originally going to do the event, you'll book 24-hour security for the foreseeable future and leave the rest to us, you'll be at our beck and call... Judge!" She grins, but it doesn't reach her eyes. The grin slides off her face as quickly as it arrives. "Then you'll go back about your business, I'll set you up with a burner phone, and you'll check in with us daily, and if they contact you, you'll forward everything immediately to us. Do you understand?"

"I won't be bought off and put in your pocket. I am the law. I won't be treated like some—"

"I'm sorry, Judge, I obviously didn't make myself fucking clear, did I?" she spits, pushing up off the wall. "I wasn't asking if you wanted to do as I fucking say. Either you do as I say, or I'll fucking kill you myself and save myself the bother of babysitting your fucking arse!"

I shrink back into myself as she steps forward. She's extremely intimidating and looks like she's balancing on a knife edge. Looking at her, I'm aware that she can and will snap my neck if given enough incentive.

Marcus rests his hand on her chest and glares at her. She snaps a look at him before glaring back at me. "Either we have a deal or we fucking don't. Either way, it's been a long day, and I'm done with this shit, so I will leave it with you! Some fucker will be along to find your answer in the morning. Either way, you'll be released and returned home."

"You'll release me either way?" I sigh. "Thank you, lord."

"Don't misunderstand me, Joseph. I will release you either way. On our side, you'll be released back to your family, and we will protect you. You'll also work for us and be in our pocket and only ours. Against us, you'll be released off the nearest bridge attached to a length of rope before being delivered back to your family in a body bag. Do I make myself clear?"

Marcus steps around her and opens the door as she's about to step through it without a backward glance. "Celeste?"

She stops, spinning to face me, and doesn't say a word, just stares. At that moment, I feel I've reached the end of her rope and drop my eyes as she turns back and leaves the room.

Marcus glares at me, "Think very long and hard about what these people are capable of, Judge, but be under no illusion that whatever they're capable of… she is ten times more capable. You'll do well to remember that."

He steps out of the door and locks it behind him.

Steel

Ray has come back from dealing with Joseph. She's exhausted and heads to bed after letting me strap her fingers and her shoulder. Everyone else has gone to bed, but I can't bring myself to go. Panic is now over, and reality sets in. I thought she was dead. The footage had shown her jump from the fifth-floor, hitting two balconies and then plummeting awkwardly to the ground, not moving. The other guy had already smashed into the concrete, and he, too, wasn't moving. You could clearly see his head had smashed like a watermelon. Next thing, the feed cuts out, and a couple of us headed back over there only to find a clean alleyway, no bodies, no blood, nothing.

We searched the area as stealthily as possible, but nothing, so we headed away until the dust settled. The more I think, the more I struggle to move towards the bedroom. I head towards the kitchen instead, grabbing the tequila and returning to the sofa. Kicking off my jeans, I sit in my boxers with my head resting on the back of the sofa. I throw the blanket over me and start drinking.

Hades climbs up beside me and lays his head on my lap. I fuss his head distractedly as I drink, my mind swirling with what ifs and should have beens. Halfway down the bottle, I blurt out, "I shouldn't have married her!"

Hades lifts his head, huffs and leaves the couch. He heads over to the bedroom door and lays down outside it. "I suppose she gets you in the divorce, then?" I half laugh, half grimace. I hear him shuffle, and he places his back towards me. Yep, think that's a definite. I chug some more of the tequila, my head starts to spin, and my inner monologue fucks me right over.

I should have never married her. It was a mistake. I need a divorce as soon as she wakes up. I'm going to tell her that's what's happening. *And how the fuck do you think that's gonna go, dickhead? Fuck off. It's for the best. Yep, you tell yourself that, knobhead. Good luck with that.* Why does my inner monologue sound like my fucking wife?

I thought it was supposed to be me that I heard in my own head. I can't stay with her. She doesn't deserve me. *You honestly think that's gonna wash, dickwad?* I don't know how long I sit there, but there's a soft click, and I know it's the bedroom door. I'm sitting on the couch with my head hanging on the back of it. I close my eyes. If I pretend to be asleep, she will just go back to bed.

"Baby?"

I jump as my eyes fly open, fuck, she's right in front of me. "Go back to bed, Ray," I slur. "You need your rest." I point my bottle at her, then take another swig.

"I need my husband beside me. Come to bed, baby?"

"You go, Ray. I just wanna be by myself, okay?"

"Erm, no... not okay. Talk to me. What's up?"

"Nothing, just go back to bed, please. We will talk about it tomorrow." I close my eyes and lay my head back again. I feel her move closer and reach my hand flat against her stomach. "Just go to bed, Ray."

She climbs into my lap, grabbing my jaw in her vice-like grip. "Ray, your fingers are broken. Be careful."

"Fuck my fingers, Steel. What's going on?"

Huffing out and closing my eyes. I can't look at her. Through a heavy breath, I say, "I want a divorce!" She pinches at my chin, tilting my head. It must have hurt like a motherfucker. She has three broken fucking fingers on that hand but still manages to make me wince.

"Look me in the eyes and say it," she speaks clearly but quietly.

I open my eyes and look towards her. "I want a divorce." I whisper out, I don't know what she sees when I look at her face, but I can't make eye contact with her. Leaning forward, she places the faintest kiss against my lips as she rocks her hips against my traitorous dick. Her dislocated left shoulder is strapped, and her fingers on her right hand are splinted. She's wearing one of my wife-beaters and nothing else. I can feel the heat from her core radiating against me.

She leans back and rocks again, and I can feel the warmth and wetness seeping into my boxers. I groan and place a hand on her hip as I take another swig. She leans over me again, resting her forehead on mine.

"Till death do us part... Motherfucker," she whispers. "If you want out of this marriage, either put yourself in a body bag, or I will... your choice!" She presses a chaste kiss to my lips, then backs off, rising to stand in front of me. "I will be in our room when you decide you wanna talk about what's really going on." Then she walks away, and I groan, throwing my arm over my face and downing some more tequila, which will *surely* help.

What feels like an age later, the door clicks again, but when I look over, it's Viking. "You good, Brother?" He asks as he walks into the living room in only a pair of boxers. His hair, normally tied back in a ponytail, is pushed over to one side, trailing over his shoulder and down his back.

"Fucking fantastic." I spit out, "What the fuck are you doing up?" I continue slurring.

"Car' wants a glass of water." He shrugs as he heads into the kitchen. "Want one?"

Letting out a frustrated breath. "Sure." He comes back and places it in my free hand, sitting on the edge of the coffee table. We sit there for a few minutes, ignoring each other, before I blurt out, "I asked Ray for a divorce!"

"Ha!" he barks out. "And how did that fucking go?"

"She said, 'Till death do us part, motherfucker.' And if I want out of this marriage, 'I can put myself in a body bag, or she will do it for me.' I mean, what the fuck?"

"Oh, better than I expected, to be honest."

Cocking a brow at him, I ask, "How the fuck is that better than expected?"

"Well, you ain't dead yet, Brother. At least she gave you a choice... Why do you want a divorce?"

Taking a breath before answering, I say, "Since I forced her to marry me, she's been shot... twice... stabbed... kidnapped... plummeted from a fifth-story building... blown up an MC and is amassing a body count to rival all of us put together. She would have been better off never finding me."

Viking's smug grin spreads across his face as he sits there, shaking his head, "Firstly... how the fuck do you think you forced Ray to marry you? Secondly, she was kidnapped and shot and stabbed before she met you, and thirdly... you're a complete twat! She belongs here whether you two are together or not. She was already one of us before you came back, and also, do you even know the stuff she did before coming here?" He points the glass at me, shaking his head. "Night, Brother."

I sigh. I suppose I don't know everything about Ray's past; it has never seemed important. Gulping the water down, I head into the bedroom. The door opens, and as I walk in, Ray's sitting up in bed with her Kindle on her lap, the dogs on my side of the bed lying against her body.

"Hades, get off," I say. He raises his head, looks at me, then at Ray, then rests his head back down. "Hades off!" I say with slightly more oomph. He doesn't even lift his head this time; just shifts his eyes at me, then closes them again.

"Still want a divorce?" Ray's voice is soft and quiet, glancing up at me.

"No!" I snap.

"Hades," she breathes, and he skulks off the bed and knocks into me as he strides out of the door.

Fuck that dog! I step further into the room and close the door behind me. I take off my t-shirt and slide up onto the bed where the dog had been. As she flattens her legs out, placing the Kindle on the nightstand, I curl my head into her lap, and her hand lays on my cheek. "Wanna talk?"

"No," I reply again, she starts to stroke the side of my face, but I can smell her arousal from here.

I wrap my arm around her and nuzzle at the hem of my wife-beater, running my thumb over her thigh. I push her legs apart and nestle between them. She shifts down the bed so she can lie down, and I whisper, "I'm sorry," before flicking my tongue out and licking her from back to front. I feel a shudder run through her as she takes a deep breath. What the fuck am I doing? I lick her again as I slide my hand up her thigh, slipping in a finger, and then back out to circle her clit. She moans.

I grin against her thigh, nipping down gently on it before licking her again. I start caressing her with my tongue and finger, inserting another and pumping a few times before sucking her clit into my mouth, rubbing that sweet spot inside. She arches her back off the bed. She winces slightly and stills, pausing for a second before her glare reaches me. I slide in another finger, and she groans, making me smile again.

Fuck, she's perfect. What the fuck am I thinking? Speeding up my thrusting fingers and flicking my tongue. I nip her clit, her breaths are coming in stuttered now, and her chest's rising and falling more vigorously than before. She has a slight flush on her cheeks and her chest. Sucking on her clit, I pump my fingers till I feel her still and clench down on my hand. Her breaths have come in short till they have stopped altogether.

"Be a good girl, baby, and come on my tongue." I continue my sucking and thrusting as she comes around me, groaning into her sweet pussy as I lap up every single drop of her orgasm. As she shudders, I slide up her body, kissing as I go, sliding my dick out of my boxers and pushing them down.

I want to make love to you." I close my eyes as all my emotions hit me. I don't want to lose her. I never had. I want to keep her safe. I regret forcing her to marry me. It was a dirty trick. If I hadn't married her, maybe she wouldn't have been injured so much, and maybe she wouldn't be the slightly psychotic killer I love so much, but maybe is too hard to think about. Maybes are fucking with my head.

I just want to be buried inside my wife and thank whatever force of nature has spared her this time, sliding into her soaked pussy. I slide in and out with such slow, steady thrusts as I lean up away from her strapped-up shoulder and kiss her like my life depends on her, and it does. I'm nothing without her. I can't live without her. I won't.

We've never made love before, I've fucked her a million different ways, and she's fucked me a million different more, but this is different. This is me needing to know she's still with me, still alive, still mine, still breathing, still owning my heart, my twisted black soul and my body sliding up her again. She arches against me.

I cup her cheek as I rock against her, making her gasp. "I fucking love you," I half-slur, half-whisper. I can't stop staring at her face.

As if she could read my thoughts, she kisses me gently. "I'm okay. I'm not going anywhere, but I am okay!" I sigh and rest my head on hers as I tilt again, sliding against each other unhurried, sharing a part of us we've not before. I know at this moment that till death do us part is how this life is gonna go, and I'm here for it.

I need this woman to breathe, think straight, focus, and love. Sliding up her again, her breath hitches in the back of her throat, and I smile against her lips.

"Promise me you'll never leave me?" I close my eyes and whisper out as I sink myself back inside her.

"I promise," she swears, and with that, I up my pace, slightly catching her clit as I slide against her, as she gasps again. This time, I lead with a little more force, sliding in and out while she shudders around me, slowly building into her orgasm before following her over the edge. After I'm truly empty, I reach and tuck a stray strand of hair behind her ear, kissing her till my heart stops aching and my soul feels complete.

Rising from the bed, I go into the bathroom to grab a towel to clean up my mess. After cleaning her up, I lay down beside her.

"Steel…" she lets out a shaky breath, searching my eyes for answers, leaning in and kissing her again. I pull her as close to me as I can get her.

I shake my head, "Shhh." She blinks, taking a deep breath, and I snuggle into her side. "Shhh, baby, sleep."

Pa Cade

As I leave the airport, Bernie's sitting in the lay-by waiting for me, "Is that everything?"

"Yep, turns out I don't have much stuff at all. A lot of this is for Ray and Steel. I sorted through all the old photos and got copies made." shrugging.

"Fuck, man, she's gonna love that."

I smile over at him. "How is she really?"

"Honestly?"

"Yeah, hit me."

"She's a raging *bitch*!" He exhales sharply. "Steel's taking the brunt of it, poor motherfucker, but she's tried to go to work already. It's only been a few days, and now Steel has her under house arrest, so you can imagine how that's going."

"Hades, I should have given it a bit longer before turning up!"

We both burst out laughing. "It's good to have you here, Brother. I've missed you."

"Missed you too, Bernie."

Bernie drops me at the clubhouse and disappears. "Pussy!" But then I decide to see if I can grab a drink in the clubhouse, ya know, Dutch courage and all that! As I walk in. Ares is sitting in his booth with some paperwork.

"Hey, man." I shout over. His gaze shoots up before taking a second to realise who it is.

"Cade? What the fuck are you doing here?"

"Thought I should come to check what trouble that daughter of mine's gotten herself into?" I walk over and throw my bags on the floor.

"And need a stiff one first?" He barks out a laugh. "I'm sure she's a pleasure at the moment!"

"You not seen her?"

"Not since the house arrest. Steel caught her at the garage and lost his shit."

"How long did that take to happen?"

"The fucking next day, she was even trying to get Dozer to help her take the bandage-type sling off as she couldn't do it with her fucked up fingers."

"Best make it a large one then before I walk into that shitshow!"

"Roach… Tequila! Bring the fucking bottle!" Ares laughs out. "Does she know you're coming?"

"Nah, just packed up and left."

"How long you here for?"

"Forever. I've packed up all together, JJ and Steven are running the Adventure Centre, so I'm gonna join the family business Stateside."

"You staying with Ray and Steel?"

"Nah, if she's being her usual delightful self, I'll probably crash at Bernie's."

"Steel's old room's still empty if you wanna crash there, so you're close but not too close."

"You sure? That would actually be great, man, thanks."

"Yeah, definitely. Maybe if you fancy staying, you could fix up one of the lodges. There are a couple of spares just rotting away up there. If you wanna be that close, obviously!"

"Actually, man, that would be perfect! I don't really wanna be away from her any longer. I know she's a cantankerous—"

The door swings open, and in walks Steel, looking like he hasn't slept in weeks.

"Fucking hell, Brother, you look like shit!"

"Fuck you! Hey Cade… Cade…? What the fuck, Cade?"

"Think we've established you've seen Cade." Ares barks out a laugh as I stand and hug Steel."

"Fuck, Cade, am I glad to see you! You've come to help, right? Say you've come to help? I'm not opposed to begging. I will if I have to!"

"Fucking hell, Steel, she's not that bad!"

Steel punches me in the arm and sits down. "Tag, you're it!" He sighs as he slouches into the booth next to us.

Ares bursts out laughing.

"Don't! Just fucking don't! I think I might just cry! She's… she's… she's just so…"

"Frustrating?" I ask.

As Ares says, "Annoying."

"Fuck you two! I was gonna say independent."

"Ah, yeah, she's definitely that, son. So what's the issue?"

"I promised I would take her to get some stuff for the dog, then I had to put her under house arrest, and now I haven't taken her, so she's pissed at me."

"Dog? When the fuck did you get time to get a dog?" I shake my head. Fuck—things really do move fast around here.

"When she was on the job she got injured doing, she went missing then turned up with this fucking dog in tow, and it's the dog version of her, so it's pissed at me too."

"Sounds wonderful. Look, Ray is easy, really. If you say you're gonna do something, especially if you promised, she will be pissed at you if you don't, so moral of the story kid"—I slap him on the shoulder—"don't promise anything. Always say, 'If possible,' then if you don't manage to do it, no harm, no foul."

"Yeah, that's great. But now I've already promised. What do I do?"

"Fucking take her, you idiot!"

Scrubbing a hand down his face and shaking his head, he says, "She won't leave the house with the sling on, and I won't let her leave without it, fuck's sake!"

"Come on, son." Taking a massive swig of the Tequila and wiping my mouth on my hand, I say, "Let's give you a lesson in manipulating my daughter, shall we?"

"This I need to see." Ares stands, waving to Roach. "Throw Cade's bags in Steel's old room. He's moving in. Lob some bedding and towels in there, too, kid."

Roach nods and scurries off. Slinging my arm around Steel, I say, "Come on, big lad, let's go."

Stalking through the door, a cushion comes flying and hits Steel straight in the face.

Dude doesn't even bat an eyelid, almost like he's expecting it!

"Baby, you've got a visitor." He smiles as he bends down to pick the cushion up. As Ares follows me in, there's a squeal and a flash of blonde as she dives off the sofa and runs at me.

She slams into me with an, "Oof, fuck, Squirt!"

"What are you doing here, Pa? Fuck." She hugs me as hard as she can with one arm and fucked fingers, but she gets her point across.

"So Steel was just telling me he was taking you out to get some stuff for a dog you got or something?" I look over and wink at Steel.

"You are?" She looks over at him with the biggest grin on her face, like she loves him the most.

"Well, he was… but now I'm here, I thought maybe I could take you."

"You will?" She sounds so hopeful and excited. It really is so easy to get her to do what you want.

"Sure, Squirt, whatever you want."

"Can we go for ice cream? No, wait, a milkshake, a burger, and maybe ice cream."

See, this is Ray's thing. She always wants a sweet treat at the end, so if you want to get her to do something, you need to do the thing she originally wanted; then when she asks for the treat, hit her with the condition.

"Sure, Squirt, but if we're gonna be out all that time, you need to keep your sling on the whole time so you can get better, okay?"

She looks up at me, over at Steel, and back at me. "Fine!"

Steel throws his arms in the air in exasperation. "I'll take the dog out before you go… Hades, outside." He huffs as he walks back down the stairs.

A mammoth of a Rottie comes from round the corner of the counter and saunters past, licking Ray as he goes.

"What the fuck's that? That's a fucking horse, not a dog!"

Ray just grins up at me. "Missed you, Pa."

"Missed you too, Squirt. Go get what you need, and let's go. I'll need to borrow Steel's truck."

Heading into the pet store, I'm told to grab a trolley. Fuck, this is gonna be one spoiled street dog. After getting the story of how they ended up together, this is gonna be one pampered pooch. They have a section where they put the pet names on the bowls. She picks up eight, fucking eight, bowls with "Hades" on them.

Then, she lets him pick a bed. I have to get every one down so he can try it, then put it back when he doesn't like it. He likes a grey corduroy soft pillow bed with slightly raised sides, which is fucking massive. I reckon I could fit in it, but that's what he wants, apparently, so that's what he gets. Then, a collar, leather with silver glitter inlay. Also, as we are going to dinner, apparently, he will need a dickie bow that clips to his collar in silver too.

Fuck my life. Then we spend forty minutes going through all the toy aisles so the fucking thing can test every pissing toy. He ends up with five annoying purple squeaky spiders, all slightly different, with different colour spots. They are about the size of a baseball each, a frisbee, a set of ten rubber balls, all different colours, a cuddly frog and a fluffy pink unicorn.

"Are we done?"

"Nope, he needs a tag, a lead, some treats, some food. We also need shampoo and towels, and then we're done."

When we get to the counter to pay, the lad says we can put the dog's name on the towels too, so he tannoys for someone to come get them and sort them while we check out. When we order the tag, the young lad asks again for the dog's name and then Ray's to put on it. When she tells him to put "Hades" on the front and then "The Reapers MC, Ravenswood" on the back, I think he will hyperventilate. She ends up getting a forty per cent discount, and then she leaves him that as a tip for his excellent service, even fills one of those cards out, saying how she will shop here again and he should be an employee of the month. I swear, shopping with Ray is always like a fucking pantomime!

Pulling up outside the diner, Demi comes out running at us like a deranged groupie, flinging her arms around Ray and then me, then stepping back. "What do I call you?" she asks.

"What do you mean? I'm Cade. I know there's a lot of us." Ray digs me in the ribs with her good arm. "You'll get used to it."

She starts fidgeting with her apron, and Ray rolls her eyes. "She means, dickhead, what should *she* call you? Yes, your name's Cade, but I call you Pa." she says, enforcing the "Pa".

"Oh…! It's up to you, sweetheart. I guess I don't know what to call you, either. Princess is taken, that's Scar, and well, Squirt here's Squirt, so why don't we just try a few things out and see what fits? Yeah, sweetheart's a no from me! Who's hungry?"

"You're such a dick!" Ray shakes her head at me.

So I fling my arm around Demi and drag her inside. "We'll figure it out, don't worry." The dog pushes in beside us.

Ray shouts over the counter, "George, is it okay if my dog comes in? I've told him he's got to be a good boy, or I will have his nuts chopped off!"

There's a massive laugh from the kitchen, and a head pops through the hatch, "Anything for my favourite customer!" He winks and pops his head back in.

Demi takes our orders, and Ray sits and reads the whole menu to the fucking dog. He has a cheeseburger, fries, onion rings, a chocolate shake in a bowl and ketchup on the side in case he doesn't like it.

Fuck's sake, and the twat sits there with his fucking dickie bow on like the lord of the manor. Even Demi and George join us. Ray cuts his food up into bite-sized pieces, then feeds him the whole lot while we all sit there and chat like this isn't some kind of fucked up tea party.

When we get back, Viking is just heading up to the apartment, so he gives us a hand with all the bags. Hades just wanders around the back of the garage to do his business before heading to the apartment himself.

"Eight bowls?" Viking raises a brow.

I just shake my head. "Easier not to ask."

Viking's taking Carmen out for dinner, and Roach has taken Catalina and Skye to the cinema, so I set up Hades' stuff for Ray and sit on the sofa. She snuggles up to me like she used to when she was a kid, and while we are talking, she falls asleep. I pull the blanket up around her shoulders and lean back to watch the TV.

Steel walks in about thirty minutes later. "Hey, Cade, are you okay with staying with her a bit longer? I just need to get her pain meds filled with Doc."

"Yeah, sure, son, she's only been asleep for about thirty mins. You look like you could use some sleep."

"Yeah, that's not happening any time soon." He walks through into the bedroom. I hear him rummage around in what sounds like the drawers. "Fuck!"

He storms out of the room. I can see he's angry. He's literally shaking. "What's up?"

Sitting on the coffee table in front of me, he shows me the bottle of pills. "She's not been taking her meds." Shaking his head, he says, "Fuck, Cade, she must be in agony. What the fuck's she playing at?"

"Steel! You need to calm down, okay? Ray's never liked drugs of any sort, so if she doesn't need them, she won't take them."

"Cade, you've seen the state she's in. Surely you can talk some sense into her. She listens to you lot."

Well, I can't help myself. "You're joking, right? Look, she'll take them if she needs them. You've got to trust that she will. Why don't you go get some sleep? You might feel better."

"I can't sleep… every time I drift off, I see her… falling… dying… I just can't bring myself to trust she's here, that she's safe. I don't know what to fucking do."

His eyes glaze over. He looks like he's fighting back with everything he has.

"You trust me? Yeah?"

Cocking his head to the side with a questioning glance, he asks, "Yeah, why?"

"I've got her. She's safe! I'm not going anywhere till you wake up, however long it takes… okay?"

"You sure?"

"Yeah, go, son, you look dead on your feet. I've got this."

Steel thanks me and heads towards the bedroom. "Cade?"

"Yeah?"

"Is Hades wearing a fucking bow tie?"

"Apparently, it's a dickie bow!"

"Sure… does he need eight bowls?"

"Apparently, two each for here, the bar, the garage and Ray's office."

"Ray's got an office?"

"Apparently."

"Thanks, Cade."

And he steps into the room, shaking his head.

Fuck knows how long we were asleep, but the door opening wakes me up as Steel comes back out of the bedroom. "Sorry, didn't mean to wake you."

"Nah, you're good. I should get off and get settled in. I'll see you tomorrow, yeah?"

He nods as I slip out from under Ray, "Don't be too hard on her, okay? She's never really been looked after. We were rubbish when they were ill. Marie used to do it, but Ray, she would always tough it out like the rest of us."

He nods as I leave and head to my new room to settle in. I didn't even put the bedding on. I was asleep before my head hit the pillow, fucking jet lag!

Steel

With everyone's help, we manage two weeks before she convinces me she's well enough to leave on her own, take the dog out for a walk and stay around the MC land. Cade promises he will stay with her even though she's convinced me she's well enough to leave on her own. Cade really needs to teach me how to get her to agree. It's priceless.

They are gone for hours, and when they come back, Ray's knackered and goes to bed. Cade tells me they've been up to his lodge. Ares's letting him fix one up. Ray's gonna go up there to help and sort out what he needs to order to get cracking, and he promises he will ease her in gently. She's chomping at the bit, and Dozer has refused to have her anywhere near the garage for six weeks. He says if she turns up, he will shoot her.

Whatever works, really. Ray and Cade spend the next two weeks up at his lodge. She leaves in the morning, strapped up in the sling, and returns at night that way. Cade promises she's helping but not overdoing it. He's doing all the heavy lifting. I've been so busy filling in the new role as Lieutenant and covering as Enforcer, too, that I've needed extra time and help from Cade.

I decided to go grab some lunch and surprise Cade and Ray. When I knock on the lodge door, there's no answer. When I try the door, it's locked. Looking in through the window, there's no one there. The place doesn't even look like anyone has been in it to do any work.

"Brother," I call Ares. "Have you seen Ray?"

"Not today. You lost her again?"

"Too fucking soon, Brother, too fucking soon!"

"Sorry man, no, not seen her."

"Is she in her office?"

"Her office?"

"Yeah, she said you gave her an office."

"Well shit, yeah." He laughs out. "Kinda, I'd forgotten about that."

"Well, has she got an office or not?"

"Office? No! Space to work in, yeah."

"Ares, where the fuck is it?"

"I'm coming to you, Brother."

"I'm at Cade's lodge."

As Ares walks up to me, he has a massive grin on his face.

"What the fuck you smiling for?"

"The office. I can't believe she was being serious. She mentioned it, and I kind of fobbed her off. Now she's actually got an office."

"Ares, I've got a fucking headache, man. Where the fuck is she?"

"Barn." He laughs.

"I'm not gonna fucking like this, am I?"

"Probably not, but I can't wait to see. Come on, Brother, your wife's entertaining as shit!"

"Fuck you, Brother. I'm too old for this shit. I think I need a vacation from my wife."

"Don't fucking let her hear you say that. She'll give you a permanent one! You'll be spending it in a body bag."

"Just shut the fuck up!"

As we push through the barn doors, there's no one here. There's some clutter, bits of metal, and rubbish in bags dotted around the barn, but nothing. Ray's missing, Cade's missing, and so is Hades.

I call her phone, but there's no answer. I call Cade, but there's no answer. I bring up the tracker app Dice added for me.

"Does she know you've got that?"

"Shut up!" Glancing at the phone again, I say, "It says she's here."

"Where?"

"In the barn, look." I shove my phone at him.

Ares takes it and walks around. He's standing near the doors. "I'm right on her phone icon. Do you think she's in the grain storage?"

"The fucking what?"

"The grain storage, it's underneath!" He shrugs, and I snatch my phone back and start dialling again.

"Shit, sorry, Steel. I didn't hear my phone!" Cade answers, out of breath.

"Cade, where the fuck's Ray. I'm in the barn?"

"Hang on!" Then he hangs up.

"Motherfucker." We stand there like a pair of spare pricks and wait. After about five minutes, I'm starting to lose my shit when a whirring sound follows a click. Next thing, the hay bale in the corner starts moving and tips up ninety degrees, leaving a hole in the floor.

Walking towards it, Ray's head pops out of the hole as she climbs some stairs. She's filthy and in her underwear with her boots on.

I stop dead, and I'm standing with my mouth hanging open. I mean, what the fuck am I supposed to say to that?

"Erm... nice outfit?" Ares looks between us both like he's not sure what to say while I'm trying to process the whole... whatever is going on. I pinch the bridge of my nose and close my eyes, taking a breath for a minute. Next, a hand on my chest runs up to my cheek.

"Hey, baby."

I sigh as my arms automatically slide around her and pull her towards me. She slides her arms over my shoulders and behind my neck, her unbandaged hand and shoulder pull me in, and I sigh into her. "You're not wearing your sling!" I breathe into her neck.

"No, I'm good." She kisses along my jaw and across to my mouth, diving in with the softest sensual kiss she's ever given me, and I melt into her. Fuck, this woman is my kryptonite!

"Hey." Cade breaks the moment as his head pops out of the hole, too.

"Do I want to know why you're both underground in your underwear?"

Ray doesn't say anything as she grabs my hand to pull me forward.

"This seems more like a... family thing. I should head back!" Ares says as he backs away.

"No way, Boyband! You need to see my new office. It's gonna be so great when it's finished!" Ray says as she pulls me along. "Okay, just remember it's not finished yet."

As she drags me down the stairs, the heat is stifling, which explains the underwear. There is a set of steel stairs welded to the wall, which looks to be steel, too. As we walk down the stairs, there's a massive, dimly lit room about fifteen feet high and the size of the barn above. Against the wall is an old steel sink and table. Against the far wall is what can only be described as a prison cell.

Two prison cells, to be exact. There's a pallet with rolled steel bars and lengths of flat steel sheeting that looks like two either low tables or possibly cot-type beds made of steel.

"Ray… what is all this?"

"It's my new office." She spins around with her arms in the air as if encompassing the entire space. "It needs a lot of work, but it's gonna be epic! I realised when we had Miguel here that it wasn't a… longer-term solution and thought sometimes these things just take… time."

"So, let's be clear. When you said office, you meant kill room?" Ares questions cautiously.

Ray barks out a laugh. "No, knobhead, it's an interrogation room!" She waggles her eyebrows at him.

"Jesus!" He rubs a hand down his face

"You know as well as I do that the barn just isn't sufficient. We had to let Joseph go the next day. If I'd had this up and running, we could have kept him secure for weeks, months, even years." To this, she just smiles.

"Baby, you're still injured. You're supposed to be strapped up for six weeks." I shoot a look at Cade, who raises his hands in defence. "This isn't what Doc meant by taking it easy!"

"I've been good. I was strapped up and under house arrest for two weeks apart from the little "Talking to" I had with Joseph. Cade did all the heavy lifting last week, and this week, I've been welding. Cade still lifts everything. I've been doing rehab at the gym, look I'm fine." She starts rotating her shoulder like there was never an issue and then wiggling her fingers at me.

I turn and glare at Cade. "I thought you were gonna help, ya know, keep her in line?" I cock a brow at him in frustration.

Everyone bursts out laughing at that, and I just shake my head because why the fuck would I think that?

"What help do you need to get this up and running? I'm kinda seeing the benefit to this, especially with how things have been going recently... well, since you arrived!" Ares seems genuinely on board with this *American Horror Story* basement.

"My brothers, if they're not busy!"

Ares looks at Cade, then back to me, then at Ray, and grins.

"You can have your brothers for a week if you pack up now. You've been here all day. You need to take it steadier, okay?"

"Deal," she says, slapping her hand out to shake his!

I throw my arms up in the air and stride out of the place, up the incredibly well-made and strong sturdy steps my wife has erected, with a dislocated shoulder and broken fingers, all in her fucking underwear.

As I come out of the barn, Hades is sitting waiting. "Come on, let's get some food ready!"

As we head back down to the apartment, he trots alongside me, still wearing that fucking dickie bow. I mean, seriously? I reach down to unclip it, and he growls. I back off, and he stops. Reaching for it again, he growls harder this time.

"You look like a dickhead; you know that, right?" He just barks at me. I'm not sure if he knows or if that's just a fuck off from him. What the fuck happened, and how did this become my life?

Ray

After arriving back at the apartment and showering, Steel has dinner ready for us all. Viking, Carmen, Tali, Skye, me, Steel and Cade.

"I wanna talk to you all. I know I've been a little bit…"

"Bitchy."

"Vile."

"Cuntish."

"Desquiciada." *Unhinged.*

"Challenging."

"Distant?"

"Thank you, Skye. I was going to say distant since I got back from the job, but being under house arrest hasn't been very fun for me, so I appreciate you tolerating my… moods."

They all share looks but nod as if they don't want to comment further.

"Carmen, I just wanted to let you know that I've been looking into the situation at yours. I've checked all the footage from before Tali got taken, and while you've been away, Dice has helped me go through everything. I believe we've found two guys who I'm pretty convinced are responsible for everything with Tali, and I've got all the information together." I slide a folder across the table to Carmen. "Let me know how you want to... proceed with everything. I've still got Dice monitoring the situation, so we can be ready to move when you are. If you need us."

"When the fuck have you had time to do anything like this?" Steel arches a brow at me.

"You had me under house arrest for two weeks, two long fucking weeks. What did you think I was doing, sitting watching TV all day?"

"Kinda, yeah."

"Seriously?" I shake my head. "Husband, you have so much to learn."

Everyone sniggers, and we carry on chatting as we eat. Tali tells us about the movie they went to see. And it feels... normal. I sit and smile and thank Hades himself for how lucky I feel right now to be surrounded by people I love.

After dinner, Carmen takes me to one side. "Thank you, Hermana loca!" *Crazy sister!* She grins and hugs me. "I need to go back and deal with this myself, they need to know I'm still in charge, and I've not gone soft."

"I totally understand. You know I'm only a call away, yeah?"

"I do, Ray, thank you."

"At least tell me you're taking my brother home with you. I'll feel better knowing he's there."

"I am." She smiles sheepishly. "I don't think I can be without him now, Ray. I'm how you say... screwed!"

"You're so fucking screwed!" I laugh, and I hug her.

"We'll leave tomorrow. I'm sure Roach will be coming with us too. It's like this MC has burned its way into our hearts."

"They say you can choose your friends, but you can't choose your family. I beg to differ on that, Carmen. I've chosen my family, and you're a part of that. I knew it from the first moment we spoke."

"I love you, Hermana!" *I love you, Sister!*

"¡Yo también te amo mi hermana!" *I love you too my sister.*

Carmen heads off to pack, with Viking and Tali close behind her.

Warm hands slide around my waist from behind, and I'm pulled into that all-encompassing embrace that I can't help but melt into. "Don't worry, baby, the apartment won't be empty for long."

I chuckle at that. "Maybe we should have a revolving door installed?"

"Maybe." He kisses me on the head and steps back, my body missing the heat of his already. "Maybe you should go see Skye. She's been quieter than normal since you disappeared."

Nodding, I head to her room and knock on the door. "Hey Skye, it's me. You got a sec?"

"Come in."

"Hey, how are you doing?" Looking around the room, I see she's put some pictures up on the wall that she's drawn. "Did you do these?"

"Yeah!" She nods, almost embarrassed.

"Skye, these are wonderful. I can take you shopping for supplies if you need anything."

She flushes with embarrassment again, "It's just a silly hobby. It's not important."

"Says who?"

"My mum used to."

I sit on the edge of her bed. "You've never really talked about your life before you came here?"

She shrugs. "I like to try to forget it. Some things are easier to forget than others."

"You wanna talk about it all?" I crawl up to her bed and rest my back against her headboard. She's quite small, really, about five-foot-two maybe, with mousy brown hair, freckles across her nose and chocolate brown eyes with gold flecks in, she is pretty when she smiles, but it doesn't happen enough.

She shrugs again. "When you're not so busy, ya know, saving the world and stuff!"

I bark a laugh at her. "Saving the world and shit? I'm definitely no superhero, kiddo!" I shake my head. "I'm kind of an arsehole, in case you haven't noticed!"

She smiles sadly at me.

"Ya know, when you're ready to talk, I'm here to listen no matter what. I'm never too busy! No judgement, No questions asked, if you don't want me to."

"How many people have you killed?"

"Shit! Too many!" I shrug at her. "Does that upset you or make you feel unsafe? I'll never hurt you, ya know!"

She's shaking her head. "I've never felt as safe as I do here, but what happens when I have to go back? What then?"

"Why would you have to go back?" I ask. I've never made her feel like this has to be temporary. I've tried to make her feel at home as much as I can.

"I just can't stay here forever." She sighs. "You'll get fed up with me being a drain on you soon, and I'll have to go."

"Why don't you tell me what's going on? Honesty, start to finish, and then we can decide what you want to do, but I told you, you can stay as long as you want!" I pinch her chin between my finger and thumb and lift her face to look into my eyes. "No secrets now, but you can stay no matter what you tell me, okay?"

"I know you'll look at me differently when you know it all. You'll see me as broken and damaged and send me away!"

"Skye, look around. We're all broken and damaged, but the only way you're leaving here is if you want to, simple as that. Come on, trust me, and if I can help, I will!"

Looking away from me, it's barely a whisper. "I think I'm pregnant."

A lonely tear slides down her face, and she looks at her hands in her lap. I slide my arm around her and pull her to me.

"Just tell me, was it consensual? Was it someone from the club?"

Dropping her head to my shoulder, she shakes her head, and a small sob comes out.

"Skye… I need you to tell me, did one of the guys here force you?"

"No! It was before I was… sold." She lets out a breath as tears fill her eyes and track down her cheek, pooling at her lips before trailing over her chin and dripping down her neck. "My mum's boyfriend."

"Did he force himself on you?" She nods, unable to hold my gaze, grabbing her chin again and raising it up to look me in the eyes. "Don't do that! Don't be embarrassed about what someone took from you without your consent! Don't ever be ashamed of surviving."

"What am I going to do on my own with a baby?"

"Firstly, you're nineteen— "

"Twenty-four," she interrupts.

"Twenty-four? Okay, secondly, you're not on your own." I pinch her chin harder to stop her glancing away. "What do you want?"

"I don't know!"

"Whatever you need, I'll help you, but if you're pregnant, then we need to get you checked out by a doctor, okay?"

"What if they tell him where to find me? I can't go back! I… " she trails off and sobs a little more. I pull her closer, holding her to my chest as she sobs some more. Once she's done, she screws her hoodie sleeves into her hand and wipes her face.

"Firstly, we have a clinic on our payroll. I'll take you there, you'll be safe, and I won't leave your side while we're there, okay? Secondly… you want me to kill the bastard?"

Her eyes shoot to mine, searching for the truth in my question. Would I do it? Yep. Would I enjoy it? Yep. Would I let her watch? Hell yep!

"You'd do that?" she asks with a shaky breath.

I wink at her. "Of course not. What kind of person would do that?" I grin at her, and she physically relaxes.

She shakes her head, smiling. "I wish I was strong enough to kill him myself."

I grin at her. "That I can help with, but you need to tell me everything!" I grip her tight and kiss her head. "Get some sleep, kiddo. We'll go to the doctor tomorrow, and then we can talk about everything else, okay?"

She nods and scoots down into bed as I get off the bed and reach the door. "Ray?"

"Yeah, kiddo?"

"Thank you. I'm glad you found me! And even though I'm older than you, you're still going with kiddo?"

"Yup! Me too, kiddo! Now, get some sleep. We're gonna have a busy few weeks, okay?"

"Night." She huffs a laugh.

"Night, Skye."

Finally, I'm back at work. It's been a busy few days with doctor appointments with Skye and a little extracurricular research on her mum's boyfriend, but I'm mainly back because Dozer has to go on a job with Dice and Steel; they are gonna be away for a few days. He's only taken a few light jobs for me even though I'd tried to convince him I'm fine. I've almost finished my office with all the time off I'd been given.

My stomach starts to growl. It has to be nearly lunchtime. I'm just gonna pull my phone out and give Barbie a call when I hear the familiar voice sail through the garage.

"How's my favourite girl?"

"Holy hell, are you psychic, Barbie? I was just gonna call you!"

He shakes a bag at me, winking.

"Fuck, I think I Definitely-Married-The-Wrong-Guy Barbie. I mean, Steel didn't even call last night, and here you are delivering all my favourite things."

There's a big yawn from behind me as Hades stretches and strolls on over.

"There's a cheeseburger in there for you too." Barbie grins down at Hades and scratches him behind the ear as he rubs against his leg before coming and nudging the bag.

"Thanks, Barbie, you're the best." I give him a kiss on the cheek as he leaves. I lock the doors down for the day and head upstairs for my late lunch. Apparently, it's mid-afternoon already.

While eating, I check my phone. Still nothing from Steel. I've sent him four messages, but no replies. I'm starting to worry it isn't like him to go more than a few hours without some kind of message. I mean, me, on the other hand, if I'm working, I'm working, and that's that, but him, it's odd.

Wife: Travel safe, baby. Miss you already. x

Wife: Hey, baby, let me know when you get there. x

Wife: Night, gorgeous. x

Wife: Morning, handsome. Sleeping on my own sucks. Call me when you get a chance. x

I read and reread the messages, but fuck knows what's going on. I throw my phone on the counter while I tidy up and give Hades some fresh water. I'm done for the day, so I'm gonna go up to the office for a few hours. Maybe that will distract me enough.

As I'm heading down the stairs and across the back of the clubhouse, my phone blings in my pocket. I'm smiling like a fucking teenager on a promise before I even pull it out. My grin only gets bigger when I see his name. It says, "Steel sent a video" on my home screen. Opening it up and pressing play, I freeze. It's Steel naked on a bed. Although I can't see his face, the rest of him is in clear view. I can hear giggling, and that's when the need to vomit hits me.

Then the phone starts shaking as whoever's filming climbs onto the bed. I catch a glimpse of the side of a woman's face as she climbs up his body, still aiming the camera at him. She slides her hand up and around his dick, licks it, then plunges it into her mouth.

I drop my phone while I throw up my dinner against the back of the clubhouse. My eyes start to stream. I buckle to my knees and continue to heave till nothing else is left. Flopping back onto my backside, I collapse against the wall. The video has stopped playing, and I snatch my phone off the floor, take a deep breath, and hit play again.

I see the woman slide up his body again and grab his dick. She licks, then plunges it into her mouth, making all sorts of sloppy sounds. *Wait a minute...* I play the beginning again. Now I'm mad, not just mad, fucking livid. She's sucking at his dick, moaning around it, and then she pops it out of her mouth and starts talking.

"Oh honey, I'm still so sore from you fucking me so good all night. You're such a dirty boy." Then she kisses up his abs and back down again. "Oh yeah, honey, you want me to suck you again, huh?" And she does.

This isn't right. There's something way off. I wipe my mouth and take in a deep breath, sliding my phone into my pocket. I storm into the clubhouse. I go straight to Ares' office, throw the door open and storm in.

"Where the fuck is he?"

"Oh hey, Boyband, how are you? You look so good today! You done something new with your hair?" Ares says in a girly voice.

"Are you shitting me right now! Where. The. Fuck. Is. He?" I grab my phone and throw it at him. "Play the fucking video."

I snatch the phone back, put the code in, and toss it back. "Play. The. Fucking. Video!"

"Chill, Ray. What's crawled up your butt?"

He presses play on the video, and his face pales. "Look, Ray, it's probably not quite as bad as it sounds. I mean, they're away from home, it's — "

"Are you seriously making excuses about cheating right now?"

"Look, it won't mean anything. I bet there's a good explanation."

"Look closely, dickhead! There's a fucking great explanation. Firstly he isn't even fucking conscious. Secondly, I've never seen his dick that soft, like ever, so I'll ask you again. Where. The. Fuck. Is. He?"

Ares plays the video again as my phone rings in his hands. "It's Beauty."

"Hey, Mrs! It's not a good time. Can I call you back?"

"Ray, fuck, I've just received a video from Dozer... Ray, he's with another woman." She sobs into the phone.

"Beauty, say that again!"

"Shit, Ray, this video just came from Dozer's phone. He's in bed with another woman. She's sucking his dick and everything... Ray, what the fuck am I supposed to do?"

"Beauty, listen to me real close, okay? Lock the doors and windows, and pack a bag. I'm sending someone to get you. It's not real, Beauty... the video, it's not real... Ares, who's here?"

"Tank's in the bar."

"Beauty, I'm sending Tank. Don't go anywhere with anyone else. Pack a bag enough for a week. You're coming to stay at mine. I'll wait till you get here. I'm gonna get our men back! I got a video, too, okay? Just lock up and pack up. Tank's on his way!"

I'm already storming down the stairs towards the bar. "Tank, emergency! I need you to get Beauty from home, bring her back to mine, don't go anywhere else! Grab her and bring her back, and be on high alert. Something is going on!"

Fuck, I love my brother. He grabs the truck keys and runs out the door! "What the fuck's going on, Ray?"

"Where the fuck have they gone? Is it just Steel, Dozer and Dice?"

"They went to a meeting with a new supplier, testing the waters."

"What new fucking supplier, Ares?"

"The Armoury! They set up a meeting like an interview to see if we qualify, if we fit their criteria to supply us."

"Shit!" I storm out of the clubhouse and towards the apartment.

Opening up my phone with my "alternative" PIN number, the automated voice answers.

"VERIFICATION?"

"Sierra 8674463," I recite.

"VERIFIED! … IDENTIFICATION?"

"Black Queen, Delta 1."

"CONFIRMED! … REQUEST?"

"Patch to White King Alpha 1!"

The disguised male voice comes across.

"White King Alpha 1."

"Request Team. Full Tactical. Availability?"

"Black King and Black Rook available!"

"Request immediate pick up from HB going in hot, going in blind."

"Affirmative pick up request accepted, on the ground in twenty!"

Hanging up, I run up the steps. I'm vaguely aware of Ares shouting from behind me, but I don't stop. Flying into the weapons room, I dig into the bottom drawer and drag out all my gear. I've created a false bottom in the base of the drawer. Stripping off, I pull on my thick, black socks, black combat trousers, black combat boots with knife sheaths on the outside, tight black long-sleeve jumper, and bulletproof vest. I strap on my gun holsters and my thigh holsters, and I slide my knives into the sheaths attached to the back of my combat belt. I load my pockets with ammo and grab my balaclava and gas mask. I load my ammo belt with grenades, flash bangs, and tear gas.

"Skye!"

"Yeah.

"Don't leave the apartment till I get back. Beauty and Tank will be there with you." I don't wait for an answer.

Grabbing the dog's tactical harness and dog gas mask, I storm out into the apartment. "You ready, boy? Shit's about to go sideways. Wanna test that training out?"

Hades barks at me and lets me put on his gear. "Work mode, Hades. Toilet!"

Hades runs down the stairs and round the back to do his business. Skye comes out into the apartment, takes one look at me and just nods. I hear a screech of tyres. I head out down the stairs. Tank is pulling up with Beauty. They both get out of the truck, and Beauty runs to me.

"Ray, what's happening?"

"I'm not sure. I just know they're in trouble! Do not leave my apartment till we're back! Tank, stay with them. Skye's inside!"

There's another screech of tyres, and everyone spins around. Ares and the rest of my brothers are standing in front of the clubhouse, mouths open. The screech is from a black military armoured vehicle. Black King is behind the wheel, and Black Rook gets out from the back, both dressed in full tactical gear, balaclavas and gas masks.

"Hades, come!" I shout as I slide my gas mask on and pull my balaclava on over the top, tucking it into the neck of my top. The only skin visible is our hands. Black Rook opens the boot. "Hades, in!" I tell him as I approach the vehicle. Hades jumps into the back. Ares is still standing there catching flies as I dive into the front seat, and Black Rook climbs into the back. Tossing him my phone.

"Video from Steel, trace it!"

We screech out of the car park, leaving the guys from the MC with more questions and no answers.

"Head north, Black Rook. Find me my fucking husband."

He doesn't say a word, just flips the tray down with his laptop attached and goes to work after about fifteen minutes of driving blind he informs us.

"Got him! Uploading coordinates!"

The map screen on the dash springs to life and starts puking out directions. We're about forty minutes out.

"Wanna talk about it?" Black Rook asks.

"Nope, stay on mission. Emotions will get us killed. This has to go down like any other job! It can't be personal!"

"Ray— "

"I said it can't be personal, Black Rook. That's when things get sloppy! I can get fucking emotional when I'm home, with my husband, in my arms, in my bed. Till then, it's business as usual!"

"Affirmative!" Black Rook says, and we drive in silence for the next thirty minutes.

"Ten minutes out!" Black King breaks the silence.

Black Rook leans over, clips the cameras and mics to Hades' tactical harness/bulletproof vest, and adjusts his gas mask.

"You ready, boy?"

He barks in reply.

"Boots on the ground in seven minutes, dog in, surveillance mode only. I want to know what we're up against. If it's the so-called 'Armoury', capture the main players for interrogation. Everyone else… Eliminate!"

"Site images show a cluster of four warehouses, suspects potentially in the northeast corner," Black Rook informs us.

"Park in the trees to the southwest, approximately one klick from the target building. Go in on foot!"

We load up and move out, checking the other three warehouses, and we move closer to the fourth.

"Visual on two targets, move around extinguish from the rear."

Moving into position, I nod as Black King grabs one guy. I grab the other, plunging the blade into their carotid and tossing them aside. Black Rook opens the door.

"Hades, find them. Stay dark!"

We pull up the footage on Black Rook's screen on his forearm. "We have visual, three hostages bound to chairs, unresponsive centre of the room, five targets close by, swapping to thermal, seven heat signatures plus three hostages." Glancing over, we take note of where everyone is, speaking into the mic. "Hades, silent. Back to the car!"

We wait till Hades is clear, and then we slip in. There are two targets patrolling what looks like the mezzanine level, one on either side of the building. "Black King, stay low. Black Rook, mezzanine left, I'll take right, meet back here." Slipping into the shadows, we both take out our targets, slipping back to Black King.

Getting closer to the guys, we can see they're unconscious, bound to three chairs in the centre of the room. There's one guy who is more animated than the others giving instructions and one who looks to be more under his command than the other three. This one's nodding at each piece of information he's giving. Maybe he's younger, a little greener, a new guy. These are the two coming with us.

I pull out my tear gas. "Three, two, one." I launch it straight over their heads. Black Rook takes the left, Black King the right, and I go straight down the middle. The five targets are further towards the back, so hopefully, the guys won't suffer too much from the tear gas. Who am I kidding? It's gonna sting like a motherfucker!

We reach out to the guys and lay the chairs down that they're on, to keep them low, shooting off one round each. We eliminate the three we don't need for interrogation, double tap between the eyes. The guys' eyes are already tearing excessively, probably burning, and they'll definitely be suffering blurred vision. Their noses and mouths will be burning, and they'll have difficulty swallowing and drooling.

One target shoots off a couple of rounds before I get to him, luckily, he can't see for shit, and they go wide. I take out my taser and spark him out. "Oooh, shocking!" I laugh. Black King does the same, taking the rope from our pockets and tying them up while they're sputtering and coughing before they can retaliate.

Dozer

I can hear mumbles, boots scraping, everything fuzzy and muffled. I try to open my eyes, but they seem too heavy. I move my hand to rub my eyes, but nothing happens. I barely register a twitch of my index finger. I try to take a deep breath, but my breathing seems laboured, and my chest is tight. I concentrate hard on opening one eye, just one. *Come on!* As it opens, it flutters shut again. What the fuck's happening? It feels like I'm floating, like I'm in someone else's body. I try again.

I hear a voice closer than the other voices, a female voice. "Three, two, one," she says. She sounds familiar, but I can't quite place it. I try again. Both eyes flutter open. There are a few sparks near the voices, and then smoke plumes out from the floor that doesn't make sense. The world tips 90 degrees, and now everything's at a different angle, and I'm lying on what I think is the cold floor. There's a series of bangs in quick succession almost simultaneously, followed by three thuds. Coughing and spluttering are going on, a few more bangs sounding further away, and everything is confusing, and then there's a zapping sound and a growl. I hear her again.

"Oooh, shocking!" Then laughter. I try to concentrate on her voice, but my eyes are blurry and stinging, and my throat is burning. My breathing is becoming a problem. The darkness starts batting at my heavy eyes, and I can't help but give in again.

Black Rook

Black King and Black Queen tie up the targets while I check on the hostages. They're all still out. Whatever they've been given has kept them wiped out. Dice has a cut or maybe a gunshot on his bicep, but it's just a scratch. Steel and Dozer look okay, although Dozer's eyes look red and puffy. I pull back his eyelid, and he must have had them open at some point for the tear gas to kick in.

"Dozer needs an eye irrigation." Black Queen nods, Black King tosses me the keys to the truck, and I jog outside to bring it around.

Hades is laid under the truck, and I signal for him to jump in the back. Pulling up at the warehouse, I open the back up. Hades gets out, and we throw the targets in the back. Hostages get water thrown over them, and Dozer's eyes are rinsed off, which makes them start to stir.

We concentrate on getting the hostages into the back seat and piling Hades in. Black King dives in the driver seat, and I climb in the passenger seat. Black Queen climbs onto my knee, and we set off as moaning and groaning starts from the back seat. "Your call, Black Queen," I say, and she nods.

"Safety first." She presses the button on the dash, filling the vehicle with general anaesthetic.

Pulling into our underground bunker, we exit the vehicle.

"All good," White King says as we head on over to him. He's standing with White Knight.

We all nod. "Like Clockwork," I say.

"How'd Hades do on his first mission?"

"He's a natural!"

"Good, you know the drill."

We all nod. White King, White Knight, and Black Queen get into the vehicle with the hostages, and we carry on with the next step of our mission.

Black Queen

Pulling into the parking lot in front of the clubhouse, I climb out of the vehicle, remove my gas mask and walk to the back, letting Hades out from the boot and removing his gas mask and harness. "Good job, boy!"

Ares stands glaring at me. "Don't fucking start, Ares. Now is not the time."

His jaw flexes and strains, but he nods. There's a screech of tyres, and Bran and Dane pull in at the side of the armoured vehicle I've just got out of.

"What the fuck's going on? You said to get here fast. What's up?" Dane barks out in slight panic.

White King and White Knight get out of the vehicle in their full tactical gear and gas masks. They open the doors and start dragging Steel, Dice and Dozer out of it, laying them on the ground still out cold.

"Bran, Tank, Priest, Blade, I need Dozer and Steel taking to my place, straight to the bathroom and stripping. They need scrubbing. They're covered in tear gas. Then put them to bed and keep an eye on them. They do not leave the apartment till I get back. Dane and Ares, can you take Dice to his room and do the same?" I turn to head back in the vehicle.

Ares asks, "What the fuck's going on, Ray? Who are these people?"

"Ares, I love you, Brother, but can we do this later? Much later? I've got people I need to secure in my office. And I need my boys taken care of."

"Sure!" He isn't happy about it, but we don't have time to go at it right now.

Placing my hand on his arm, I give him a tight smile, and he nods.

I jump in, and we head up to the office, driving into the barn and securing the doors. We get out, open the back and drag the targets out of the van. I head over to the rusty panel on the wall, lifting it to reveal the retinal scanner beneath. There's a clunk and a whirring sound as a hay bale moves, revealing the stairs. We drag the targets down the stairs, dropping them at the bottom.

The lights flicker on automatically. White King looks around the room, whistling, "Nice set-up you've got here, Black Queen. This is gonna do just fine! Where do you want them?"

"Just one in each cell and shackle them to the wall. I'll get what I need out of them."

White Knight and White King drag the targets into the cells, locking the doors behind them and heading back up to the armoured vehicle. "I'll let you know when I find anything. But right now, I'm gonna check on Steel."

The guys pile into the armoured vehicle, and I jump on the side, hanging on as they drive down towards the clubhouse with Hades running along beside us. Slowing down as they drive towards Ares, who's stood between the garage and the clubhouse, I jump off as they accelerate away and out onto the road.

"Well, that was excessively dramatic!" Ares still doesn't look impressed. "What's the situation, Ray? You're gonna need to give me something."

"I will, just not right now, Ares. I need to check on the guys, and then I need to get to work finding out what the fuck's going on. I've got two guys in my 'office' waiting on a chat when they regain consciousness. Until then, I can't really tell you anything!"

I head towards the apartment to check on Steel and clean myself and Hades up before heading over to visit with our friends.

"Ray?" Ares stops me. His voice is off. He doesn't sound right.

I turn and cock a brow at him. "What's up, Ares? You're worrying me with your tone!"

He casts his eyes down, then back up to meet mine. "Who's side are you on, Ray?"

Turning and stepping back towards him, I put my arm on his. "What are you really asking me, Ares?" I glance around. We're alone. There's not a soul in sight. "Talk to me!"

"Are you with us, or is taking you in gonna come back and bite me in the ass? Bite us in the ass? I'm asking, Ray, are you gonna rip my best friend's heart out?"

I sigh. "I think we need to talk, and we will. I'll tell you what I can. Can you give me forty-eight hours? That's all I ask. Believe in me till then. I will have answers for you by then. But I love Steel. I love you, I love you all! I'm not gonna do anything to hurt any of you. You're my family!"

He nods as he pulls me into his arms and hugs me like he loves me back! "Why the fuck are you… spicy? …What the fuck is that? Jesus, I can taste it… Ugh, why are my eyes stinging?"

I laugh as I pull back. "Sorry, tear gas!"

"Do I want to know?"

"Maybe some other time. Now go shower and get those clothes off, or you'll be sorry." I wink and walk away.

Stalking into the apartment, there's no one around, so I head straight into the bathroom, strip off in the shower, and start scrubbing Hades down. The door creaks open, and Bran walks in. "Hey, you good?" He steps in and closes the door.

"How is he? How are they?"

"They're all good. All decontaminated and asleep, they stirred quite a bit and mumbled but didn't fully come back around. Should be out for about another half hour, give or take, so I'll ask again, you good?"

"Yeah!" I breathe out. "I am now. Thanks, Bran… ya know, for everything!"

"Love ya, Sis." He opens the door, "I'll grab you some clothes."

"Bran, I love you too. Make them work clothes. I'm heading up to the office to get this shit squared away and figured out. Ares has given me forty-eight hours before he wants answers." Bran nods and leaves the room.

After scrubbing us both clean, I head out to the kitchen, grab Hades some steak and chicken and drop it in his bowl. "Stand down, Hades. Good boy. Eat and sleep, pup. You did good today!"

I knock on the spare room door. "Beauty, it's Ray." The door flings open, and I'm thrown into the wall by the tiny redhead, arms thrown around me with a big sob! "Hey, is Dozer okay?"

"Fuck, Ray. Yeah! How the hell did you manage to get them all out? Dice is the only one with a small scratch! Who the hell are you?"

Grinning at her, I squeeze her harder. "I'm the motherfucking Reaper!" I whisper, and she barks out a laugh.

"Fuck, girl, I love you forever."

"Back at ya! Now go look after my brother while I go check on my husband."

She squeezes me again and slides back into the room. Heading into my room, Steel looks so peaceful. *Fuck.* I take a shaky breath as Bran steps in behind me, sliding his arms around me.

Taking another shaky breath, I ask, "What if they make me choose?"

"They won't!"

"You don't know that." I close my eyes and drop my head back onto him for support. "I can't lose him, Bran. I just can't!"

"You know we've got your back, always."

"It's not as simple as that, Bran, and you know it."

He squeezes me tighter and says, "I won't let you lose him. Stay here. I'll go to the office to get this sorted."

"No, I need to find out. I need to get the answers. It's fucking Gerald, of all people. Just stay with them, yeah. Message me when they wake up. I'll be back when I know something."

He hugs me again before I turn and leave. I can't even hug or kiss Steel if I do I know I won't leave, and shit is hitting the fan already, it looks like I'm on cleanup!

Dane

The tires screech as we pull in at the side of the armoured vehicle Ray has just got out of.

"What the fuck's going on? You said to get here fast. What's up?" I bark out in slight panic.

Two guys get out of the vehicle in their full tactical gear and gas masks. They open the doors and start dragging Steel, Dice and Dozer out of it, laying them on the ground still out cold.

"Bran, Tank, Priest, Blade. I need Dozer and Steel taking to my place, straight to the bathroom and stripping. They need scrubbing. They're covered in tear gas. Then put them to bed and keep an eye on them. They do not leave the apartment till I get back. Dane and Ares, can you take Dice to his room and do the same?"

Ray turns to head back into the vehicle. But Ares stops her. I don't listen. I head over to Dice and start to lift him, Bran helps me get him up, and I throw him over my shoulder.

"I've got him," I say to Bran once he's secure on my shoulder.

"Yeah, I'm sure you do, little brother!" Bran grins at me before heading over to the other guys to grab Steel and Dozer.

Walking into the bar, there's a guy cleaning some glasses. "Hey man, can you show me where Dice's room is and let me in?"

"Sure, kid!" He steps in front of me till he gets to Dice's door, then opens it for me to walk in. "You need a hand?"

"Nah, I'm good, thanks. Can you get someone to make a sandwich for us both, but wrap it up and send some fizzy drink or orange juice, something sweet if possible? That would be great. Thanks, Barbie."

He grins at me. "I didn't know you knew my name!"

"I make a point to know who's important to my sister." I smile back.

"I'll have everything brought to you straight away, kid!"

Walking into Dice's room, I kick my way into the bathroom, leaning him against the wall on the toilet. I step into the shower and get it running, rinsing my hands while I'm in there, grabbing some towels, pulling the duvet back, and laying them on the bed. *Fuck, how the hell am I gonna do this?* I grab some boxers from his drawer, placing them on the bedside table. What else do I need?

I spin around as Barbie walks back in. "Hey, kid, here's what you wanted. I'll put it down over here. My number's next to the sandwiches in case you need anything. Drop me a text, and I will have it sent over!"

"Thanks, Barbie, I appreciate it!" He nods and steps from the room. I lock the door behind him and head back to the bathroom. I strip off down to my boxers, grab a bin bag from under the counter and throw my clothes in it. I've only picked Dice up, so it shouldn't be too bad, but it's better to have them clean than risk it!

I take Dice's top off, tugging a bit where the blood has dried from the graze, trying not to perv. I lean him back, remove his boots and socks and undo his belt and his fly, resting my head under his arm and lifting him onto my shoulders. I slide his jeans and boxers down. I gulp as his dick springs free. Fuck, why do I put myself in these situations? I may or may not have a tiny crush on Dice from the wedding. What can I say? Dude is hot in a suit! And now I'm realising it's not just in a suit! And maybe it's not a tiny crush.

I let out a shaky breath as I lift him into the shower. I pin him with his back against the wall. I slide my knee between his legs, supporting him and letting the water run over his head and face. He starts moving and mumbling, stirring as he's coming around.

"Hey, Dice! …It's Dane! Can you hear me?"

His eyes flutter, and his head lolls to the side. I lean in closer, holding him against the wall. "Dice… Hey… Dice." He smiles a little and flutters his eyes again, mumbling something intelligible. His head starts to loll forward, but he stops himself, almost like he's drunk.

He mumbles again and lifts his hand up, slapping me in the face before dropping his deadweight arm again, his head lolls forward, and I lean my head against him to hold him up. "Dice, are you with me?"

"Mmm, yep."

"I'll take it," I grin. I lift my hand to his cheek and tilt his head so he's eyes are level with mine. We're about the same height. "Dice?"

His hand comes up and hangs onto my wrist. His head tries to loll again, and I keep hold of him. We're about an inch apart at this minute, and I glance at his full lips, with droplets of water dripping off them. I take a breath and blink the water off my lashes as a grin tugs at the corner of my mouth.

"D-D-Dane?"

My eyes shoot up to find him watching me, although I'm not sure he truly sees me. His eyes look unfocused. "Hey, you good?"

He closes his eyes, takes a deep breath again, and tries to flutter them open. "Come on, let's get you to bed." I pick him up again and take him out to the bed. I lay him on one towel and pat him dry with the other, sliding on a fresh pair of boxers.

I head to the bathroom cabinet, grab some painkillers, and leave them and the drinks on the bedside table. I grab myself a pair of boxers and lay down next to Dice, pulling the cover-up over him. He's mumbling again, and he looks purely exhausted.

I turn on my side to face him. "Get some sleep, Dice. I'll be here when you wake up." I stroke his hair back away from his face, his soft tan skin still glistening from some of the water I didn't manage to dry, his dark hair still glistening wet from the shower. Hades, this man is fucking attractive. Shame he's into women. I run my fingers across his cheekbone and jawline before tucking myself up next to him. I can just close my eyes for a minute.

Gerald

It's dark... I think it's dark, or my eyes are closed... Why can't I open my eyes? What happened? My head hurts... My throat hurts... My eyes feel scratchy.

I try to open them, and it burns. I wince at the pain. I know that feeling, that smell, that taste, fucking tear gas! Who the fuck used tear gas? No one knew where we were. I can smell it and taste it, fuck. I try to open my eyes again. I lift my hand to rub my eyes, but there's just a twitch to start with. My limbs ache, and everything feels spongy. Sounds fluffy. Where the fuck am I?

I try to open my eyes again, only to wince, taking a deep breath. I force them open. They feel so dry and scratchy. I try to talk. "H-hello?"

Fuck, that's like trying to swallow razor blades. I start rolling my eyes, trying to get some moisture in there when I hear a choked-out cough. Managing to force open one eye, it's too blurry. I need to rinse my eyes. They're too dry.

"Who's there?" another scratchy voice wheezes out.

"Liam, is that you?" I try blinking again, and my eyes start to come into focus. "Liam, it's Gerald. Are you okay? Are you hurt? Where the fuck are we?"

"Gerald? Shit!" Theres a clunking, almost like chains, before I hear another curse. "Fuck."

I try to move and shuffle to rub my face. That's when I hear the chains fuck this is bad.

"Liam, where are we?"

"I don't know, man… I honestly don't know. They can't know we're The Armoury. They wouldn't take us if they knew that. We would be set free or dead." Liam tries to… I'm not sure what he's trying to do, but it's not reassuring.

I start trying to stir, shaking my arms to get some movement in them and blinking like my life depends on it. There's a clunk and whirring noise, then footsteps. "Shhh, don't fucking say a word. Leave it to me!" I bark at Liam.

I glance around, and bars come into view. I think we're in a cage, maybe. Blinking like mad, I hear footsteps coming closer down some metal steps before there's a gasp from Liam.

Blinking again, I see the figure walking towards us, then stop to grab a chair and drag it over to the front of the cage. The noise is grating as they drag the chair across what sounds like a concrete floor. They spin the chair, and the guy sits on it backwards and slides it forward slightly. They cock their head to the side.

I start to see more clearly. It's a woman, yeah, definitely a woman. "Hey, sweetheart, you need to let us out. We can help you. Do you know who we are? Sweetheart? Do you know who we work for?"

She scoots the chair further forward, and I squint and blink again through my dry, scratchy eyes. The chair scratches across the floor, and she's walking away. "Wait, what do you want? We can help you."

I hear something dragging across the floor, and the next thing I know, there's water crashing into me, knocking me back into the wall. It's moved up from my chest to my face, causing me to splutter and try to catch my breath, choking on the freezing water. The water's shut off, and I can breathe easier, freer. I blink back the dry eyes, and they feel so much better.

Taking a few blinks and rolling my eyes around, I start to see more clearly. The girl is back on the seat, glaring at us both. "Do I know you? I ask her seriously, confused. She looks so familiar, that blonde hair, the scowl on her face, those blue-grey eyes. Where do I remember her from? She smiles at me, and that's when I remember. It's *her*. What the fuck was her name…? "Mary? Marny? …Madi?" I shake my head. I just can't quite place the name. She grins again and, in that subtle Southern accent, says, "Well, looky what we have here."

"M-Madison?" I breathe out, fucking Madison! She was at The Armoury training camps. She was pathetic and got booted out at least a few times. I think we even fucked once. I lie to myself, truth is I know we fucked.

"Madison!" I bark at her. "Let us out now. You know who we work for, and you're fucked if you don't let us go… NOW!"

"Well, bless your heart, Gerald, ain't you just about fixin' to be madder than a wet hen?" She laughs out, that Southern twang irritating as ever, that too sweet voice, that too kind, too soft girl that never amounted to much is sitting on the outside of a cage grinning like a cat that got the fucking cream.

"Madison, listen. I will call our employer. I can put a good word in for you. I can get you back into the training programme. I can help you make a real shot at it this time! I can help. You need to let us out before they come back."

"Bless your heart, Gerald." She smiles again.

"Is that a yes? You'll let us go?"

Barking out a laugh. "Ahh, Gerald, ain't you just the sweetest, and what makes you think I need your help, sugar?"

"You didn't get in! I did… that must right piss you off, Madison!" I spit her name at her, and she just grins again.

Fuck. I need to stay calm. I'm supposed to be professional and reveal nothing in this situation, but it's her, its Madison. I haven't thought about her in years. Well, that's a lie. I may have misplaced her name, but I remember the feeling of her under me and on top of me. I've played it over on more than one occasion, fuck, she's still sexy.

"Who are you really working for, sugar?" She glances over at Liam, and he's watching us both like hawks. "You and I both know you ain't in The Armoury, sugar!"

I glance over at Liam and back to Madison. She's still got that apple pie smile and those flushed pink cheeks. I remember her sucking my dick at one point.

That sweet way she has about her always drove me crazy. There's something in her eyes, but as I try and study them more, she blinks and moves away! Rising from the chair, she steps closer to Liam.

"What about you, honey? What's your name?"

"Don't talk to him!" I spit out. "This is between us, Madison!"

"Why did you want those little biker guys, sugar?"

"Madison, just let us go. You know we're The Armoury. They will come for us, and I don't want to see you get hurt. You know I always had a soft spot for you."

"Bless your heart again, sugar. The Armoury will come; you and I both know that! And as far as your 'soft spot', we fooled around, sugar. No harm, no foul!"

I glare at her, then back at Liam. His eyes are wide, his breathing patchy. He has no clue what's going on, but me and Madison have a history. I just need to twist it to scare her to let us go. "Where are those redneck brothers of yours, Madison? What were their names? Milton and Milo? If you don't let us go, I'll make sure they're tortured or worse." I push up from the cot I'm sitting on and lunge forward to grab the cage bars. She doesn't even flinch, so I slam my hand through the bars and grab at her, but she's sat just slightly out of reach. She rises from the chair, stepping over to Liam. "Who do you actually work for, honey?" She smiles at him.

"The Armoury," he says, standing from his cot, too.

She shakes her head at him. "Who told you you work for The Armoury, honey?" He glances at me and back at her, then at me again.

"I recruited him!" I straighten my shoulders. "I'm his superior. I'm in charge. Let him go, Madison."

"Y'all have torn up my last nerve. I'm gonna pray for you, sugar!" She points at me in disgust.

She shakes her head and turns to grab a... tranq dart, shit! She jabs it into my thigh, and there's a pain that feels like burning or freezing. It's excruciating, and my leg goes numb. I feel foggy and stumble. It feels like only minutes before I give out, and as I crash to the floor, my eyes roll into my head. I hear her laugh.

Liam

Gerald drops to the floor and is out cold. She just laughs. "Okay, kid, are you gonna cooperate, or am I gonna have to get creative?"

The accent's gone, well, the Southern one, anyway. Is she British? She opens a drawer full of knives, screwdrivers, and all sorts of weird-looking clamps. I glance from her to the drawer and back again. "I'm not cut out for this. If I tell you what you want to know, you'll let me go?"

"Of course, honey!" she drawls back at me, slipping back into that Southern accent. She grins, and I shake my head, trying to make sense of what she's up to.

"Please, I only took this job to pay for my grandma's residential care home. I need the money. Gerald said it was quick money."

She drags the chair over to my cell. "Look, kid, I just want to know what's going on. Answer my questions honestly, and I will get you picked up and taken out of here, okay?"

Dropping my head to the cell bars. "Okay… just, please. I need to get back to my grandma. I need to pay for her care."

"Who do you work for?"

"The Armoury."

"Who told you you were working for The Armoury?"

"Gerald."

"How long?"

"Three months."

"What training did you have?"

"Training…?"

"Why did you go after the Reapers?"

"There was a job, one of Gerald's guys died, and the bikers came looking around the area after. He wanted information. Gerald said they were a rival group, so we were gonna ransom them back after we had the information he wanted."

"What do you think The Armoury does?"

"What?"

"The quicker you answer, the quicker you go!"

"We run security for events, protection."

She grips the bridge of her nose and shakes her head.

"Does Gerald have a boss?"

"There's a guy he messages, but they never speak. I don't know anything more about him!"

"When you went on the job where the guy died. What was it?"

"Security at an event, some people were kidnapping a judge, so we went in to secure the place while the other team rescued the judge."

She shakes her head again. "Why do you keep shaking your head?"

"Because, kid, you've no fucking clue who you're working for or what they actually do. You've been made to be a fucking mug, but why? That's what I want to know. What the fuck is Gerald playing at?" She stands from the chair and grabs the dart stick.

"Please just let me go. I don't know anything—" There's a scream. I realise it comes from me as the dart penetrates my thigh. I rip it out as quickly as I can, but the pain is immense, the warm, then the burn—or is it cold?—then it's freezing, I can't tell. I stagger as I try to stay upright, tears streaming down my face, and I stagger again, dropping to my knees after what seems like about five minutes. I'm face down on the floor. My breathing shallows, and my vision is limited and patchy. It's going black, going, going, gone!

Black Queen

I drag Gerald out of the cell and dump him on the table. God, I'm a genius. That hydraulic table makes life so much easier. I can just roll him onto it and jack the twat up!

Stripping him to his underwear and strapping him down with the leather straps, I pull up my toolbox. It's the same as the one we have in the garage, but this one contains my "other" tools. I grin to myself as I sort through the drawers, familiarising myself with the positions of things and moving things I'm not happy with. It will take a while to have everything just where I want it.

I start taking notes of things I want and things I need for my kit, writing in my little notebook so I can place my order. I have a penchant for blades. I have every shape and size you can imagine. I had to start my collection again when I moved here, but I have a very, very long list of contacts over here, so it hasn't taken me too long to gather a relatively adequate collection at this point.

There's always room for improvement, though. I pull out my scalpel. I'm gonna start intricate and work my way up to deranged. There's no point starting out that way, as then you have nowhere to go. And Gerald still thinks I'm that sweet Southern belle he railed as a teenager. Oh, someone is in for a surprise.

Gerald starts to stir. "Well, hello there, sugar," I drawl in my fake-as-fuck Southern accent, "looks like you drifted off there for a minute, sugar." I grin down at him. His eyes start to flutter as his body starts to wake up.

His eyes slowly drift open and grab onto mine. "How ya feelin', sugar?"

He tries to move his head, but I've got him strapped to the table by it, and his biceps, wrists, torso, thighs, and ankles. Ya know, just to make sure there's minimal movement.

"What do you want?" he spits.

"No need to pitch a hissy fit, sugar. I just wanna talk."

He flattens his lips together as if to tell me he won't, but I know differently. "I'm gonna ask you a question, sugar, and if you answer correctly, I won't cut ya. If you lie or refuse to answer"—I waggle my scalpel and then point to the toolbox in his peripheral—"then we're gonna see just how many cuts it takes to kill you deader than dead!" I smile sweetly at him.

"Madison," he tries to reason. "You really don't want to do this. You know how powerful The Armoury is!"

"That I do, sugar." Grinning at him again. "But The Armoury don't scare me. So let's start small, shall we?" I twist the scalpel in my fingers. "Who do you work for, sugar?"

He takes a breath and sighs like I'm an idiot. "The Armoury!"

I smile and push the tip of the scalpel into his forearm just enough to cause a grimace. "Well, heavens to Betsy, looks like this is gonna be a long day. I hope you didn't have any plans, sugar. That's your only warning." I twist the scalpel in my fingers again. "Who do you work for, sugar?"

"The Armoury!"

Standing over him, I press the tip of the scalpel into his bicep and drag it slowly, about three inches, causing him to clench and grimace in pain. "Who do you work for, sugar?"

Through gritted teeth, he says, "The Armoury."

I nod and smile, digging the scalpel deeper, this time into his chest and dragging it five inches across his pec. "Who do you work for, sugar?"

I can see the sweat starting to bead on his forehead, it is warm down here, and he's tensing like a motherfucker trying not to show how much it hurts. "The A-a-armoury," he stammers a little.

"Who do you work for, sugar?" I smile down at him again. He always hated my sweet smile.

He closes his eyes. "The Armoury," he breathes out. His eyes fly open as I push the scalpel into his cheek, and he yells out!

"Eyes on me, sugar! Who. Do. You. Work. For?" Before allowing him to answer, I start to drag the scalpel along his cheekbone, and he grits his teeth and tries not to move. "Think hard before you answer, sugar. My patience isn't what it used to be!"

His eyes stare into mine, trying to find some resemblance to the girl he remembers, the sweet Southern girl who tried her hardest to fit in, who they ridiculed over and over for her failure to be tough enough, fit enough, ruthless enough, clever enough, she never quite cut it, but did it all with a sweet apple pie smile and that really gripped him, he tried to take advantage and fuck it out of me a few times, but needless to say, you can't change someone when they're not that person to begin with.

The funny thing is, I never was that girl. "Who do you work for?" I dig the scalpel in this time, dragging it down his thigh roughly as he screams out in pain. "Who do you work for, Gerald?" I stab the scalpel in again, dragging down his shin without waiting for an answer. My actions are aggressive, but my voice is calm and sweet, with that Southern accent front and centre. "Who do you work for?"

Again, I stab into his stomach and drag across his abs as he clenches and screams out. "Who do you work for, sugar?" I stab into his other peck, drawing down towards his nipple. "Who do you work for, sugar?" He's panting and screaming, but I don't give him a chance to take a breath.

I stab into his ribs and drag it down towards his stomach. "Who do you work for, sugar?" Eat, sleep, rave, repeat, I stab, I drag, I ask who he works for, then again and again till he starts hyperventilating and passes out. "Shit!"

I sit back and wait, cleaning my blade and keeping an eye on my other prisoner. He came around at least an hour and a half ago and hasn't murmured a single word. Even when he pissed himself fifteen minutes ago, he didn't mutter anything.

"Who do you think he works for, honey?" I ask, spinning my head towards him as, in shock, he stumbles back onto the cot. I rise and go to stand at his cell. "Who do you think he works for?"

"I-I-I d-d-don't kn-n-now!" he stammers out.

"Do you still think he works for The Armoury?"

He shakes his head and hangs it down to the floor. "I-I-I d-d-don't know what's h-h-happening." He looks up at me and back down again.

There's a murmur as Gerald starts to come around again. "Well, hello there, sugar." I walk over to him. "Ready for round two?" I say in my sugary, sweet voice. I've swapped my scalpel for my skinning knife. "So, sugar, I thought we could ramp things up a tad."

I slide my skinning knife into the wound on his thigh, and as he screams, I slide it parallel to his skin just under the surface and start to slice a patch of skin off. He starts sobbing and crying out, "P-p-please don't, pl-l-ease?"

I hear heaving from the other guy as he starts to puke as I remove my first piece of flesh. "Bless your heart, honey. You might wanna look away. It's only gonna get worse from here."

Gerald still screams and sobs as I remove another piece, then another. "S-s-stop p-p-please!" He sobs. "P-please!"

"Just tell her what you know, Gerald, please. It's not worth it. Just tell her!" the other guy yells out toward Gerald.

"They'll kill me." He sobs.

"Ahh, sugar, you're already dead. The only thing you'll change by talking is how long before you take your last breath and how painful it has to be. Tell me what I ask, and I'll make it real fast, sugar!"

He closes his eyes. "I thought we had something? What happened to you?"

"Ah, sugar, there ain't time for my life story. The bit you can have is we fucked, we lost touch, I found you, you die, the end!"

"Okay!" he shakes out.

"Okay?" I've been at this for a good six, maybe even eight hours or so, and my boys have woken, kind of and passed out again from possible sheer exhaustion and the cocktail of drugs, probably. I just want to hold my husband, but this motherfucker is dragging this out!

"I work for The Armoury." He sighs, and as I slam the knife into his thigh, he screams, "I do… I just work for Dante Crane, too!" He screws his eyes up and lets out a shaky breath, followed by a sob as tears roll down his face. "Dante recruited me a year ago. I don't know why he wanted the Reapers. My team thinks they work for The Armoury. I don't know anything. He just gives my team jobs, and we do what he says."

"What does Dante have you do?" I ask in my normal accent, and his eyes bug out of his head. "Gerald?" I snap.

"Normally just stalking, kidnapping or security for important people so he can get something on them, and I inform him on The Armoury. That's all I know. I swear that's all I know!"

"You sure?"

He nods and then closes his eyes. While his eyes are closed, I hit him with another tranq dart, and his eyes bug out again as he cries out.

"See you on the other side, sugar!" I wink. He's still a handsome guy, the kind of guy I used to fall for before I quit guys and had whatever it was I had with Jer. Gerald is the kind of guy I thought I wanted, I thought he would accept me, but he never knew me. He knew her, Madison, fucking Madison. We met a long time ago, a different life ago, a different person or ten ago. He served his purpose back then, but now he doesn't have a purpose. He's surplus to requirements. Once he's out again, I lower the table and drag him back to the cell.

"You're not gonna kill him?"

"Not yet!"

Stalking out of the room, I lock up and head towards home. I log into my app on the phone and bring up the CCTV of my office so I can listen and watch.

Dice

I can feel his breath on my face, the heat of his body against mine, his hazel eyes and dirty blonde hair. He's been haunting my dreams for a while now. I can never quite place him when I wake. He's so real, so familiar, but also not. This feels more real today, though. I shuffle closer to his heat while I still can. Once I wake, I know he will be gone.

I reach out and groan as I feel his hard abs under my fingers as I slide my hand up his chest. I can almost feel his muscles bunching under my touch. I slide closer to him. I rest my head on his chest, sliding my hand back down his abs, hitting the waistband of his boxer shorts. I slide my leg up his leg and over his hip, grinding myself into him.

I feel a hand slide up my arm and neck, cupping my cheek. "Dice?" His voice almost questions me. "Dice, can you hear me?"

"Mmhmm." I nod and then sigh. I'm so content I'm not sure I want to wake up.

I feel a hand slide down my cheek to cup my jaw, "Dice? Hey, Dice."

I freeze, my eyes fly open, and I gasp as a look of concern crosses his face. "What the fuck? I scurry back like I've been burned.

"Hey, Dice, it's okay. You're safe. It's me, Dane, I'm here!"

I slide up, slamming my back against the headboard, and let out a shaky breath, screwing my eyes up and scrubbing a hand down my face. "What are you doing here? What happened?"

"What do you remember?"

"Did we…?" I trail off, slightly panicked. *Shit, if I fucked Ray's brother, she's gonna string me up.*

"No! …Dice, what's the last thing you can remember?"

"Erm… the meeting with The Armoury… I don't remember anything after that."

Nodding, he sighs. "They weren't The Armoury! Whoever they were, they drugged you all and took you." He pauses as if he's looking for the right words. "They sent a video of Steel and Dozer to Ray and Beauty of them with a woman… Ray lost her shit and came and got you all, but you were all out of it, so I had to stay with you to make sure you were okay. We got you back yesterday."

"Shit!"

"Yeah, that about covers it." He grins at me. "Here." He reaches around, grabbing a couple of pills and a glass. "You need to take these, and I'll get Barbie to send some food down. We don't know what they gave you, so we need to keep an eye on you for a few days." He grins again. "Looks like I drew the short straw." He winks and slides off the bed.

Is he flirting with me? Nah, fuck it, I must have been totally out of it and drugged well and truly to be thinking that. He's totally into girls; he has that cheerleader thing, and he's a kid, and he's Ray's brother, Ray's kid brother at that. Fuck, whatever they gave me has right fucked me up.

" ...Did you hear me? Dice?"

"What?" My eyes shoot up at him. I blink again and shake my head. "Sorry!"

He leans over with some orange juice. "Here, drink this. It should help. Food will be here soon. If you wanna shower, just get up slowly, but leave the door unlocked in case you need me, okay?"

I reach to take the glass and wince, glancing down at my arm. There's a small bandage around my bicep. I take a gulp of the juice, swing my legs off the bed, and take a deep breath. I stand, a little shaky, but I make it to the door of the bathroom. Turning to face Dane, my eyes skate up his body, taking in his physique. He's lean like an athlete, ripped but not bulky like Bran. He's clearly packing, which makes me subconsciously lick my lips as my gaze rakes up the V, dipping into... wait, are those my boxer shorts?

I cock a brow, and a frown of confusion must flash across my face. I continue my gaze up his abs and his pecs; his arms fold across his chest, which breaks me out of my trance, and my eyes fly up to his. He has a smirk across his face, and his hazel eyes are glinting at me in amusement. He's about my height with dirty blonde, dishevelled hair. I swallow as I glance down at his smirk and back to his eyes.

"You good?"

"Hot... really hot!"

The smile that spreads across his face is fucking sexy as fuck, and that itself elicits a gasp of surprise as I feel my dick stirring.

"You need a…" He quickly glances down at it and back up to my gaze. "Hand?" He bites down on his lip.

I fumble for the handle and go back into the bathroom, shaking my head. As I step into the bathroom, I close the door and lean against it. What the fuck just happened?

Steel

I wake up feeling queasy and slightly groggy. I go to sit up but grab my head. "Motherfucker!" A body moves at the side of me, and I glance over to see my wife only to find… her fucking brother… in my bed… with me in my underwear! "What the fuck, Bran?"

"Morning," he replies sleepily.

"Morning?" I question. "Bran, why the fuck are you here? Where's my wife? And why the fuck does my head feel like I've got a herd of fucking elephants tap-dancing to a drum band in it?"

He grins over at me. "Ray told me to be here, she's in the office, and that's a longer story, here!" He grabs some pills and a glass of water and hands them to me. "Why the fuck are you wearing my clothes?" I shout after him as he leaves the room.

A few minutes later, he comes in with a glass of juice and a bouncing Rottie, who dives up on the bed and licks my face before looking at Ray's side, whining and laying down, resting his head in my lap. I rub my fingers behind his ear as I drink the juice. Bran slides back onto the bed, sitting against the headboard and crossing his legs at the ankles.

"What do you remember?"

"The meeting with The Armoury. Where's Dice and Dozer?"

"They're fine. Dozer's in the spare room with Beauty, and Dice is in his with Dane. They weren't The Armoury! You were drugged and taken. They sent a video of you with another woman to Ray and one of Dozer to Beauty, they—"

"What the fuck do you mean with another woman, Bran? I wouldn't. Where's Ray? I need to see her… " I dive up but then stagger and fall back.

"Fucking steady, you daft twat! We don't know what they gave you. You need to take it steady for a few days!"

"Where's my phone? I need to call her… Bran, my fucking phone?"

"Listen, you don't really want to talk to her while she's 'working'…" He makes stupid fucking air quotes around "working". "She's not herself at the minute and needs to work through some things!"

"Fuck, Bran, she doesn't think I would, does she? I wouldn't! I couldn't! I… " I trail off as I drop my head back to the headboard and drag my hands through my hair. "How bad is it? Does she hate me? Can I salvage anything?" Letting out a sigh, I ask, "How fucked am I, Bran? Give it to me straight."

He's grinning at me like a motherfucker when my eyes meet his.

"Aww, you're just so fucking adorable. You honestly believe that if you had cheated on my sister, you would be sitting here now talking about it... with me? Cute, Steel, real cute."

"Bran, I know you'd kick my ass—"

He barks out a laugh at that and shakes his head. "You're such a fucking clueless dick. You all are!" He shakes his head again. "You've no idea who you've married, do you? You poor motherfucker!" He huffs a sigh and puts his hand on my shoulder. "Steel, I love you like a brother, mainly because you're married to my sister, and she loves you more than anything.

"I've never seen her like this... ever... but Ray is like the puppy you get from the pound that's cute, adorable, loyal, and loves you almost unconditionally. She will do anything for you, but the second she feels any kind of betrayal, she will rip your throat out in your sleep! And then go right back to sleep herself. If she believed for one second that you had cheated, she would have killed you in that instant. Don't let her love for you cloud the reality of who she really is."

"Who is she really?"

"That, Brother, is for you to figure out, but she's not cross with you. She is working, and this she has to do on her own. Trust me, you don't want to see her like this! She will do whatever it takes to get the answers she needs, and she will stay there till she does. I'm here till that happens. My sister trusts me to look after you and keep you safe. Don't make that difficult for me, Steel, or I may have to kill you myself!"

"I don't need a babysitter, Bran. You're just as ridiculous as she is if you think that."

"You keep telling yourself that." He winks at me. "Breakfast?"

"Sure."

Dozer

I take a deep breath as I wake up. Everything feels fuzzy, like a hangover from hell! I take another deep breath, wincing at the headache that's pounding in my brain. There's a murmur beside me, and I lean over. Beauty's next to me, but we're not at home.

I slide up against the headboard, and Beauty turns over. "Hey. You're awake. Thank the motherfucking Reaper!"

"What?" I scrub my hand down my face and through my beard. "Where are we?"

She slides up to sit next to me, leaning over and cupping my cheek. "You okay?"

"I don't know… what the fuck happened?"

She looks a little sheepish. "I don't know… we're at Ray's. Something went wrong with the deal. You were all drugged and taken. Ray lost her shit! They brought me here, and then she took off after you with two guys in an armoured truck, armed to the back teeth, decked out in all black balaclavas and gas masks and came back with you all unconscious. Shit,

Dozer, I don't know who that girl is, but I'm glad she's on our side."

"Dice and Steel? Are they okay?"

"Yeah, Dice has a small graze, but just the effects of whatever drugs they used."

"Where's Ray?"

"I don't know. They dumped you all in the parking lot, unconscious, drove off up the back road, and came back later. Ray showered and left again and hasn't been back since. That was yesterday."

There's a knock at the door, and Beauty tells them to come in. Bran and Steel step through the doors.

"Hey, you good?" Steel asks.

I nod. "You?" He nods, and we just stare at each other. "Do you remember anything?"

He just shakes his head. "You?"

"I vaguely remember some tear gas and three people dressed in black. I remember a woman laughing, and I… fuck, I don't know?" I shake my head and scrub my eyes.

Beauty leans over, drops some pills in my hands, and gives me a glass of water.

"Apparently, we're under house arrest here until my wife shows her face!" Steel says, glaring at Bran. "Apparently, we are to be babysat till she graces us with her presence."

"Don't get pissy! Think yourself lucky she trusts you enough not to kill you when she saw that video!" Bran spits at Steel.

"Video?" I frown at Steel, then glance at Beauty as all the colour runs from her face, and she starts to shake. "Sweetheart, what's wrong? What video?"

She climbs out of bed and over to her phone. She pulls up the video, holding the phone to her chest. "I love you, but I can't hear that again. I'm going for a shower. Just wait till I'm out of the room before you play it."

She tosses the phone on the bed, grabs the towel and her bag and walks out the door, not looking back.

Taking a deep breath, I press play. I watch, my stomach turns, and I close my eyes and shake my head before screaming out and throwing her phone across the room! My heart is racing. I can feel the bile in my throat. I feel sick, angry, and violated, but most of all, I feel guilty.

Steel picks up the phone and presses play. I keep my eyes scrunched up as I hear it all over again. When I look up, I see the sheer look of horror on his face and the rage that's there.

"Did she get one like that as well?"

Bran nods.

"Fuck!" he roars as he throws the phone back across the room and he storms out. There's a clatter and a scuffle before Steel bellows out, "Get. The. Fuck. Off. Me. Bran!" There's more scuffling, and the dog starts barking. "Bran! You motherfucker let me go!" I step out of the room on shaky legs, and Bran has Steel face down with his arms wrenched behind his back, pushing the side of his face into the floor. I mean, Bran's a big lad, but Steel's a fucking mountain, and yet Bran's holding him down.

"Guys, come on. We need to find out what's going on, not fight amongst ourselves, fuck's—"

The door opens into the apartment, and all our eyes fly up to find Ares, Dice, and Dane standing there. "What the fuck's going on?" Ares barks out.

"What the fuck are you doing here? She told you to keep him in his room. She really doesn't need anything to get in her way right now!" Bran barks at Dane.

"Yeah, I'm sure she'll be thrilled if she walks in and finds this whole… situation… like, seriously, man, get off him." Dane bends down, shoves Bran off Steel, and gives Steel a hand.

The door opens again, and Priest, Tank and Blade walk in. Just as the bathroom door opens, Beauty steps out. She lets out a small gasp at seeing us all there, then walks past me with her head down and into the bedroom. "Beauty…" I sigh. "Give me a minute, guys."

"Scar will be here in five minutes. She's taking Beauty back to our room. We all need to talk about what the fuck's going on, and the only people I trust are in this room. Well, you two …" He points at Bran and Dane. "I'm not sure I fucking trust either you or your sister, for that matter!"

"What the fuck, Ares?" Steel barks out as he crosses his arms over his chest.

"Brother, don't, you have no idea —"

The door opens again, and Scar walks in. She walks straight over to Steel and wraps her arms around him, looking up at him. "You okay?"

"I'm okay." He places a kiss on her head and gives her a squeeze.

I turn to go to the room Beauty's walked into, but she's already coming back out dressed with her bag in her hand. She walks past me with her head down and walks toward Scar. She grabs her wrist and heads towards the door. "Beauty!" I gasp, so much pain in one word. She turns to me, giving me a tight-lipped smile, and walks out the door. Closing my eyes, I sag into the door frame.

Brans is in front of me in a second. "Hey, come and sit down." He helps me to the couch, sits down, and passes me the blanket. "You good?" I just shake my head. What else can I do?

Dane's in front of me a second later with a glass of juice. "Here, it'll help. You all need to eat something." He walks to the kitchen and starts rummaging in the cupboard. Grabbing out the bread, he starts making sandwiches before walking over and placing a massive pile in the middle of the coffee table. Everyone sits down and starts eating. No one says a damn thing.

Ray

When Gerald wakes up, he's groggy at first, and then he panics.

"Madison?" he murmurs. I sigh.

I've been sitting, waiting for him to wake up. The other guy, Liam, has been quiet as a mouse and keeps his head down. I don't have any answers for anyone other than Dante Crane. I mean, who the fuck is he really? He's the one making waves. He's the one who is linked to the Hellhounds and Tali, but who the fuck is he? I need more. I can't face Steel until I have a reason for what happened to him.

"Well, nice of you to join us, sugar!" I smile at Gerald. He physically shakes as he scooches back to the cot and craws onto it. "You feeling any more helpful? Sugar?" He winces as he moves, as the tugging from the wounds pulls with his movements.

"I-I-I don't k-know anything else, please!" he gasps out.

"I must admit, sugar, I'm massively disappointed in you! Dantes is going to be very dissatisfied too when I tell him my report on how well his 'recruits' …" I use the air quotes to emphasise my point. "Hold up…" I shake my head. "There's definitely no promotion for you, Gerald. On the other hand, Liam here hasn't squealed at all!"

"Y-you work for Dante?"

"Sugar!" I shake my head. "You're just a major, major disappointment to the whole organisation. I'm gonna have to make an example of you." I step up and turn around, whistling while I rummage through my toolbox, grabbing out my blow torch and lighting it up, firing it up a few times. I switch it off, and I set it next to the table!

I stand and head towards Gerald, sliding the gun out of my pocket. "Only one of you is gonna make it out alive, sugar." I point to Liam. "You snitch, you go, you don't, he does." I turn to Gerald. "Same for you! You've got till the count of five to start talkin'!"

"Please, I don't know anything. My grandma needs me!" Liam begs.

Gerald looks at Liam and back at me, then back again. "I'm sorry, Liam!"

Gerald takes a deep, shaky breath. "Where do you want me to start?"

"I want you to start at the beginning, sugar, as all good stories should. Dante must check every ounce of information to ensure nothing is leaked or compromised!"

I train the gun on Liam as he whimpers and begs. Gerald starts talking, and bless his heart; he leaves no stone unturned. He lays everything out for me clear as day, going into the finest detail about Dante's organisations, the jobs he's pulled, the information they gathered, and the passwords to his encrypted sites. He gives me everything. The thing is, Gerald was always a rat who only looked out for number one.

Once he's done squealing like the little pig he is, I pull my phone out of my pocket. "Is that everything, sugar?" He nods and glances back at Liam. My gun is still trained in his direction; the slight smirk that slides across his face makes this a whole lot easier. "I'd like to say it's been a pleasure, sugar, but... fuck you, Gerald!" I pull the trigger, and he crumples straight to the ground.

Liam just gasps. He's splattered in Gerald's blood, but he just stares at me in shock. "B-b-but?" He glances at Gerald and wipes his face with the back of his shaking hand. "B-b-but?"

I attach the surveillance footage with audio to my report and send it all in with the instructions. "Dinner for one at Cletus's, request pick up in thirty minutes." I let out a steady breath, you're gonna have to hang tight Liam, till I get my orders!" I say, accent dropped. Now, there's no point pretending anymore.

I grab one of the bags I've made. It's a huge, almost tarpaulin, with hooks on the corners and around the sides. I lay it down on the floor and open Gerald's cell, dragging the piece of shit onto it. I slide my toolbox and table to the side and head to the bottom of the stairs. There's a winch attached to the ceiling. Releasing the cable, I drag it across to Gerald, hooking every hook into the multiple carabiners hanging from the end. Starting the winch, it drags the bag all the way to the bottom of the stairs. There's another at the top of the stairs in the barn for when I need to get him up the stairs. I mean, work smarter, not harder, am I right?

I grab the hose and clean down the cell. The whole room is like a giant wet room. I give Liam a little spray down, too, while I'm at it because I'm nice like that, and by the time I've cleaned the room down, I can hear the rumble of the truck.

I check the feed from the camera in the barn and click the release to open the door. As the door swings over, White King and White Knight have arrived, coming down the stairs.

"Good job!" White King acknowledges as he arrives at the bottom of the stairs. I nod and walk up the stairs to grab the other winch. I connect it all up and click the button, and it drags the bag up the stairs.

"Ooh, I like that." White Knight nudges my arm. "You've made a few modifications to this kill room."

"Stop calling it the kill room. It's my office!"

"Sure it is." White King chuckles. "Nice office!" And then he winks at me. That's all I can see through the balaclavas and gas masks they wear.

Hauling Gerald into the back of the truck.

"Hey, I want my tarp back. I had that specially made. Drop him at Cletus's. When's White Rook gonna look at the footage I sent?"

"He's still on a mission. He and White King have requested a three-day extension, so they'll be on their assignments till then." I nod. "What about the other guy?" I nod in Liam's direction.

"We're taking him."

I nod again. "As is?"

They both nod, so I head over to Liam and unlock the cell, un-cuffing him. He hangs his head and walks towards them. Pulling out handcuffs and a bag, they cuff him and put it over his head, leading him to the back of the car and locking him in. White King walks around, pushes the button on the dash and shuts the door. The general anaesthetic floods the car, and it's not long before he's out.

"What are you gonna do with him?"

"Depends what the footage shows. He will be kept in holding until we declare whether he will be a liability. Then, we will proceed accordingly." Again, I nod. They climb into the vehicle and head out.

I grab the hose and clean everything down again: the table, the cells, the floor, my tools, everything. Taking a look at myself, I'm covered in blood. "Fuck's sake, it's a good job I like red," I mumble to myself!"

As I get to the door to the apartment, I slip off my boots and socks, choosing to go barefoot as my boots are covered in... Gerald, along with the rest of me, really. All I can hear is arguing through the door and multiple raised voices. I don't have the patience.

I've used it all up, and I've no fucks left to give, so I slam the door open glaring at every motherfucker in that place! I haven't eaten in fuck knows how long. I'm hangry, I'm tired, and I'm still reeling from the video. I need a moment to myself to process everything, and I can not be held accountable if I flip and kill one of these motherfucking dickheads, so I do the one thing I can do. I continue glaring as they all spin to face me, the look of sheer horror on some of their faces as I hold a single finger up, close my eyes, take a deep breath, and storm across the room into the bathroom.

After cleaning myself in the shower for nearly an hour, I wrap myself in a towel. As I go to leave, there's my joggers and t-shirt on the counter. I slide them on and take a deep breath before I leave the room. As I walk out, the room falls silent again, and all I see is mistrust, trepidation and nervous energy.

Steel's just coming out of the kitchen area with a sandwich and a drink. He puts it on the counter, walks straight over to me, picks me up, and clutches me to his chest.

He whispers into my ear. "I'm so sorry you had to see that... I would never... I could never..."

I kiss him like I can't breathe without him when we finally pull away. "That's how I knew you were in trouble!" I rest my head into the crook of his neck and just breathe him in! "I will always come for you!" I breathe into his neck. He leans back at me and smiles a sad smile, which I return—cupping my cheeks in his hands and turning my face from side to side, staring into my fuzzy eyes.

"When did you last sleep? What about eating?"

"What day is it? Fuck knows, the last time was when you went!"

"Bed, eat. The vultures can wait." As he says this, he glares at them all. "Everybody out! We're done till she's rested."

"But..." Ares trails off.

"Bran, Beauty, and Dozer stay. The rest of you can fuck off till I tell you otherwise!"

He grabs my hips, turns me to face the bedroom door, and slaps my arse. "Bed!" He walks over, grabs the food and follows me into the bedroom. "Bran, lock up when they've fucked off!"

Dice

After Steel tells us all to fuck off, we head back towards the clubhouse. I turn to Dane. "You can fuck off! I don't need a babysitter! Especially when said babysitter is a fucking child!" I mean, it's an insult, really. He must be about fucking twelve.

"Ahh, if this was about what you wanted, I wouldn't be here. Until my sister tells me otherwise, you best get used to it, roomie." He slings his arm around my shoulders and walks alongside me.

"Argh, fuck off, will ya? You're such a dick!"

He just laughs and shoves his hands in his pockets, following along beside me. I storm through the clubhouse into my room and shove the door shut in his face.

He pushes through the door. "Real mature. Who's the dick now?"

I strip off my jeans and slide into bed. "I'm fucking tired. Keep it down, dickhead."

"Sure thing, Grandad. I'm going for a shower."

I must have been tired. I don't remember falling asleep. I just remember him, those hazel eyes, that dirty blonde hair artfully dishevelled. I can never make out the rest of his face or anything else for that matter, but as the man of my dreams leans over and kisses me, I don't ever want to wake up. I'm here; I'm free to just be, and he makes me feel… everything.

He slowly runs a hand over my cheek and down my jawline, rubbing his thumb over my lip before devouring me. His hand slides down, pinching my nipple and my back arches off the bed into him. He grins at me, even though I can't see it. I know it's there.

He rubs himself into my thigh as his hand trails across my stomach, abs, and velvety shaft. His thumb rolls over the head, causing an involuntary thrust into his hand. I groan into his mouth. Those eyes remain on me like he's trying to reach my soul. I grind against him, needing some contact, needing some release.

"Dice," his voice is but a whisper, but I love the way it sounds from his lips. I groan again as his hand travels up and down my aching cock. I buck again, "Dice." It's slightly louder this time. I groan again as I thrust up into his hand. I'm so close.

"Dice!" My eyes start to roll back in my head and then flutter open, meeting his beautiful hazel eyes. His artfully dishevelled hair is now wet. I'm vaguely aware his body weight isn't on mine. Why has he stopped kissing me? My eyes flutter closed as I pull him down and smash my lips into his again. There's a clash of teeth, and he stiffens as I slide my tongue along his lips, tasting the coppery tang before plunging my tongue in.

I reach up and grab his hip, pulling him down onto me again so I can grind into him. I'm so lost in him. He's everything I've ever wanted and more. I kiss him more aggressively, and he groans into my mouth, and I try to devour him the way he does me every night. I reach down and cup his ass, grinding into him and causing a groan from both of us. "Dice." His hand comes up to cup my cheek, and I melt into it. "Dice!" Fuck, I love the way he says my name. "Dice!" my eyes flutter open. "Dice." His face is full of concern as he tries to pull back from me. I pull him in and crash our lips together again... wait. I gasp and scurry up the bed, slamming my back to the headboard and scrubbing my hand down my face. "Dice?" He's staring into my eyes now with a slight smirk. "There you are!"

"What the fuck, Dane?" I gasp out as he stands off the bed, droplets of water slipping down his tanned, muscled body, doing little to help the raging, aching boner I have. He is totally naked as he stands at the side of the bed, hands on hips, sporting his own rather impressive boner. I can't take my eyes off him. I can't take my eyes off *him*. I let out a shaky breath. "What the fuck happened?"

"I thought you were having a nightmare. I came to help you, only you grabbed me, kissed me and started grinding yourself into me. I thought I was saving you from a nightmare. Turns out it was a dirty dream, real fucking dirty by the sounds of it!" He smirks again. "So, you gonna finish what you started?" He gestures to his dick.

Glancing down at it, he twitches it at me, standing with his hands on his hips and dick pointing my way. He shakes his hips from side to side. "Well?" He nods down at it again.

"You're such a fucking dick!"

He laughs and walks backwards to the bathroom, snatching the towel off the floor, "I'm gonna take care of this…" He's gesturing to his dick again. "All by myself! You know where I'll be if you wanna join!" He winks and backs into the bathroom, pushing the door to.

I groan as I thrust a pillow in his direction, only it pushes the door open. I slide back down into the bed, trying to slow my heart rate that's trying to pound out of my body. As the shower fires up, I glance that way and have the perfect view of the back of him. He looks like he's sculpted by one of the greats, Michelangelo. As the water runs down his body, he raises his arm to the wall and rests his forehead on it, and his other hand slides around and takes hold of his cock. I can see his muscles bunch and his cheeks clench as his hand pumps. I can't look away. It's like a car crash; you know you shouldn't look, you don't wanna look, but you find yourself slowing down and rubbernecking to take in every available view. I can't believe he's been the man in my dreams. He's a fucking kid, I feel disgusted, but I still can't look away as he continues to pump his dick. He spins around, slamming his back into the tiles, and his head falls back against them.

He picks up his speed. Nothing could ever happen between us, that's exactly what it would be, a fucking car crash, but I still don't take my eyes off him. He puts his forearm on the glass screen and rests his head against it, looking down at himself as he pumps faster. His thighs bunch and his hips thrust, and still, I can't look away. He comes all over the glass with a shudder, and his thumb slides across his head, causing vibrations through his body. I subconsciously lick my lips, and he wipes the come onto his thumb, raising it up. I follow that thumb, wanting to suck it, lick it clean as he pushes it between those luscious lips and the sexy as fuck smirk slides across his face, causing my eyes to shoot up and meet his, those hazel eyes boring into my soul. "Shit," I gasp out as I slam my eyes shut rolling slightly on my front to trap my aching pulsing cock between my hip and the bed.

I hear the water shut off, and I keep my eyes closed. There's a soft chuckle, and a moment or two later, the covers pull back, and the bed dips behind me. I try to keep my breathing calm, but my heart is hammering in my chest, my mouth is suddenly dry and as he slides in behind me. Feeling his warmth against my back, I hold my position when all my traitorous body wants to do is relax into him. His fingertips lightly graze the bottom of my back, between where my boxer shorts sit and where my t-shirt has slid up. I bite my lip to try and stop any reaction to him.

This is not happening! This will not happen! He's a kid! He's Ray's kid brother! He's my best friend's kid brother. She would fucking kill me and then drag my ass back from hell just to kill me all over again.

I feel his breath skate across my neck as he slides closer so his body's flush against mine, and I freeze. "Playing hard to get?" he whispers. Another breath flutters across my cheek. "Game on, Dice… I'm coming for you!"

The heat from my back eases as he rolls away, and all I feel is empty. I feel… I feel… lost. I've found the man of my dreams, the man in my dreams, and I know I can't have him because he's a fucking child and my best friend's kid brother, to top it all off. I let out a sigh as I relax, and he chuckles from behind me. "Sweet dreams!" I can hear the grin in his voice, the fucking dick!

Waking up, now I know it's him. He's in my dreams again. I can see all of him, feel all of him. He consumes every sleep-filled second, and my mind has filled in all the blanks, all the missing pieces and every agonising moment of that kiss, the feel of his hands on me. I groan and flip onto my back. He's next to me. Still asleep. I turn slightly to take him in. The covers are bunched up around his waist. He has one arm behind his head and the other under the covers. One leg has snaked out and is resting on the bed on top of the covers. He's all long muscled limbs and firm. Everything's so toned. He looks strong but young, far too young. I groan as I slide out of bed. Grabbing some clothes, I head to the shower.

As I slide into the shower, I rest my forearm against the tiles and rest my head against it, resting the palm of my other hand at shoulder height, and I just lean into the spray of water and close my eyes. He's all I can see now, I screw them shut, but that sexy smirk he gave me when he caught me watching is all that's there.

It's not until a hand slides over my stomach and the other slides up to my throat that I feel his front press against my back. My initial reaction is to relax against his touch, but as I feel his hand slide around my cock I grab his wrist.

"What the fuck are you doing, Dane?"

"Morning." he whispers as he kisses my shoulder, trailing kisses and nibbling along it, squeezing his wrist tighter.

"Dane?" I gasp out. Even though I have his wrist, he still strokes his hand enough to make me shudder. I feel him grin against my shoulder as he kisses along it and up my neck. "Dane!"

"Let me show you what we could be like together."

"Together?" I laugh. "Dane, we will never be together."

He squeezes me and ups his pace a little, causing a groan and my grip to relax. I feel him smile against me again as his other hand runs all over my body, causing goosebumps to break out everywhere he touches me. He pumps harder, and he pushes against my back, pushing me forward a little so my other hand pushes into the tiles to stop him from crushing me against them. He starts pumping harder now my grip is totally free, and I groan and relax against his body, looking down to watch his hands all over me. My breath hitches. My heart pounds in my chest, his hand pumps harder, and shit, it feels like heaven.

I screw my eyes closed as I groan my release against the tiles. While I pant and try to regain what little self-respect I have, he lazily kisses my shoulder. I can feel his rigid cock pushed into my ass cheek, but he's not trying for any more. He slowly runs his hands across my stomach, and as I come down from the high I shouldn't have had, all I feel is betrayed, betrayed by life that I can never have him.

I push back and turn around. "I can't do this with you. I just can't." I step to the side and go to leave the shower.

He grabs my hand. "What do you have to lose?"

Looking down at his hand around mine, I look back up to his face. "Everything!"

Stepping away, I grab my clothes and disappear into the bedroom.

There's a knock at the door. Swinging it open, it's Priest. "Hey, what's up?"

"She's ready!"

"Dane, get your ass out here. Ray's up."

The bathroom door opens, and the twat scrubs his hair dry with the towel, stark bollock naked! I scrub a hand down my face. "Will you put some fucking clothes on."

He stops rubbing his hair and glances in our direction, leaning on the door frame. "Oh hey, Priest." He waves and stalks through the room, grabbing my grey sweats and wife-beater and sliding them on.

"Seriously?"

"What?"

"Under-fucking-wear!"

"She's my sister. I don't think she's gonna notice my lack of underwear." He shoves past me and slings his arm around Priest. "So, how's it going?" I swear if he wasn't Ray's little fucking brother and sexy as hell, he totally wouldn't be getting away with this shit right now. I seriously need some space.

Ray

When I come out of my room, everyone's here, well, except Viking. He's still with Carmen, but there's Steel, Dozer, Ares, Priest, Tank, Blade, Dice, Bran and Dane.

Dane stalks over to me and scoops me up into his arms, hugging me tight. "You good?"

I nod, resting my hands on his cheeks. "I'm good!" He kisses my cheek and places me down.

Dice scoops me up next. "Thank you for coming to get us, Ray!"

"I'll always come to get you!" I give him a kiss on the cheek. "I don't want to appear ungrateful, but when can the 'child' babysitter leave? I'm good!"

I spear Dane with a look that tells Dice he is already free to leave.

"Motherfucker," he grits out between his teeth, and Dane just smiles before dropping onto the sofa right at the side of Dice and popping a cup of coffee in his hand. "Fuck's sake, can you get any closer?"

"Yeah!" Dane grins. "But then I thought it would be uncomfortable."

"It's already fucking uncomfortable!" He scrubs his hand down his face and turns to me. "I love you, Ray!" And I smile back, clearly his way of apologising for my brother.

Ares has been really quiet until now. "Can we get on with this." he barks out, and Steel slams him with a glare. I walk to the other side of the coffee table while they all sit on the sofa.

"Before I start, I want to say… I love you all. You are my family, and I will tell you what I can. There are some things I can't share and that's not because I don't trust you, but there are bigger things out of my control. Also, I'm on your side, and I will never hurt or betray any of you. You're my priority. That being said, if keeping things from you is in your best interest, you better damn well believe I'll do it." I glare this last bit at Ares as he shifts.

"So I… detained two of the guys who kidnapped you lot!" I nod to Steel, Dice and Dozer. "They were part of an organisation run by a guy called Dante Crane. I'm gathering information on him at the moment and will let you know as soon as I have anything. Apparently, you were taken as a vendetta against this club, the details of which we don't know either. The group is trying to pass themselves off as The Armoury, but I can assure you they have nothing to do with them… one hundred percent! Dante knows you would be excited to finally get in with The Armoury and be on their list of preferred clientele. I can also confirm this is all bogus.

"I can confirm that they did, in fact, think that Ares was one of you; therefore, this was a direct hit against him. All we know is they went through your phones, looked for 'wife' as a contact, and then hired a hooker to make the videos with your own phones. I've had my tech guy look through your phones, and there's nothing on them, so they're clean. I've also deleted the videos, and we've wiped them. They weren't distributed elsewhere, which makes us think this is personal. So, Ares, you must have had dealings with Dante at some point."

"I don't know anyone called Dante Crane."

"As we thought, but we're trying to get background and a photo as he could be anyone and be going by any name. I need you to stay vigilant while we're unsure what's happening, and don't let your wives, girlfriends, boyfriends, life partners, dogs, cats or hamsters out alone… okay, any questions?"

"What did they actually want?" Dice asks. "It seems a little petty sending those videos."

"It was petty and vindictive, which makes us think it's personal, definitely some sort of revenge."

"You keep saying us, we, who is that? As it's not us?" Ares gestures around the room.

"Me and my colleagues, when I can give you more info than that, I will… trust me when I say I'm working on it."

Ares opens his mouth and closes it again before changing his mind and saying, "So what you're telling us is nothing!"

"Respectfully, Ares, I don't have to tell you fucking shit! I'm giving you the courtesy of sharing what I can, but most of what I know is above your pay grade!"

"What the fuck's that supposed to mean?"

"It means we're fucking done here! Bran, Dane, I need a word before you go. The rest of you, I'm glad you're safe, and be careful. As soon as I've found something I can share, I will." I fold my arms over my chest. I stare at each and everyone one of them as they walk out the door, chuntering to themselves.

"I'll head over to the bar with the guys and give you all some privacy." Steel nods as he walks out the door, too!

"Fuck!" I flop onto the sofa.

"Hey, it's gonna be okay!" Dane tries to assure me.

"I need to call them."

Bran nods as I pull out my phone. I enter my "alternative" PIN and fire up the app.

The automated voice comes through the speaker
"VERIFICATION?"
"Sierra 8674463"
"VERIFIED, IDENTIFICATION?"
"Black Queen Delta 1."
"CONFIRMED!"
"Patch to White King Alpha 1."
"UNAVAILABLE."
"Patch to White Knight Alpha 1"
The disguised male voice comes through.
"White Knight Alpha 1,"
"Black Queen Delta 1! Requesting Status Request for The Reapers MC Ravenswood?"
"Standby… Level 3."
"Request full disclosure, request vote."
"Target?"
"Colby Steel!"

"Separate partial disclosure request vote inner circle The Reapers MC Ravenswood?"

"Request accepted. Submit your votes by the normal channel within seventy-two hours and await confirmation of outcome."

"Affirmative."

Hanging up, I say, "And now we wait!" I flop onto the sofa.

"And now we wait!" Dane smirks.

I punch him in the arm. "So why have you been torturing Dice? You didn't have to stay this long,"

Shrugging, he says, "I like him… like, like like him! He thinks I'm a kid, and you'll have a problem with it."

I shake my head. "Just be patient, okay? He'll come around. Maybe stop winding him up. No underwear's a nice touch, though." I laugh out at him, and the motherfucker grins back. "So while I've got you here, I want you close. How about you come to stay for a bit? We need to get this moving on our end. Dane, you can get on with that level 3 while you're here, and I need some help in the office."

"Can Demi stay, too? We're still trying to find somewhere, and Demi's had some news that she's not thrilled by." Bran shakes his head. "George is selling up."

"What the fuck? She could buy him out if she wants. She's loaded now, even with only the legit stuff."

"Yeah, she wants to be closer, though."

"How much closer?"

"Why?"

"I may have an idea. Gonna need to get on Ares's good side, though. I might have to give him a little something."

"Make it happen. Whatever it is, we'll back you." Bran grins. "I love it when we're devious and stick together!"

Bane of my existence: Meet me in thirty mins at the gym. Don't tell anyone!
Boyband: K

I'm in the gym when Ares stalks in. "What's going on, Ray? Huh?"

"Sit!" I gesture to the bench as I slide on, too.

"I can't answer all your questions, and certain things can't be told to the rest yet, but ask what you want to know, and I'll answer what I can, just me and you!"

"Seriously?"

"Yup!"

"How do you know it wasn't The Armoury?"

"We've done a full check, and I swear it wasn't them on my life!"

He lets out a shaky breath. "Who do you work for?"

"I can't tell you that… yet! I am requesting information for you, but I've got to go through the proper channels."

"Are you here under false pretences?"

"No."

"Is this the first time you've been here?"

"The States? No. This area? Yes."

"How many times have you been to the States?

"Too many to count."

"Just how dangerous are you?"

"I'm deadly. I'm meticulous and overly protective of those I love. You are one of those people."

"Are we safe with you? And this organisation?"

"Me? Definitely. Them? Probably."

Huffing out a breath, he asks, "What do I do, Ray? I have a club to protect and families relying on me. If The Armoury decides to wage war on us, we'll all die!"

"Firstly, it's not The Armoury— "

"How can you be so sure?"

"I know The Armoury, Ares. Trust me when I say this isn't them."

"Can you keep us safe?"

"I'm doing my best, Ares."

"So you're not an ordinary girl that just wandered in off the streets and ended up here accidentally?"

"Not an ordinary girl, no. Just wandered in, yes, definitely. This wasn't planned, and I never intended to stay."

"Scar?"

I smile at him. "Scar knows bits. She's not ordinary, far from it, but not in the same way I'm not ordinary. I think you already know that, though."

"How many men did you take out to get them back?"

"About seven, got two back here, one left alive, one in a body bag."

"I'm sorry I tried to pass it off as an affair or bit of fun while they were away. I know Steel would never do that. I just panicked. If you tell anyone that, though, I will be… very upset with you."

I laugh as I punch his arm. "Are we good, Ares? You're… important to me!"

"Yeah, we're good. You're important to me too!"

"Seriously?"

"Yep."

"Good, I need a favour!"

"Fucking typical!" He laughs as he shoves me in the head. "What do you need?"

"I want to move my brothers closer. Dane can stay with me, but Bran wants to bring Demi, and I need somewhere safe for them, like maybe a lodge if you have one spare. And also, what's in the room at the side of the garage?"

"Sure, there's a lodge left, but they fix it up themselves, and it's just random storage. Why?"

"I have an idea that I think you'll like." And then I tell him my plans, really selling the shit out of it. Finally, he agrees, and I can't wait to tell Dane, Bran and Demi the news. Standing, I hug him, and he pulls me in tighter.

"Are we gonna get through this okay, Ray?"

"I'm gonna make sure we do, or I'm gonna die trying!"

"Fuck, don't say that." He squeezes me tighter.

The door creaks open, and Steel walks in with his gym bag thrown over his shoulder. "Oh, the horror… my best friend and my wife, how could you?" He grins at us both as he stalks in.

"Brother, she's all yours. She's too much work and trouble for me to contemplate it."

I punch him in the arm as I shove him back. "Arsehole! You'd be lucky to have me!"

"Well, if there ever comes a time when I want you, feel free to call the asylum and have me committed."

Steel barks out a laugh, drops his bag and opens his arms wide. "Come here, baby. I love your crazy. You're perfect."

I stick my tongue out at Ares and jump into Steel's arms, wrapping my legs around him and smiling at him, taking in those swirling grey orbs and his beautiful face and dimples.

"How much of a workout are you looking for, baby?"

"Ew, gross. I'm leaving! And Ray, do what you want, you will anyway just keep me in the loop, yeah?" Ares heads for the door.

"Aye, aye, captain!" I salute him, and he shakes his head as he heads out of the door.

"So, this workout." I grin at Steel, winking. "How hard do you wanna go at it?" He groans as he kisses me and backs me up against the wall.

"So fucking hard!" My back slams into the wall. "I wanna do dirty, dirty things to you. Are you gonna be a good girl and let me do what I want to you?" He grinds into me, biting down on my lip and causing me to clench and groan around his tongue that he's just forced into my mouth to taste the blood seeping out of my lip. "Gloves or bare knuckles?" He drops me on my ass.

"What the fuck?" I laugh as he stalks over to the cupboard and grabs some boxing gloves. He throws a pair at me.

"Come on, wife? Show me what you got!"

Demi

Bran picks me up and tells me he has a surprise for me. He won't tell me what it is, but as we pull into the MC and around the side towards Ray's, I think we are visiting them. Ray is standing halfway down the steps to their apartment as Bran slows down. As we pass, there's a thud in the back of the truck and a double bang on top of the cab. Then Bran hits the accelerator.

"Jesus. Did she just jump in? Your sister is insane!"

Laughing at me, he says, "You're only just noticing now?"

I shake my head as we follow the track around the back of the clubhouse and up towards the gym. As we pass the gym—that's as far as I've been before—I say, "Where are we going?"

"Ray's got a surprise for us!" He shrugs.

As we clear the trees and around the track, I see a lake with cabins. The lake is in the shape of a heart, and there must be ten cabins around it, all with their own fishing docks.

We pull up to the cabin on the end and jump out. "Wow, it's nice up here," I say as Ray jumps down from the bed of the truck.

"Then, hopefully, you're gonna love my idea!" She grins and throws her arm over my shoulder. "You know when you said you wanted to be close? Is this close enough?" She points across the lake. I can see the apartment across the field.

I look at her and back at the apartment. "Eh." She spins me round to the cabin and pushes me forward.

When I turn to ask her what she's on about, she throws a set of keys at me and points to the door. "Close enough?"

"Seriously?"

She just nods. "It's gonna need some work doing as they've been sitting empty for a while, but go inside and have a look." Putting her hands on my shoulders, she pushes me forward.

With shaky hands, I open the door, and a tear rolls down my cheek.

"Oh, fuck! It's not that bad, a lick of paint and a bit of elbow grease!" She hugs me into her.

But I'm shaking my head. "No, No, it's not that. It's perfect. Can it really be ours?"

"If you want it." She beams at me.

"Can we move in straight away? We can do the work while we're here. I love it. I just want to be here now." I blurt out, and Ray laughs.

Bran walks in behind us, hugging us both. "Whatever you want, beautiful."

"Can we go get some stuff now? Can we stay here tonight? Please?"

"Sorry, no can do!" Ray butts in and pulls me back out of the door towards the truck.

"Wait? What? You can't be that mean; show me my dream home, then drag me away from it." I'm trying to pull back inside, but Bran sweeps me up from behind and walks me towards the truck. "Hey, you're supposed to be on my side."

They both just chuckle as we drive off back towards the garage. I cross my arms across my body and pout. I can't believe they would do that to me.

Climbing out of the truck in front of the garage, Ray throws another set of keys at me. "What're these for?"

"That door!" Ray points to the door next to the big garage doors. A big window at the side of it is boarded up. "Open it!"

I open the door and step in. Ray flips the lights on. It's a big space full of junk. There are two doors on the back wall. "I don't get it." As I turn around in the space, Ray and Bran are grinning at me.

"You wanted a bakery, maybe a coffee shop? Well, how about here?" Ray grins again.

My jaw hangs open, and tears swell in my eyes. "Seriously? Here? And the cabin? Seriously?"

Bran sweeps in and hugs me. "Only if you want."

"I want, I want so bad." I start bouncing on the balls of my feet, and Ray grabs my hand and drags me to the door on the right. It's a large cleaning cupboard with a little sink in it.

"I thought you could make this into a bathroom for your customers." She drags me to the other door, and as we push through, the space is as big as the front portion. "And here's your kitchen." She grins.

"There's enough room for a counter and a few tables out the front, and here is a kitchen to bake everything you want!"

"How much? Where do I sign? When can I start?"

Ray barks out a laugh. "Ares, no doubt, will want free coffee and apple pie for life, but you fix it up. It's yours, same with the cabin."

"Fuck, Ray."

"Demi!" She gasps at my language.

"Shut up and hug me. I can't believe it."

"Knock, knock." Steel comes strolling in with Ares In tow.

I bounce up and down again. "Did you know? Did she tell you? Oh my god, I'm so excited!" I throw my arms around Steel, then Ares. "Oh my god, are you sure? Is this really real? I can have my own store, business, and home?"

"That smile is totally worth it. You're the sister I always wanted." Ares grins at me and hugs me again.

"What about me?" Ray cocks her head and rests her hands on her hips.

"You're the sister none of us wanted!" Ares grins back at her.

"Dick face!" Ray spits back.

"When can I start?" I ignore them both.

"Where are you all?" Priest shouts from the door to the outside.

"In here!" I yell.

Priest walks in with Tank, Blade, Dice and Dozer. "Where do you want it all going?" Tank asks.

Ares rubs his chin. "The barn for now." Then, he turns to Ray. "Is that okay?"

"Yep, to the left, inside the doors. Don't go anywhere near the hay bale at the back, but other than that, it's fine. Watch out for the rolled steel. There's some on the ground, so be careful!" she tells them.

"You're moving this stuff now? Like right now? Oh my god." I start bouncing up and down like a three-year-old.

Steel pulls out a tape measure pen and paper. "Let's start measuring up."

It only takes an hour to empty the place, and then Steel hands me a roll of tape. "Start marking up where you think you want units and counters, islands in the kitchen, oven, dishwasher, whatever you want, then lock up and sleep on it. Tomorrow, we can come back in and have a look, then I'll take you to the hardware store, and we can get started."

I hug and thank everyone, and then they leave, leaving me and Bran standing in the middle of my new coffee shop. "I can't believe it. It's really happening."

"You deserve it, beautiful."

"Can we go now? I want to look at some baking equipment and sizes before I return tomorrow!"

"Sure thing, beautiful." Bran grins as he spins me and kisses me. You wanna camp out in the cabin tomorrow night? We can start doing up the coffee shop and stay in the cabin. Ray says the water and electric work!"

"Really? Can we really do that? Bran, I'm so excited. This is everything I've ever wanted! I can't believe I get to have it all with you."

Dane

I'm grabbing a box of stuff from my truck and about to head up the stairs to Ray's place. Well, I suppose my place now, too.

"What the fuck are you doing here?"

I grin as I turn. "Hey, Dice! What's crawled up your butt?"

He scowls and steps forward. "What the fuck are you doing here? I thought you went home?"

"You know what thought did, don't you?" I grin like the child he seems to think I am.

Puzzled, he cocks his head to the side. "What?" he asks.

Grinning, I say, "Shat himself and only thought he did!" I blob my tongue out and walk up the stairs. "You want to treat me like a child? I can act like one."

When I drop the box in my new room and come back down, he's waiting, leaning against my truck. "What are you doing, Dane?"

"I'm moving in."

"Like fuck you are!" He spins and slams my back against the truck.

"The thing is, Dice, this has nothing to do with you."

"I don't want you here." he snarls. "I can't have you here."

"Tell that to your dick that's trying to burrow into my thigh." I push him back slightly, "You want me, you know you do. Just be honest. If not with me, Dice, at least with yourself." I shoulder-check him and grab another box, stalking up the stairs. I hear a growl and something getting kicked across the concrete.

After I'm unloaded, I head over to the bar where everyone is. Priest and Tank shout me over, and Dice sits at the table with his face screwed-up like he's chewing a wasp.

Pa walks through the bar. "Hey, kiddo, what are you doing here?"

"Hey Pa! Just moved into Ray's for a bit. Where are you off to?"

"Going out with your mum and dad, don't wait up." He winks as he strides out the door.

"That's still so weird." Blade shakes his head. "I mean, five dads that brought you all up and treated you all the same? I didn't even have one."

"Well, if you ever wanna borrow one to go fishing or camping, you're welcome to any of them." I laugh out loud.

Blade looks really serious. "I've never been fishing." He pouts before realising he said that out loud.

"Seriously? Holy shit, my dad and pa would totally drag your arse fishing if you wanted to go with them, anything. They love that whole dad bonding thing."

"Really? They would?"

I fling my arm around him. "Yeah, you're part of the family now. Once Ray says you're her brother, that makes you my brother. Therefore, my dad and pa are yours if you want them too."

He grins, wraps his arm around my waist, and pulls me into his side, and we both laugh. I catch sight of Dice out of the corner of my eye. His face is like thunder, and he stands, shoving his chair across the floor with a screech. "I'm knackered. I'm gonna go to bed."

And then he's gone.

After an hour, I make my excuses and leave, heading out the front door. I head around the back of the clubhouse and into the back door. I grab my wallet and drag my picks out of it, grinning to myself as I pick the lock on Dice's door.

Soft snores and heavy breathing are coming from his room, and as the light from the hall shines across him, I can see he's asleep on his back. His covers are only pulled up to his waist, and one hand is tucked under the covers and the other behind his head. I slide in and shut the door, gently pulling the covers off him. He murmurs as the sheets slide against his lower half, he has one leg straight and the other bent, and he's totally naked.

"Score!"

I gently nudge his legs further apart and slide in between them, sliding my hand around his dick, then licking my tongue from bottom to top, licking it around the head and back down again, eliciting a filthy moan from his beautiful lips as they part with a gasp.

I lick again and slide my lips around his head, this time sucking his dick slowly into my mouth. With another groan, his hand reaches into my hair as his hips buck up to meet my mouth, and he groans again as his dick bottoms out inside my throat.

"Dane?" he gasps.

"Mhm," I hum around his dick, and I slide it in and out of my mouth, rolling my tongue around the head.

When I reach the top, leaning up on my elbows, I cup his balls and start massaging them as I slide my hand up and down his dick. His hand grips tighter in my hair as he pushes harder into my mouth. I slide my hand up and suck my fingers in my mouth with his dick before sliding them down between his cheeks and entering him. He groans again and bucks harder this time.

"Dane." he grinds out between a clenched jaw as his thighs start to tense, and I can feel him clenching on my fingers as he grips my head tighter as if he thinks I might pull back, but I push harder and faster with my mouth and my fingers as he groans his release down my throat and I swallow everything he gives me.

While he's panting and trying to figure out what just happened, I slide up his body and kiss up his chest, around his neck and jaw until I slam my lips into his and force my tongue between his lips. He groans again, giving in to me. I grind my fully clothed self into his gorgeous naked body and groan into his kiss as I slide my hand back down his body. He freezes. I stop kissing him. "Dice? What's up?"

"I can't do this, Dane. You need to go. I won't let this happen anymore. You need to leave now!"

"Dice, come on, you know we could be great together. We—"

"No, Dane. There's no we! There never was and never will be! I don't want you. Why the fuck won't you listen to me?"

Sitting back on my knees, I say, "Seriously? You couldn't have said that before you came in my fucking mouth?"

"Just go, Dane, and don't come back. Ever. Stay the fuck away from me!"

Rising from the bed, I shake my head. "Message received, Dice. Loud and clear! See you around, yeah."

He doesn't say a word as I slam the door behind me and stalk to the back of the clubhouse "Motherfucker." I kick the door open and stalk through it.

Heading towards the stairs of the apartment, I pull out my phone and message Steel.

Dane: Hey, I'm gonna head back to uni for a bit. Let Ray know. Cheers!.

Steel: Sure thing, kid. Drive safe.

Fucking kid! Fuck's sake. I messaged Steel as Ray would try and talk me out of it, and I just needed to be away from him. As I slide my phone back into my pocket, it chimes, and I freeze. "Fuck!" I click in my "alternative" PIN.

Rendezvous base pending immediate departure.

"Shit." I hear clunking on the stairs as Ray exits the apartment, "I thought you were with Steel?"

"I was, just popped back to see Skye. Come on, we'll take your truck." Diving into the truck, I peel out of the parking lot and tear down the road. "I need to call Steel. Fuck. I can't disappear and not tell him."

"Call him on the encrypted line. That way, they can't track it either. Be quick."

"Shit, it's voicemail!"

"Then say what you need to before we get any closer."

"Steel, baby, it's me. I'm sorry, so sorry! I've been called away on a job. I'm not supposed to let you know, but I couldn't go without speaking to you. I don't know where or when I'll be back or if... just know that whatever happens, I love you and hope you'll forgive me. I'll try and come home soon. Take care of Skye and Hades for me. I love you. I'm sorry."

She punches the dash. "I'm out, Dane. After this job, if I make it back in one piece, I'm out. If I can't tell him... I need him to know everything."

"Let's just get this over and done with, K?"

She nods, staring out the window. When we pull into our base, we hop out, slide our phones into the dead boxes, and head to the offices. White King, White Knight and Black King are already there,

"It's all hands on deck. White Rook and White Bishop are meeting us there," White King says, and we both nod.

Shit, this is fucked up if we're all heading out.

"Full tactical ready to leave for the airfield as soon as possible. Debrief on take off."

We nod again, racing out of the office and to The Armoury.

Geared up, we load the armoured truck and head off, full gas masks, balaclavas and everything. It's more of an identity protection measure most of the time. We run interference on all surveillance cameras within a 7-mile radius, so we're virtually untraceable.

As we head to the airfield, we pull into the hangar. White King and White Knight head out to taxi the plane in while we unload everything near the doors. Once the plane has been taxied to the hangar, we load up. Everyone's on the plane now. It's just Black Queen and me at the bottom of the steps. She's glancing around before finding the security camera. She turns to face it, pointing to her eye behind the mask. She holds her hands together over her chest in the shape of a heart and then points straight at the camera.

"Why?" I ask.

"Dice will find it and show Steel; then he will know I love him. If it's all that's left, at least he'll know."

I turn to the camera and flip it off. Dice can find that fucker, too. I stomp up the steps and onto the plane.

Steel

My phone rings, and I glance down at it on the table. I don't recognise the number.

"You gonna get that?" Ares nods towards the phone.

"Nah, it's probably nothing. If it was someone important, the number would be saved in my phone."

After an hour or so, I grab my phone and text Ray. She's been gone for ages. After another twenty minutes and no reply, I call her, but it goes straight to voicemail. *That's odd.* I dial the voicemail to listen to the message that the random number left.

"Steel, baby, it's me. I'm sorry, so sorry! I've been called away on a job. I'm not supposed to let you know, but I couldn't go without speaking to you. I don't know where or when I'll be back or if… just know that whatever happens, I love you and hope you'll forgive me, take care of Skye and Hades for me. I love you. I'll try and come home soon. I'm sorry."

I drop the phone onto the table, mouth open in sheer panic and shock

"You okay, Brother?" I slide the phone to Ares, and he picks it up and listens. "Shit." He stands from the table. "Get Dice, surveillance room now!" He grabs my arm and pulls me up from the chair.

Dice is at the desk, firing up the computers, listening to the message. "Fuck." He pulls up Bran's number on his phone and calls it. "Voicemail." then Bernie's. "Voicemail." Dane's. "Fuck voicemail."

Then Demi's. "Hey, Dice, everything okay?"

"Yeah, hey, Demi, I was just trying to get hold of Ray. Is she with you?"

"No, sorry."

"How about Bran? Is he there?"

"No, he's away with Bernie, some gun convention or something out of town. I'm staying with Marie till they're back."

"Oh, okay, do you know where Dane is?"

"Nah, I thought he was with you guys? He was moving in at Ray's today."

"Yeah, he did. I just haven't seen him since. No worries, Demi. See you soon."

"Bye, Dice."

"Dane told me he was going back to uni for a bit!" I tell him, and Dice seems to relax slightly at that information.

Dice pulls up the footage of the clubhouse, and we see Dane and Ray talking, then get in Dane's truck and leave together.

"So she's with Dane?" Ares asks. "So, has she gone to uni with him, or does Dane work for whoever she does?"

"Fuck, fuck, fuck!" I start pacing. "Ares, keep trying Bernie. I'll keep trying Bran."

After about thirty minutes or so, Dice shouts out, "Fuck, that makes no sense."

"What makes no sense?"

"I've tracked their vehicle, followed it, found it on every camera, then it just vanishes."

"They must have turned down a side street or—"

"No, look, it just vanishes here!" He points to the screen, and sure enough, it just disappears.

"How the fuck is that even possible?"

"I'm scanning all the cameras outwards from that point to see if they reappear, but there's something funky going on. Trucks don't just vanish."

After another hour, he says, "I've got nothing. I've tracked every truck, ignoring the number plates in case they changed them, nothing!"

"The armoured truck!" Ares shouts out. "When she went after you guys, they had an armoured fucking truck. What if they swapped it out somehow?"

"I'll pull up the footage from that day and see." Dice starts tapping on his keyboard.

"Go back to when she left," Ares says, giving Dice the day and time to search for.

"Who the hell are these guys?" I ask. This is the first time I've seen this and shit, that's a professional team setup. "What the fuck is she involved with?"

Dice pulls up the footage of when they brought us back. "That's at least one different guy, possibly two different guys!" Dice says. "Look!"

He's pointing towards the screen. "The one that puts Hades in the back is about the same height as Ray, and when they bring us back, they're both taller and physically bigger." He pulls up a screen grab and lays them side by side.

"So she's working with at least three different guys, possibly four."

We sit there for what feels like hours, just trawling footage. Blade, Priest and Tank join us, and we're all huddled in this box, just waiting.

"There!" Dice yells. "Is that the armoured truck?" Scanning back. "It just appears, look."

He points at the screen.

"Shit. Follow it, find where they are." I stand up and start pacing. We lose them on one camera and pick them up on another. We track, lose, and find, and I'm going out of my mind.

"Private airfield." Dice breathes out.

"Do they have any cameras inside that you can hack? Can you get a closer view?" I ask him, hoping we can find them.

Flicking around, he finds one. "There, look, that has to be her. Same outfit." We watch five of them loading gear onto a plane, and then she and a guy head towards the steps. They're the last to get on. She stops and looks around, then makes eye contact with the camera. "I love you."

"Fuck, that's Ray. She knew you'd find her!" Then the guy behind flips off the camera, and Dice winces. "What's up?"

"That's Dane. And the others on the plane are Bran, Bernie and Cade."

"How can you be so sure?" I ask Dice.

"Look at how they move. They're so in sync with each other. Also, who else do we know who is built that way? I mean, come on, Bernie and Cade are built like brick shithouses, and Bran's not far behind. And that's definitely Dane." He points to the one flipping the bird.

"Can we track the plane?" I ask, already assuming it can't be done.

"I've no idea. I can try."

"Keep eyes on the airfield. I want to know the minute they're back!" I say as I grab for the door.

"Where are you going?" Ares asks.

"I'm going to the airfield to see if I can find anything. I can't just sit around here. Tank, can you stay at mine and keep an eye on Skye and Hades?"

"Sure, Brother."

"Fuck!" I yell as I stalk out the door. As I jump on my bike, Ares, Priest, Blade, and Dice are right behind me.

Skye

I'm in the living room watching TV when Tank walks in. Damn, this guy is hot! They all look at me like I'm a kid, though. I suppose I've only got myself to blame. I thought if they thought I was nineteen, they would be more likely to help me. The thing is, I'm twenty-four. Ray knows this since the whole come clean about my past thing, and especially with the whole baby thing, I may have a little crush on Tank, but he would never be interested in me. I'm just some knocked-up kid Ray and Steel took in.

Although no one else knows about the knocked-up bit. Well, yet, anyway, Ray's given me time to think if I want to keep the baby or not, but I'm so confused.

"Hey, you okay? Ray's gone away to work for a bit, and Steel had to head out, so he's asked me to stay. Is that okay?"

"I don't need a babysitter, Tank. I'm not a kid! But sure. You wanna watch TV?"

"Sure." He grins and slides in beside me on the sofa. The guy is a total unit. "What are you watching?"

"It's a show about painting." I blush as I flick my gaze to him, then pass him the remote. "You can change it if you want."

"What kind of painting?"

"Watercolours."

"I like charcoal myself." He drops out in conversation with me like it's not important, but my heart skips a beat or ten at the thought we have something in common. *He likes drawing?*

"What do you draw?" I sit up at the side of him, turn into him and cross my legs under me to give him my full attention. This is the most we've ever spoken, and I can feel the butterflies fighting to get out with him this close.

He turns to face me, kicks his leg up under him and drops his arm onto the back of the sofa, resting his head against his hand. His bicep is bulging from under his t-shirt, and it's suddenly really hot in here, and my mouth is suddenly dry.

"I like to draw the ravens in the woods, out the back. It's peaceful out there. We rescued a raven, me and Ray. She called him Odin." He smiles at the memory, and damn it, I've not seen him smile much, but it's the most beautifully perfect thing I've ever seen.

"You want a drink?" I say, diving out of the seat, fully aware that I'm becoming aroused. I don't think I ever have been before, and the hot tingling sensation between my thighs distracts me. I'm blaming the pregnancy. I've never fancied a guy before, ever. I've never even had a sexual thought, but now it's all I can think about. Well, when it comes to him, it's all I can think about, and sitting with my legs crossed in front of him isn't the best way to hide it.

"Sure."

I grab a Pepsi Max Cherry for me and a beer for him. "Can I have one of those?"

I swap it out for the same as mine. "Sure."

"Do you paint or draw?"

"I like anything. I've done a bit of drawing. Ray says she'll take me to get some supplies. I suppose we'll go when she gets back."

"We can go tomorrow if you like. There's a tiny art store in Ravenswood, and if they don't have what I want, they order it for me. We could go for coffee after."

"I'd really like that." I grin back at him. *What the hell am I thinking? Dude's not interested in me. He's just babysitting for me while Ray's away. Calm yourself down.*

I snuggle down on the sofa beside him, and we silently watch the show. He doesn't say much anyway, but I'm always comfortable when he's around. He makes me feel safe, but he has a gentleness about him, which for a man of his size is surprising; he's not really tall, but then again, I'm only five-foot-two.

After watching the show and learning all about watercolour techniques, I must drift off.

I feel weightless. There's a weird sensation of being carried and warm, strong arms around me. I loll back and forth, almost like I'm in water. It's really soothing. The next thing I know, the heat disappears immediately as my back hits the bed. I feel his fingers brush my face as he sweeps my hair back off my cheek.

"Night, love, sweet dreams." he whispers, and I feel a smile tug at the side of my mouth as I burrow under the covers.

I slept so well last night, and I can smell bacon, so I throw on my bathrobe and trudge out of the bedroom only to find Tank cooking shirtless. I mean, my mouth was watering before, but I'm done for. I'm not sure if it's my hormones making me feel like this or the man in front of me, just that every inch of him, from the neck down to his jeans, is covered in colourful tattoos, and I want to lick every inch of them. I slide onto the stool by the counter.

"Morning. That smells so good." Then I blush as I think I may be drooling.

"Good job I made you some then, huh?"

"Are Ray and Steel back yet?"

"Nah, it might be a while, so you've got me till they're back. That okay?"

"Keep cooking me bacon, and I won't let you leave." *Fuck, why am I flirting with him? Jesus, get your libido under control, woman.* I mentally scold myself!

"Ah, bacon's your kryptonite, duly noted." He grins again, and there's a little twinkle in his hazel eyes that takes my breath away. He leans down on the counter so I'm staring straight into his eyes, "So, rather than flowers and chocolates you prefer bacon?" He chuckles to himself.

"I mean, if you wanted to get me chocolates and flowers, I wouldn't turn my nose up, but you can't go wrong with bacon." I blush as I realise I'm still flirting with him.

He barks out a laugh, and it startles me. "Shit, sorry." He chuckles.

Smiling at him, I tuck my hair behind my ear and glance down at my other hand on the counter. "Don't be. You should laugh more often, it's … nice."

"Maybe I will!" He winks and goes back to the bacon. Pulling open the cupboards, he grabs the ketchup.

"Can I have the brown one?" I point into the cupboard.

Pulling it out and looking it over, he spins to face me. "What's this?"

"Try it. It's amazing! Ray bought it from the UK. She just calls it brown sauce." I shrug. "It's kind of fruity? tangy? Just try it."

"You're not trying to ruin my bacon, are you, so you can have it all?" He casts a suspicious grin at me.

"Me never." I give him my best innocent face.

"Come on then, let's try it." Loading up his bread with bacon and lashings of brown sauce, he leans in his elbows onto the counter in front of me. He takes a massive mouthful and then groans. "Shit, that's good." He moans around his mouthful while he chews.

I'm suddenly finding it hard to swallow, and my brain has short-circuited. I reach up and wipe my thumb across the side of his mouth where he's got a dribble of sauce, and before I can stop myself, I put my thumb in my mouth and suck it. My eyes flutter closed, and as they open, Tank is staring at me.

"Oh my god, I'm so sorry… I… I have no idea why I did that… sorry… erm, I'll—"

"You really like brown sauce, huh?" He laughs at me, and I blush like the fool I am. Jesus, Ray and Steel need to come home soon before I end up dry-humping my babysitter. Mentally facepalming myself, I eat my breakfast with my eyes down, but I can feel Tank watching my every move like he's trying to suss me out.

Finally, he breaks the tension. "You should go and get ready, and then we can head off to the art supply store if you still want to go?"

"Erm, I should probably wait for Ray… I've…" I trail off. I'm such a loser. I've got no money, nothing without Ray.

"Don't worry about money." He grins like he can read the embarrassment on my face. "I've got some stuff I need to pick up. Maybe I could get you something instead of chocolates and flowers?" He smiles at me.

"Really?" I'm sure I'm misreading the signals, but is he flirting back, or are my hormones through the roof, making me think he's saying things?

Go on, scoot. Get ready." He wafts me away while he clears the plates.

I grab a quick shower, and four outfits later, I'm finally ready: a pair of skinny jeans tucked into combat boots, which, thank god, the jeans are stretchy, and a t-shirt with a skull on, which I actually think is Ray's, which I tie to the side to hide my small bump. I'm starting to show, but not much. I'm aware my body's changing, and it won't be long before my boobs are busting out of my bra. I throw my damp hair up into a messy bun and let a few messy bits fall around my face.

"You look cute." Tank smirks as I walk out of my room.

"Cool. Cute. That's definitely what I'm going for." I pull my lips into a flat line but can't force a grin out. Cute is something you say to a kid, a girl in a cute dress with cute pigtails and a cute name like Matilda or Jessica. Sighing, I ask, "Shall we go?"

He looks hurt by my snarky remarks but brushes it off as he grabs Steel's keys out of the bowl.

Watching the world go past, I can feel him keep glancing over at me, but I don't say anything. I just take in the view.

As we park in the centre of Ravenswood, I hear a yell across the square. "Skye, Tank, what are you two doing here?" I turn to see Scar walking towards us.

"Hey, we're shopping for art supplies. What are you doing here?"

"Just finishing off getting the law firm up and running, my dad's finishing up transferring the day-to-day running to his lawyers he has working for him; they're gonna run the firm for him, then he's moving here. I'm trying to get the apartment above it ready. You wanna take a look?"

I turn to Tank. "Can we? Please?"

"Sure, kid, why not?"

My heart sinks, and I'm sure Scar just sees it all over my face when I feel the grimace it causes. Here's me thinking he was flirting earlier, and he really does just see me as a kid. Scar flings her arm around me. "Come on, I'll show you around. Tank, you wanna grab some coffee and pastries?"

"Sure."

I turn to look at him over my shoulder, but he's already stalking across the parking lot.

"So you've got a crush on the big guy, huh?"

"Please don't say anything. I thought… we were… oh, I don't know."

"Come on. You can tell me all about it while he's grabbing the coffee."

While Scar's showing me around the place, which she's done up lovely, it looks so professional. We talk about the flirting. I thought he was flirting back, but then he called me kid, and I'm so confused, and god, I've no idea what's going on with me. Scar takes pity on me and offers me some advice, which I most definitely will not be taking, but I thank her all the same.

Tank turns back up, so I drink my coffee and stuff two doughnuts in my mouth. Scar and Tank talk about what needs doing. He's so dreamy, the way his muscles bunch and flex under his tight black t-shirt and the way his dark blue jeans hang on his waist and are tight across his bum and thighs and slack across his calves before they tuck into his biker boots. He's as big around as he is tall. He's got the physique of a weightlifter.

"Don't you think Skye? …Skye?"

"Huh?"

"I was just saying…" he trails off as he steps towards me and wipes the corner of my mouth, staring into my eyes, there must have been jam and sugar there from the doughnuts, and he does the same as I did this morning and sucks his thumb clean then glances down and steps back before looking back at me with a look that says, "What the fuck did I do that for?" He scowls and steps back. "We should get going." He reaches down, grabs my hand, and drags me out of Scar's office.

"Bye, thanks for the tour!" I shout over my shoulder as Tank just sticks his arm up in the air and waves. His hand feels red hot, and I can feel my skin scorch under his touch, and little zings of electricity zap along my wrist where his big hands engulf my tiny hand and wrist in his.

He doesn't stop dragging me till we wander down a little side street away from the centre, and he just stops dead and spins to face me. His head cocks to the side, and he looks confused and surprised. By what, I'm not sure, but after what feels like hours of just staring into each other's gazes, but mustn't have been more than a minute at most, he turns and grabs my hand again, dragging me along.

Pushing through the door of this quaint little shop, I stagger to a stop and just stand there with my mouth open, gazing around at the most beautiful selection of art supplies ever.

My eyes tear up, and the next thing I know, Tank is in front of me, cupping my face in his hands. "Hey? You okay?"

I just nod.

"What's wrong?"

I shake my head, and he grabs my hand to drag me out of the shop. "No, please… I'm fine… it's just I've never been anywhere like this. I've never had any art stuff. I went to a birthday party at Chuck E Cheese once and stole the crayons so I could draw. I used to colour on the inside of cereal packs." I have no idea what made me blurt that out. He's wiping my tears away with his massive thumbs so delicately, like he thinks I will break.

"Then let's change that." He smiles down at me. "Grab whatever you want."

I smile at him, and he smiles back. He still has hold of me, and it could just be the two of us, and I know it's my hormones screwing with me, but at this moment, I think I'm falling in love. I'm not sure as I've never been in love before. I never really had a chance to, but right now, I feel my heart is handing itself over to him whether he wants it or not.

"Come on." He pulls me further into the store. "Where do you wanna start?"

I hang my head in embarrassment; my heart is pounding in my chest, and I'm so overwhelmed by his generous offer that I'm taken aback before I can think about it too much. He's dragging me over to the counter. He grabs a basket from the woman behind and gives me a shove. "Whatever you want." He nods.

I grab watercolour paints, paper, charcoal, pastels, a sketchbook, some paintbrushes, and crayons. When I head back to the counter, Tank frowns at me. "Is that it?"

I look into my basket and back at him and nod! He glares at me and snatches the basket off me. He glances around the shop before grabbing acrylic paints, different sets of brushes for the different paints, another pack of charcoals and pastels, and some better paper for the different types of paints I've got. He grabs a large case to store everything in and an easel, along with some rubbers and pencil sharpeners, rulers, and a few different pencil cases for the pastels, charcoals and crayons. Looking around, he grabs some beginner guides to the different mediums. He's like a whirlwind, and then he stops and taps his lips with his finger. "Hmmm, I'm missing something?"

"Tank, I think you've put the entire shop in that basket. I can't accept all that! It's too much."

"Pftt!" he spits out as he's spinning again, then he grabs a smock, a table covering, a stool that goes with the easel, a paint pallet, a set of knives, and oil paints, then the paper for that too!

"Tank! Stop!" I breathe out. "Please, that's too much."

"Okay, we can always come back if we need anything else, right?"

"Sure! What about what you need."

"We could just share yours. Maybe we could go for a walk and take it with us when we get back." He grins at me; he's like a kid in a candy shop, and I've never seen him this excited.

I lean up and give him a chaste kiss on his cheek as I whisper, "Thank you, Tank!"

After spending a small fortune, we head back. I must have fallen asleep in the truck as I have that feeling of weightlessness again, and as my eyes loll open, Tank says, "Shhh, love, sleep." He kisses my forehead as he carries me upstairs to the apartment.

When I wake up, I'm on the sofa wrapped up in the blanket. I'm a little disoriented as I sit up.

"Hey, you okay? You coming down with something?"

I glance around as Tank comes from the kitchen with a glass of water for me. "I'm good, just tired, I think!" God, these hormones are kicking my ass today.

"I've put some food in the oven, and then you can have an early night. Hopefully, you'll feel better tomorrow."

"Can we go paint then?"

"Sure we can."

After we eat, I go straight to bed. I can't keep my eyes open.

Tank

It's the middle of the night, and I'm woken by whimpering. I automatically think it's the dog, but it gets quieter as I walk to the living room. I turn back and head towards Skye's door, pressing my ear against it. I can hear her crying.

"Skye? You okay?" Nothing. "Skye?" Nothing. "Skye, it's me, Tank. I'm coming in, okay?" As I walk through the door, she's curled up on the bed, clutching her stomach. I gently touch her shoulder. She's wet through. I touch her head. She's sweating and grimacing.

"It hurts." She grasps at her stomach.

Wrapping her up in her blanket, I head for the door.

"Where are we going?" She gasps out.

"Hospital."

"No, wait… I can't … please don't take me there."

"Skye, you're sick. I need to get you to a hospital."

"Bedside drawer, there's a card. I need to go there."

She grimaces and starts crying. I snatch up the card and head for the truck. I lay her in the back and pull up to the address on the sat nav. It's a private clinic. I'm unsure as to why she needs to be here. I mean, I already know she's got no money, but I bring her anyway.

Pulling into the clinic, I grab her from the back and walk as fast as possible to the doors. As we walk in, the receptionist asks for her name. "Skye… " I trail off. I don't even know her name.

"Alice," she croaks out. "Alice Montgomery."

"Okay, Alice, hang in there, okay? What's your date of birth?" She gives it, and I frown. Wait a minute… that makes her… twenty-four, not nineteen. I look down at her, but she's got one hand gripping her stomach and the other fisting my t-shirt while her face is screwed-up in pain.

"This way, Mr Montgomery." She leads me through a private room. "I've got Alice… sorry, it says here she prefers Skye?" I nod. "Pop her on the bed, and we'll be with her shortly."

I place her down and pull up the chair beside her, grabbing her hand. I smooth my thumb back and forward over the back of her hand, lifting it to my lips and placing a kiss on it. "It's okay, love. You're gonna be okay."

Ten minutes later, the doctor comes in, looks over her charts and orders some tests. She's asleep for the minute.

The doctor comes back in to start the tests. "Mr Montgomery, would you like to wait outside while we run the tests on your… wife?"

I raise an eyebrow at the doctor, but I nod and rise to leave. But Skye tightens her hold on my hand, fear skimming her eyes. I sit back down and tighten my grasp on hers. I ignore that fact they keep calling me Mr Montgomery and have decided we're married and look at those beautiful big chocolate brown eyes staring at me with so much fear. "I'll stay if it's all the same." He nods and starts the tests.

"So, Skye, we've drawn blood and need a urine sample." The nurse wheels in a machine. "Let's do an ultrasound, see if we can't hear the baby's heartbeat."

Her hand grips mine tighter, glancing at her. Her eyes plead with me not to flip, to not say anything, so I bring her hand to my lips and give it a gentle kiss. "Don't worry, love. It'll be fine, okay." She nods but doesn't take her eyes off me till the doctor speaks again.

"I'm going to move your gown and put this gel on your stomach. It will be cold, okay?" She glances at him and nods, then stares straight back at me. I can't take my eyes off her till I hear that baby's heartbeat, and my gaze flies to the screen as hers follows. I glance back at her as tears fall from her eyes.

"That's my baby?" She sniffles, and the doctor points out the little bean on the screen.

"Would you like a picture, Dad? We can print one off for you?" I nod as I smile at the screen, and I can see her gaze upon me, out of my peripheral, but I can't take my eyes off that little pulsing bean.

They print a few pictures of the scan, and the nurse takes Skye to the bathroom for the urine test. They need to run that and the blood tests to ensure everything's okay.

"You can head home if you want to, Dad," the nurse says. "We'll watch Mum and baby closely for you."

I shake my head. "Sorry, I'm not leaving her. Can I have a pillow and a blanket if you have one? I'll make myself comfortable here if that's okay."

The nurse nods and heads out of the room.

"Tank, I'm sorry, I didn't… I can't." She sighs. "I'm sorry."

"What're you sorry for, love?" I cup her cheek as she gazes into my eyes. Hers fill with tears. "Is it someone at the club?"

She shakes her head. But drops her gaze to her hands, which are twisting around themselves in her lap.

"Then who?"

She shakes her head and starts to cry.

"Did they make you?"

She glances away, but I hold her chin in my grasp and gently turn her face towards me. "Did they make you?" She drops her eyes again, and I lean forward and kiss her forehead. Her eyes flutter closed as I hold my lips there before pulling back, wiping my thumb under her eyes to wipe the tears. "I won't let anyone hurt you again, okay?"

She nods. "But what if he finds out and tries to come for my baby?"

"Do you want him to be a part of the baby's life?" She shakes her head.

"Does anyone else know who the father is?"

"Ray… Ray knows everything."

I nod in reply. "As far as anyone's concerned, this baby's mine, got it?"

"What?" She gasps.

"This baby's mine. We can be together. We can not be together. I will support and protect you whether you want to be with me or not, but this baby is mine."

"Tank… I—"

The nurse walks in and brings a blanket, a pillow and a jug of water.

"Get some sleep, love. You don't have to decide now." I pull the picture off the table, stroke my thumb over the grainy image, and can't help but smile. I'm gonna love this child with all my heart. It's gonna be my missing piece, my family. Hopefully, Skye will feel the same. There has definitely been some flirting, which I tried to stop, but now that I've found out her real age, I don't feel so creeped out by my feelings towards her. She could be my forever.

Skye

As I wake, he's still asleep in the chair, the picture of our child clutched to his chest, and a smile tugs at my lips. Can I have it all, the guy I can't stop obsessing over and our child? Well, my child, but does he really want this? What if he just wants the baby and not me? What if he's only saying I can be a part of it so he can keep the child? I mean, I barely know him, but there's a pull, and I can't deny there's an undoubtedly strong attraction, and I can't stop thinking about him.

"Morning, love," his gruff voice comes through my thoughts, and my eyes snap to his.

"Hey, handsome." I grin at him.

"Handsome, huh?" He grins. "I like it! Now, how are you feeling?"

I sit up straighter in bed. "It doesn't hurt anymore, not like before. It's a little tender, but I'm okay."

Sliding onto the edge of the bed, he takes my hand in his. I'm not sure what he's searching for, but he takes in every detail on my face. Bringing my hand to his lips, he gives it a kiss, and I'm sure my cheeks blush. He's so gentle it's a complete contradiction to his gruff voice and his sheer size. He's only about five-foot-nine, but the guy is built! And he's so handsome with his hazel eyes and golden brown hair, all tousled with sleep. I want to run my hands through it, so I reach up, and as my hand touches it, I grab it back. "Sorry, I …"

He grins at me. "You can touch me. I won't bite,"

I slide my hand to his cheek. "I can't ask you to do what you said yesterday. That's a massive commitment, and we barely know each other. I can't tie you to me for my own selfish gain." I sigh as my eyes drop to his lips and back again to his eyes. His tongue flicks out and licks his lips again as my eyes drop back down as he smirks,

"Kiss me, Skye." He smiles at me, and my hand drops away from his face.

"I… I… c-c-can't. I…"

He cups my face with his hand, and I soften into it. "You don't have to. Just if you want to, you can. I'll wait for you." He brushes his thumb across my cheek back and forwards and just stares into my eyes. It's not weird; it's not uncomfortable; it just feels safe. I close my eyes and just lean into his hand.

The door clicks open. "Morning," the nurse says as she blatantly checks Tank out. I scowl at her, which makes him grin, but he doesn't move his hand from my face or his gaze from my eyes. I smile and roll my face and kiss his hand. "Doctor will be in shortly with your results." She nods and leaves when neither of us acknowledges her.

"Okay." The doctor walks in smiling. "All the tests came back good, nothing to worry about. Just take things easy, and if anything else happens, come straight back in, okay?"

I nod.

"Do you want to know the sex?" the doctor asks. "When we did the blood work, we tested for abnormalities and did a full work-up."

"You can tell the sex?" He grins.

"We can." The doctor holds his tablet to his chest.

I glance at Tank, and he smiles back. "Your choice."

"Really?"

He just nods but can't stop the beaming smile across his face. I chew at my lip, glancing back between Tank and the doctor. "Yes... No... Wait! Yes. Yes, I want to know."

The doctor flips the pages over on the screen. "Congratulations, it's a boy!"

"A boy?" I gasp.

"A boy!" Tank whoops as he lunges forward and sweeps me up in his arms. His eyes land on mine, and his lips curl into a smile. "A boy." He grins.

It's at that moment I know I want everything he offered. I want him, the baby, the family. I want it all, and I lean in and smash my lips to his, taking him and the doctor by surprise. I pull back and throw my arms around his neck. "A boy." My voice cracks, and my lip quivers, and I know I've never felt happiness like this.

As we leave the clinic, I'm so content and actually excited. I didn't know if I wanted this baby with everything it stood for and what it meant, but Tank erased all that with those words. "This baby is mine." He erased every speck of doubt, and now I see a future, a good one, hell, a great one, and I'm finally looking forward to having something good.

As we pull at the club, I take a breath, but as I go to leave the truck, the door is ripped open, and Tank pulls me out and into his arms. I gasp in shock, and he whispers, "Second thoughts?"

I shake my head as his lips crash to mine. I throw my arms around his neck and melt into his firm body, screwing my hand up into the back of his hair and holding his mouth against mine while his tongue invades mine. I sigh and moan around it, and he pulls me in closer, which I didn't think was possible. He pulls back and whispers, "Are we telling people?"

"Telling people…?"

"About us, about the baby?"

"Erm… I don't know, why?"

He spins me round in his arms, and the rest of the Psycho Six bar Ray are standing there, staring, right along with Ares. "Just wondering." He grins at me.

"Oooh," is all I can get out before I'm placed on my feet. His hand grips mine as we head towards them. I'm aware that I'm still in my PJs from leaving at night and some flip-flops I got from the clinic.

"What's going on here?" Ares snaps. Dude scares me a little, and I drop my head.

"Nothing." Tank says as he pushes past his brothers towards the stairs and tugs me up them.

"You can convince Ray of that when she gets back. Good luck with that, Brother!" Priest says.

I'm dragged up the steps. As he closes the door behind us, he grins. "Well, the cat's head is out of the bag. It won't be long before the rest of it follows!" Then he drops to one knee. "Marry me?"

"What?"

"Marry me. Let's do this properly. We can go to The courthouse, change your name so you never have to use that one again, and we can get married. We can start this properly unless you want a big wedding like Ray and Steel, and we can do that too!"

"Tank, this is all so… sudden. I don't know."

"Sure you do." He winks at me, and I do. I really do know. I've never had a boyfriend. I've never even had sex, well, consensual sex, anyway, not with someone I've chosen. But at this moment, it's him. I want him forever, and I can't imagine it not happening.

I laugh. "Yes!"

"Yes?" He grins as he lifts me off my feet and spins me around as he lets me slide down his body till my feet dangle and my arms wrap around his neck. He looks into my eyes. "I promise to make you and our son happy every day. I promise to protect you both forever."

He grabs my hand and drags me through to my bedroom. My heart starts pounding. I don't know if I'm ready for this. It's all happening so fast. As he pulls me into the room, my mouth dries, and my heart's hammering. "Now, bed." He lifts the duvet and taps the bed. "You need to rest. I'll go get you food and a drink, okay, love?" I slide in, and he tucks me in, leaning down and kissing my forehead. The panic is soon replaced with disappointment, and I chuckle at myself for the complete 180 in my emotions. Clearly, my head's all over the place.

Tank spends the next few days waiting on me, hand and foot. He holds my hand and kisses me but never pushes for more. He's told me to take some time to figure out what I want wedding-wise, but other than that, he's been a perfect gentleman, and I'm falling in love with him more every day. We haven't told Steel yet as he's busy helping Demi with the coffee shop-come-bakery while Ray's away, but he's not himself either, so I'm going to wait till Ray's back to talk to them both.

After a good few days of house arrest. God, now I know how Ray felt. Tank asks me to take a walk with him. We head out on the lane past the clubhouse, up past the gym and the barn. As we round the trees, there's a lovely lake in the shape of a heart with some wooden cabins around it.

"Ah, it's so pretty up here, Tank."

"You like it up here?"

"Yeah, it feels so remote and free."

He pushes some keys into my hand. "Fourth one down." He nods. "It's ours if you want. It just needs doing up a little."

"Really?"

"Really, love."

I run off towards the cabin, and a boisterous laugh follows me as I glance over my shoulder. Tank is chasing after me. Getting to the door, I unlock it, and as I swing the door open, I'm swept off my feet and carried in through it. Resting me down and sliding his arms around me, cupping my stomach with both hands and resting his chin on my head, which seems to be his new favourite position, I grin up at him. "This is ours?"

"If you want it." He takes my hand and leads me through the open-plan kitchen, diner, and living room. There are three doors on the side wall. The first and last are bedrooms, and the middle is a large bathroom. The back bedroom has patio doors leading out to a deck, and Tank points out a mezzanine level above the bedrooms. "I thought I could make that space into an art studio for us. We'll need to secure a yard with Bean coming soon, but what do you think?"

"Bean." I laugh and shake my head. Ever since that day at the clinic, he's called the baby Bean, poor kid. "I love it!" I turn and face him. "I love you!"

His eyes widen slightly, and he grins the biggest shit-eating grin I've ever seen on his face and pulls me to his chest. "I love you too! I can't wait to marry you and start this family."

"What's your name?" I ask as it just occurs to me that I don't even know it.

He looks away like he's embarrassed. "Thomas, Thomas Pershing."

I cock a brow at him, "That's where the name Tank comes from, as in Thomas the Tank Engine. I thought it was because of your size?"

He bursts out laughing, then when my face scrunches in concern, he stops. "Oh, you're serious?"

I slide my arms across my chest and glare at him. "Why wouldn't I be?"

"My name's Pershing, as in the make of a tank." He grins at me.

"Ooooh." I did not know that was a thing.

He squeezes me back to his chest. "I think the Thomas the Tank Engine thing is cuter." He smiles and drops a chaste kiss on my forehead, and I gaze up into his eyes.

"It's a family tradition that all the men's names begin with a T. I'm Thomas after my grandpa, and my dad was Trevor, my great grandpa was Theodor and before him was Trenton."

"I like that. We're gonna be happy, aren't we?" I question, a moment of reality hitting me like a baseball bat to the face.

Sensing my unrest, he says, "I promise to try to make you as happy every day as you've made me, allowing me to be this child's father." A sad smile forms across his face. "I don't have any family left, and I can't… have children of my own." He looks away as if ashamed. "I should have told you that before. I understand if that changes everything, not being able to have more children."

"Honestly, I didn't intend on keeping this one. Just the panic that I might lose him at the clinic and your excitement made me excited, so I will accept our little miracle boy and be more than happy with our life."

I cup his face and kiss him with all the emotion I'm feeling, all the love, the hope, the excitement and most of all, the contentment that this man has brought to my life over the last week. *Hell, is that all it's been?* I carry on kissing him like my life depends on it until my stomach growls, and he laughs.

"Come on, gotta keep Mama's strength up! Let's get you fed." He kisses my head and leads me out of the cabin. Locking it up, we head straight across the field back to the apartment.

Steel

I'm in the bar after a long day helping Demi get the coffee shop sorted. It's been over a week and a half since Ray went, and we've heard nothing. I'm barely able to focus, but Demi thinks Bran and Bernie are at a fucking gun show, of all things. She has no idea, so me and the boys are getting the coffee shop fitted out. We just need a lick of paint and the furniture, and she's good to open. We've been pulling long days trying to distract us from the fact they're all missing. Cade, too.

"Steel, fuck!" Dice comes skidding into the bar. "There's movement at the airfield."

Standing so fast that my stool flies across the room, I pull out my phone and send everyone a text. As I take off after him, he's had a search running in the background, looking for any of the vehicles within a twenty-mile radius from the centre of where we lost Dane's truck to where we picked up the armoured truck. We went back to the airfield and left a load of motion detector cameras. It's one of those that's been tripped.

"It tripped while I was in the shower, so we're about twenty minutes behind," he says as he flicks through the images on the screens. "This is live, but it's all recorded, so we can go back and watch it all."

As we scan the video, we decide to start at the beginning. We're already behind them, and the airfield is over an hour away. So we wait, and we watch.

The plane is what trips the camera as it taxis towards the hangar. Three people get off the plane, and one of their legs gives out as they get to the bottom. They drop to their knees, down onto all fours. Another one comes up and places a hand on their back, and they shake their head but rise up. They head around the plane and pull out all the equipment from the cargo hold. Next, they pull a body bag out and lay it on the floor, then return and pull another out.

We're all crammed in this room again: me, Dice, Tank, Priest, Blade, Ares, Scar and Viking, who only just got back from Carmen's last night. Dozer is on his way and should be here any minute. We all hold our breath. "Can we get a closer look? Who's in the bags? Fuck!" I yell, grasping and pulling at my hair as I kick the door just as it starts to open.

"Motherfucker!" Dozer shouts out from the other side of the door.

Grabbing it and dragging it open, I reach into the hallway, grab him by his shirt, and drag him into the room with the rest of us.

Dice backs up the footage a little and starts it again. Once everything is on the tarmac, the plane taxis away and takes off. Three of them are just standing there hugging each other. "That has to be Ray, Dane and Bran. I've seen them stand like that a ton. I would bet my life that that's them." Dice sounds almost like he's trying to convince himself more than anyone else.

"Wait, what's that?" One of the other screens flares to life.

"That's the gate. There's a vehicle approaching and heading in. It's a blacked-out van. We follow it on the camera before it pulls to them in front of the hangar. Two men get out, shake their hands and load the body bags into the van before setting off.

"Set a tail on that vehicle. I want to know who's in that van and where it goes!" I spit at Dice.

"Wait, that's Ray!" Dozer shouts, "back it up." We watch as they load the equipment into the armoured truck, then Ray rips off her gas mask and throws it across the tarmac, screams into the air, then drops to her knees and sobs into her hands. The other two take off their masks and drop them to the floor before collapsing at the side of her.

My phone chimes in my pocket. Grabbing out, it's a message from Ray.

Unknown. I'm back. I'm sorry. I need some time. I'm okay. Back soon, love you.

I try to reply, but it won't let me. I tell the guys, and all we can do is watch. We watch as she drags a device out of a bag. That must be what she messages me on. Then she gets up and wipes her face, and the look that passes it sends shivers up my spine. I've seen Reaper in full swing, but this… her face just falls blank, dead eyes like her soul has just departed. They climb into the armoured truck and drive out of there like bats out of hell.

All we can do is watch. We have multiple monitors playing multiple footage. Dice is running number plates, watching cameras, and hacking into the cloud to get to the stored footage from all cameras, all before the armoured truck disappears.

"Fuck!" I bellow. "How is that fucking possible? Where the fuck are they?"

Dice leaves those screens scanning. "We'll be alerted if Dane's truck pops back up, or Bran's, for that matter. I'm gonna concentrate on the van."

After what feels like a lifetime, Dice finds the van. It's pulled onto a military base. *Of course it fucking has.* "Can we get eyes on that base and find out who's in those bags? It's pointing to Bernie and Cade, but fuck… That's gonna blow up their entire world if they lose those two."

Dice manages to tap into a few cameras, but nothing gives us anything useful. Then he tries phoning through to the base, but that's a dead end. "Send me the coordinates. I'm going there myself." I bark out. As I go to leave, Scar speaks up.

"Steel …" she lets out a breath. "That's not her."

"What the fuck, Scar? You just saw her. It is; it is her. She's back. I'm going to the base to find answers, then I'm finding her and dragging her ass back home."

"No, Steel… I mean… that's not the Ray you know. I've known them for nearly ten years. You need to let her come back when she's ready. Whatever has happened… you think Reaper is a ruthless killer? You've seen nothing yet. They all compartmentalise, but they do it with personalities. This is full-on Black

Queen, and trust me, you don't want to be near her when she detonates, because that is what's going to happen.

"Steel, please just let her come to you. Right now, they're all riding a fucking high or a fucking low, and it's gonna get way worse. When they come back, they're empty. There's no compassion, there's no humanity, and there's certainly no love for anyone. They will rip you apart and burn the pieces without a second thought. Please let her come to you. Don't force this. She's sent a message, which is more than any other time."

"They've been like this before?"

"As long as I've known them. They've spent a lot of time 'travelling' to various destinations." Scar uses air quotes, as if that's what they've told people but not what they've been doing.

"I'm going to the air base to see if I can find anything out, but I'll come straight back, okay?" I look at Scar. "I trust you." I nod at her.

She nods back. She cups my face. "She will come back. You just need to let her find her own way. Ares, go with him, please." He nods and drops a kiss on her cheek before clapping me on the shoulder.

"Come on, Brother, let's see what we can dig up."

"Dice, let me know if they show up on the cameras." He nods as we walk out the door.

"Jesus, Ares, what is she involved in? I thought all this started here. I thought this was someone she was becoming here. I thought it was my fault. I can't lose her."

Black Queen

Pulling into The Tower, I get out. I can't feel. I can't shake this emptiness. I'm trying to will myself to feel something, anything, but there's just a void, a black hole where my fucking swinging brick used to be, and I can't function. I head for the shower. I swing by our dorm room and grab my tequila on my way.

When I get to the showers, Dane and Bran are in there already. It's more like a changing room here, so I slide into an empty shower cubicle. I don't bother closing the curtain. I just turn the water on freezing, slide down the wall, and drink my fill of tequila.

It's not till the water shuts off that I glare up, and Dane is standing there in a pair of boxers with his hand held out. I slap the bottle in it, and he chugs it like it's his job. He leans down and drags me to my feet, pulling me to our room. It's one we all share. It has two double beds, but we only ever sleep in one. When we come back from what we've seen, we never want to be away from each other. Bran's already in bed in his boxers, and he tosses me a t-shirt, which I slide on as Dane grabs me some pants. I pull them on and slide into bed. Dane gets on my other side, and we drink till the tequila is gone.

Waking up the next day, or maybe the day after that, fuck knows what day we're actually on, Bran's getting dressed, looking freshly showered. "I can't do this." He gestures to us, wallowing in self-pity in bed, stinking like a five-day-old hangover, and *Stig of the Dump* comes flooding back. "We've already lost them. I'm not prepared to lose Demi. I'm going home."

I look over at Dane, he grumbles, "He's right. You should go back to Steel." He takes a swig of the tequila before rolling over and pulling the covers over his head.

"He'll understand," I say, leaning over him to snatch the tequila. I take a good chug and slam it back down, flopping onto my back. "Eventually."

Bran shakes his head in disgust as he leaves us in The Tower.

I'm not sure how many bottles of tequila we got through, but there's one left, and Dane is asleep, so fuck it. I drink it like it's my motherfucking job till it's totally empty and spinning on its side on the floor.

Dice

Steel and Ares's trip to the base is a bust. They can't get in, can't get answers, and we can't get footage from anything, but I suppose we expected that and just have to feel like we are doing something, so I've trawled through hours and hours of footage. It's been… I don't know, three days, and I can't get him out of my mind. The hurt on his face when I told him I didn't want him, the video of him flipping me off, as, let's face it, that was for my eyes only.

I know he's back, but not knowing if he's okay… it's torture. I can't be with him, but I don't think I can be without him. I watch the footage from before we were taken. I watch the footage of Ray leaving to find us. I've seen "the videos" of Steel and Dozer that were sent to the girls, and I've watched Ray's reaction to them over and over again. I feel like I've lost my right arm with Ray gone, and a part of my heart without Dane.

I'm just about to go grab some food when the alarm rings and Dane's truck flashes into view. I grab my phone, send an alert to the guys, and track the shit out of that truck.

"Let's see you flip me off now, motherfucker!" I snarl at the footage as I follow the cameras, snatching up the laptop. I run to the bar as Steel and Tank come flying into the corridor. "I've got a hit on Dane's truck. Let's go." I run past them and out to Steel's truck.

"Tank, stay with Skye, let the others know we're headed out. I'll call you when we know anything." Steel shouts to Tank as he dives into the truck.

"Just bring them home safely." he yells in reply.

"Head for Gosport Harbour. That seems to be the direction they're travelling." I pull up the cameras on my laptop and flick from image to image while Steel drives like a bat out of hell, "They've stopped!" Shit, I know exactly where they are. They've gone to the club where I took Ray. The gay club! I direct Steel to where we need to be and park up.

As we get to the club entrance, I sigh as I don't recognise any of the bouncers, so we head on inside, searching around. I don't see any of them. "Do you see them?" Steel asks nervously.

"Nah, man. I don't see any of them." Doing the rounds and heading to the bathrooms, we still don't find them. "Where the fuck are...?" I trail off as I spot him on the dance floor. I can't take my eyes off him. He's beautiful, and shit, can he dance. The look on his face is so relaxed and so... *wait, what the actual fuck?* I set off to storm across the dance floor.

Steel grabs my shoulder. "Where the fuck are you going?"

"Dane!" I spit out. "Wait here, keep a lookout."

As I storm towards him, there's a guy behind him, taller and broader than Dane, covered in tattoos. He has one hand across Dane's chest holding him to his body, the other fucking rummaging In the front of his jeans, all while he's biting and sucking on Dane's neck and kissing him.

"We're going home!" I bark.

Dane's eyes lazily open as the guy talks into his ear. "He with you?"

Dane looks at me, but not really looking at me as he shrugs and carries on grinding against the guy whose hand is sliding up to his throat. He tilts Dane's head towards him and starts kissing him while his hand thrusts further into his jeans as Dane groans into his mouth.

"Dane!" I snap at him. He turns to me, looking almost through me, and gives me a sad smile before turning his face back to the guy to kiss him again. Fuck, he's lost weight, his face is sunken, and his eyes look dead behind them.

I grab the front of his shirt and drag him towards me. "We. Are. Going. Home. Now!"

He staggers towards me as the guy drags him back. "I found him first. He's mine."

Just as I'm about to swing at him, I'm grabbed from behind in a bear hug. "What the fuck, Dice?" Steel squeezes me from behind. "You're not helping the situation, and I still can't see Ray or Bran." I spin on him, ready to get in his face and start laying down the law, when he gasps over my shoulder. "Where the fuck did they go?"

Turning back, I spin around, looking in every direction, just as I see the back of Dane's shirt disappear out the door. "There, they're going outside."

The only way out is across the dance floor, which is proving difficult for guys who look like me and Steel to escape unscathed. We are grabbed and mauled for attention as we push our way through. When we finally get outside, there's no sign of them, so we start hunting when I hear groans coming from the alleyway. I step around the corner. Dane has his back against the wall, head back, his tight, ripped, white-washed jeans are pulled down to his thighs, his shirt is unbuttoned and hanging open with his still toned perfect body on display. The guy who was with him is on his knees and is sucking off my… Dane. He's going to town on him, and I'm standing with my mouth open at the sheer look of ecstasy on his face, wanting to throw up. I stumble back as Steel grabs me, and I turn away from him to vomit.

    Steel secs what I'm looking at and storms over there, gripping the guy by the throat, pulling him to his feet, punching him, and dropping him to the floor before turning and grabbing Dane as he slides down the wall, grabbing him before his ass hits the floor. "Dice, give me a fucking hand!" As he holds Dane up, he's hammered. "You're gonna have to… put him away while I hold him!"

    "Why the fuck should I tuck him?"

    "Dice? Seriously, you've just seen your boyfriend having his dick sucked by someone else and puked, I love you both, but this one's on you."

    "Boyfriend?" I step back. "What the fuck, Steel? I'm not fucking gay."

    "Dice, we don't have time for you to hang out in the closet. Just fucking grab his legs, and let's get him in his truck. You drive, I'll grab my truck, and we'll find Ray."

My mind is racing. *What the fuck, what the fuck, what the fuck?* It's all I can come up with as we load Dane into the truck. Dude's out cold. Slapping him around a bit, trying to get him to tell us where Ray is, he just keeps saying he's locked her in The Tower, whatever the fuck that means.

Steel grabs his phone out of his pocket. I hear a guy's voice answer.

"What?"

"Fucking what?" he bellows. "Where the fuck is she, Bran? Are you with her?"

"She's safe, Steel. She's with Dane." he barks back.

"Really? Well, I must have some other fucker passed out in a tequila coma in the back of the truck, then."

"What the fuck?"

"Exactly! What the fuck, Bran? Where is she? She's on her own."

He sighs. "Steel, look…" he trails off.

"Bran, whatever's going on, I'm here for all of you, and I've got your backs, but fuck, she's my wife, and whatever she's going through, she's on her own."

"Fine… give me a sec. I'll call you back on a secure line."

"Bran—" Steel loses his shit. "Motherfucker hung up."

His phone rings again, but it's an unknown number.

"Bran?" he panic barks down the line as he answers the call.

"Steel, listen closely. I'm not repeating myself. Once you get to the address, it's an underground parking garage. Go inside and drive to the left. There's a barrier that says 'work crew only'. Do you have Dane's truck?"

"Yes?"

"Good, that needs to drive towards the barrier. It will open. Follow it around to the back wall where there's a metal sign that says 'work crew only'. Drive towards the wall, it will move, and head inside. Park up, and at the elevators, you want the top floor. You will need Dane's retina and fingerprints to be scanned to get into the elevators. Do you understand?"

"Yes."

"It's 3582 Castle Cove Road, Gosport Harbour."

"Do you need anything? Are you okay? Where are you?"

Sighing again, he says, "Yeah, I'm good. I'm home with Demi. I just can't … I just… sorry."

Then the phone cuts off. "Fuck!" Steel bellows, and Dane flinches but is still out of it.

"Look, at least he's safe now. Let's get Ray and get home."

Pulling into the parking lot we follow the directions, I'm driving Dane's truck and Steel's behind me, going through the stages Bran told us. We reach the elevator. Dane is suspended between me and Steel and dead to the world. "Bagsy fingerprints!" I laugh as Steel rolls his eyes, battling to hold Dane's head up and open his eyes.

There's a ding, and the door opens. Hitting the button for the top floor, we wait. Once the doors open, there's a long corridor. There are numerous doors along it. Glancing backwards and forwards, I look over at Steel. "Maybe we should prop him up here, and you go that way. I'll go this way and see what I can find." I shrug as I start laying Dane against the wall. Dude is so out of it.

"Sure. Shout if you find her."

I nod as I head to the first door, then the next, and so on, and so on, till I reach the last door. "Steel, she's here." I bark out as I rush in the door. She's face down on the bed, laid diagonally across it, her arm and half her head hanging off the side with her hair trailing on the floor. She's wearing a screwed-up t-shirt and underwear, and empty tequila bottles are everywhere. As footsteps come thundering towards me, I say her name. "Ray?" Nothing. I step into the room further as Steel arrives and pushes past me.

"Baby?" he growls at her, turning her over. There's vomit on the floor and some crusted around the side of her mouth. Well, it's more bile than anything. I can see she's lost weight. The bags around her eyes are dark, and her cheeks are sunken. It's the stench that has my stomach turning. Fuck knows how long she's been here like that.

"Steel, there's a shower room next door. Maybe we should get her in there."

He's lost, staring down at a face we barely recognise, stroking her cheek. She's breathing, but her breaths are shallow and tortured.

"Steel?" I rest my hand on his shoulder.

His eyes cling to mine, and he nods. "Look, see if there are any clean clothes."

I take a step back round the room. There are three sets of drawers. Diving into the first, it smells like Dane. I subconsciously pull the t-shirt to my nose and inhale. There's a huff behind me as I drop the top and turn to face Steel.

"Not your boyfriend, huh?" Steel cocks a brow, and a knowing smirk tugs at the corner of his mouth.

"How long have you known?"

"About you and Dane?"

"No, about me being gay." I sigh. That's the first time I've said that sentence out loud to one of my brothers. Ray's the only one who truly knows.

"Honestly, I thought you were bi!" He shrugs like it's no big deal.

I sigh a defeated sigh. "What's gonna happen now?" I look down at my boots and wait for it.

"You're gonna find those clothes you were looking for, and then we're gonna wash this fucking stink off her, then we're taking them home. Now, get what we need so we can get out of here."

I nod, head out, and start the shower.

Loading them into the trucks, wrapped in the bedding from the other bed in the room, we head back. Ray wakes a bit while we shower her but is rambling, not making much sense, and as soon as she's wrapped up in Steel's arms, she goes back to sleep. Getting Dane to the truck is a little less romantic and takes us both to drag his ass through the building, but we manage it.

Pulling up at the apartment, we take Ray in and lay her in bed, then we drag Dane up and throw him in his room.

Steel rests his hands on my shoulders. "You wanna stay with him?" My eyes glare at him, searching for some sort of disappointment, disgust, or hatred, but his eyes are soft and caring, and I sigh.

"You wouldn't mind?"

"Dice, I love you. I don't give a fuck who you stick your dick in as long as you are happy. Just be warned, Dane is the guy version of Ray." He chuckles. "So good fucking luck with that." He points at Dane face down on the bed, snoring.

I smile, I actually smile, and my heart feels a little less empty. "You know, I once told Ray she would be my perfect guy if she had a dick."

"Really?" He barks a laugh at me. "Be careful what you wish for, Brother. I think you got exactly that. You've just gotta allow yourself to have it now."

Clapping me on the shoulder, he goes to leave the room. "Look after him. She'll have you by the balls if you don't." And he laughs again as he walks out and leaves me there, chest pounding, just staring down at him.

I start trying to undress him and get him more comfortable when there's a quiet tap on the door. I spin around, gaping as Tank stands there. "Need a hand, Brother?" he asks as a blush rides up my neck into my cheeks.

"It's… it's… erm… it's not what it looks like." I rush out. Panic in my tone has him frowning.

"Well, it looks like you're trying to get a shit-faced Dane undressed and into bed? So, if it's not that, then … " he trails off, shrugging. "So, you need a hand?"

"Yeah, thanks, man."

I pull off his boots and socks, Tank lifts him under his arms, and I undo his jeans and pull them off. "Fuck's sake," I bark out as his dick falls out. "Dude's fucking commando."

Tank chuckles and nods to the drawers. "Check his drawers for underwear."

I find a pair and pull them on. I can hear Tank chuckling at me. "What the fuck's so funny?"

"You! You're so fucking weird. You're acting like you're offended that his dick ended up out, but aren't you two together?"

"Why the fuck do people keep saying that?"

"Sorry, dude, just a vibe I got."

I sigh and drop to the bed. "Sorry, thanks for the help, man. I appreciate it."

"No worries." He takes a step to leave "Can I offer you some advice?"

I glance up at him, dubious about what he will say. "Guys like Dane don't come around very often. Don't let him slip through your fingers because you're too proud to admit you're into him." He tips an imaginary hat and heads out the door, softly clicking it closed as he leaves.

I strip off and flop into bed, pulling the covers up around us both. He's lying on his front, but he's facing me. His dirty blonde hair has flopped over his forehead, giving him a surfer guy kind of look. I can see where he's lost weight. The angles in his face are sharper. I rub my thumb across his cheek. "I'm so sorry, Dane. I wish I could be the brave man you deserve." I get as close as I can, wrap my arm around him, and close my eyes.

Dane

I wake up groggy. *Where the fuck am I? Ouch, that fucking hurts.* My head is spinning, then I'm suddenly aware I'm wrapped in someone's arms, and I freeze. *Fuck, I'm in my room at Ray's. I don't remember coming back here. Who the fuck did I bring back? Shit, shit, shit.*

Arms tighten around me. "Shhh, babe, go back to sleep."

That voice. I recognise it. My skin pebbles as he kisses my shoulder softly, and my dick starts to stir. The smell of him engulfs me, and it's too much. I scramble out of bed, falling into the drawers as I grab for the door.

"Get your fucking hands off me. Where is she? Where's my sister?" I spit and slur as I stumble out into the living room.

"Dane, she's fine. Come back to bed?" he says from behind me.

"Fuck you! Stay away from me." I stagger further towards her door as it swings open, and Steel is there in his boxers. Fuck, my mind goes blank. Dude is ripped and hot, and fuck, I'm drunk. That's my sister's husband.

"Dane, what the fuck?" he mumbles at me, half asleep.

"Where is she?" I slur again, and he nods into his room and takes a step back, allowing me to stagger past him, heading to the empty side of the bed.

He tsks at me. "That's my side, dickhead." He nods to the other side of Ray. She's not quite in the middle, so I climb over her and snuggle in behind her, grabbing her and pulling her into me so we're facing each other.

"Go back to bed, man. Things won't be so bad in the morning." Steel speaks out into the living room. I'm assuming he's talking to Dice. Fucker can fuck right fucking off.

Steel slides into the empty side and slides as close to Ray as he can, resting his head on one arm and reaching over. He puts his hand on my cheek and pushes my jaw up so I'm looking him in the eye as best I can, but I'm pretty sure he's really blurry. "You okay?"

I pinch my lips together and shake my head.

"I love you, ya know." he whispers, and my eyes shoot to his. "I know you wanna protect her, but I'm here, okay? I've got you both. You just sleep." He reaches down to my waist and pulls us all closer together, then relaxes his hand, leaving it there, burning a patch just under my ribs as my eyes flutter shut. "He loves you too, ya know." My eyes fly open to meet his. "He just doesn't know how to be that man yet. Be patient, okay?"

"He doesn't want me." I slur again.

He huffs out a breath. "Dumb ass motherfucker, doesn't know how to tell you he wants you. Give him time."

I shake my head. "No. I... can't." I shake my head again.

"Get some sleep, kiddo. Things won't look so bad in the morning."

He tugs at me again, stopping me from pulling away, and closes his eyes. I relax into his touch, feeling safe for the first time since we got back.

When I wake, I try to open my eyes, but fuck me, it feels like they're welded shut. I feel a twitch of a big hand against my waist, and my eyes fly open before meeting Steel's grey eyes and sighing in relief. He chuckles at me and smiles. "How's the head?"

"Fuck," I gasp as I realise it's pounding and the brass band has just started the encore.

"Tablets and water on the bedside table. When was the last time you two ate?" Steel gives me a sad smile, and I just shrug. "I'm gonna go sort some food out. Shower's in there if you wanna use it, and help yourself to anything out the wardrobe, K?"

"Thanks, Steel."

He smiles as he walks out of the bedroom in his boxers. Fuck, his arse is... "Ouch..."

"Stop drooling!" The scratchy voice from lack of use crawls through my mind, making my head snap back to her gaze. There's no emotion on her face at all, just a tight lip.

I pull her in closer, dropping a kiss on her forehead.

"How are you feeling?"

"Like I've been run over by a steam roller and a lion's shat in my mouth!"

"That good, huh?"

"What the fuck are we doing here, Dane?"

I shrug, as fuck if I know how we got here. "Steel's gone to make breakfast. Come on, let's grab a shower and some fresh clothes and get some food. I can't remember the last time I ate."

"Can't remember the last time I was sober." She scoffs.

"I don't actually think you are."

"Dick!" She weakly punches me in the arm. "We'll be okay, won't we?"

I shrug again as I'll be fucked if I know.

After we both shower and grab some black sweats and hoodies each, I take her hand and pull her into the living room. Flopping down on the sofa, she folds her legs under her, flipping her hood up and pulling the sleeves down over her hands, keeping her face down. She sits there looking lost, and I've no idea how to help. I'm just as lost. Steel doesn't say a word; he just brings two plates of food and hands them to us, then walks away and comes back with some sweet black coffee. As he walks round the sofa, he squeezes my shoulder as he passes by. He smiles down at me as I look up at him, then he bends and kisses Ray on the head and walks back to the kitchen. Her eyes flick to mine, but I just smile, pick up the fork, and start eating.

Once we've finished eating, we just sit there for a while, listening to Steel wander around in the kitchen. The door clicks open, and Tank comes out with Skye behind him. Skye clears her throat. "Ray, you're back. Can I have a word… in private?"

Ray's eyes shoot to Skye's as Steel replies, "Now's not a great time, Skye."

She nods and gives him a tight smile as she leaves, heading back to her room.

Ray doesn't say a word. She just rises from her seat and follows after Skye.

Tank hovers in the doorway, and Steel hovers behind the kitchen counter. The tension is rolling off everyone, and a good ten minutes later, Dice walks out of my room and can clearly feel it, too. He opens his mouth to say something but closes it again before sighing and opening it again. But Ray pushes past him. "Dane, I need you to grab your laptop and head out with me. Steel, I will be back before morning."

Storming towards the door, she grabs her trainers, snatches the truck keys, and heads out. I shove past Dice and head to my room, grabbing my trainers and laptop and heading back into the living room.

"Dane?" Dice sighs as I walk past and storm towards the door. "Dane!" It comes out more snapped and more urgent. I spin round to face him. "I want to talk to you." He gasps at me.

"We don't always get what we fucking want, Dice, do we?" I snap back as I stomp down the stairs, climbing into the truck as Ray peels out of the gates.

Skye

Stepping out into the living room, all eyes turn to me and my puffy red eyes, my sniffling face and my blotchy skin. "Love?" Tank gasps. "What did she do?" The concern across his face lets me release a big sob. As he pulls me in towards his chest and then leads me over to the sofa, "Talk to me, love." I glance over at Dice and Steel as they both come to sit on the sofa. Steel has a bottle of water in his hands, which he passes to me.

"Whatever it is, Skye, she's not quite herself at the minute. What did you need?" Steel gives me a softened grin like he's not sure what's going on, but he'll help if he can.

"Me and Tank are getting married," I blurt out as fast as I can, and Tank grabs my hand, squeezing it hard.

"Married?" Steel roars as he dives to his feet. "She's a fucking child, Tank!"

Tank jumps from the sofa as I sob again. "Steel, please listen, it's not what you think."

"You were supposed to look after her, not start fucking grooming her!" Steel slams his hands into Tank's chest.

"Wait, it's not what you think, please. Steel, let me explain." I exhale a sob.

"I'll leave you guys to it!" Dice starts to head to the door.

"Wait, Dice, please, we need your help!" He turns on his heel and just glares between us. "Please just listen to the whole story before deciding how you feel, okay?"

Steel slides back onto the sofa, and Dice joins him. "Do you want me to start love?" Tank asks, and I just shake my head, taking a gulp of water.

Staring into his eyes, I shake my head. I need to do this for me and my family.

"I'm twenty-four," I breathe out a sigh, then look at them both as they look at me and then back at each other.

"What do you mean you're twenty-four?" Steel asks, looking at Tank and then back at me again.

"When Ray found us, she really looked after us and made me feel safe. The others were so much younger than me that when she asked, I lied. I didn't have anywhere else to go and no one to look after me. I'd never… been out in the world alone before, and I was so scared. Ray protected me and made me feel safe, so I lied so she would still help me. I didn't think she would if she knew I was older than her." I hang my head in shame.

"Does Ray know now?"

"Yes!" I breathe out, my bottom lip quivering slightly as I look between Dice and Steel. "I'm pregnant," I say, just blurting everything out and sighing with relief.

Steel's gaze shoots to Tank. "Did you knock her up when you thought she was nineteen or when you found out she was twenty-four?"

"Steel — "

"Dice, can you take Tank into the room he's been staying in, please? I need to talk to Skye alone." Steel stands and folds his arms across his chest. This guy is huge and totally scary, so I turn to Tank and nod, giving him a tight-lipped smile.

"Come on, man, give 'em a sec, yeah?" Dice puts his hand on Tank's shoulder and leads him through the door towards the bedrooms.

"Skye… I need you to be honest with me, okay? Did he force you?"

"No, God, no, we haven't…"

He nods, "Did anyone else force you?"

My lip quivers again, and I look away from him. "Tank is gonna be the baby's father." I say as I turn and meet his gaze. He nods in acknowledgement of the underlying truth in my tone.

"Why did Ray take off? What did she say?"

"She asked me if I wanted this, as I don't have to get married. She said she would support me herself. She would take care of the baby and me. I told her I wanted this. I want me and Tank and the baby to be a family. She asked what kind of wedding I wanted, and she would pay for everything, and then she said she was going out to get my wedding present."

"She stormed out of here, dragging Dane along like they were heading out on a murder spree, to get you a wedding present? That's all she said?"

"Yeah."

"Then why the tears?"

"She just told me she loved me and would protect me no matter what, and no one ever looked after me before I met Ray."

He sighs, stands, pulls me to my feet, and drags me to him, holding me tight. "Whatever you want, we will all help you, okay? But is this honestly what you want, to stay here? You don't wanna fresh start somewhere else?"

"This is my fresh start." I smile up at him. He hugs me tighter.

"Do I get to play uncle?" I gasp as I pull back, staring into his face to see the lie, but I feel so much love from him that my eyes swell, and a tear rolls down my cheek.

"You would want that?"

"Sure, Tank is my brother, and you're my... I suppose my little sister is a little weird if you're marrying my brother. Shit, now I know why that was weird for Ray."

I stare up at him, confused, but smile, as he and Ray have been the only true parental figures I've ever really known, the only people who give a damn about me besides Tank. "It's a boy!" I smile.

"Holy shit!" He beams. "Congratulations!" He spins me around, and I let out a little squeal as Tank comes barrelling through the door and stops dead in his tracks when he sees Steel spinning me round the living room.

He lowers me, and I skip to Tank's arms and throw myself into them. "Steel wants to be the baby's uncle." I beam at him.

"He does?" Tank looks over at Steel and mouths, "Thank you."

"Uncle? What the fuck?" Dice spits out.

"I'm gonna be a dad." Tank grins, and Dice throws his arms around us both.

"Holy shit." Dice laughs.

"Are you moving in then, Brother?" Steel cocks a brow at Tank as he knows we're not staying in the same room.

"Nah, I'm gonna get the lodge ready, and we're moving in there as soon as it's finished."

"Well, I've nearly got the coffee shop ready, and the boys have helped out. Why don't we just carry on and smash the hell out of that reno too?"

"You wouldn't mind?" Tank asks, looking between them both.

"Nah, just get what you want, and we will all chip in. We can have the whole thing done in a couple of weeks.

"Wait, what did you need me for?" Dice looks even more confused.

"I don't have any... documentation." Skye steps out of Tank's arms. "I also want to change my name."

"Steel, can I grab a notepad or something? Let's get to work." Dice grins at me. "I need you to write all your details, original name, date of birth, address, where you were born, and what you want to change your name to."

"Skye Pershing," I say, smiling at Tank. "Seems silly to change it, to then get married and change it again!" I shrug, and he grabs me up and slams his lips into mine, making me soften against his body as I moan into his mouth.

"Ahem." Steel grimaces. "Sorry guys, still a little weird." We all burst out laughing. "So what kind of wedding do you want? If Ray's paying, you can have anything you want. She's loaded." He laughs.

"I just want a quick wedding at the courthouse, no fuss,"

"You sure? Hopefully, you only get married once." Dice asks.

I smile. "I just want to be married. I don't care how I get there."

"Right, Dice and Tank, you sort out documentation and whatever else needs to happen. Skye and I will head up to the lodge and start measuring up. I'll call the others on the way up."

Heading up to the lodge, we walk in silence as Steel carries a bag of stuff he apparently needs. Once we get there, he pulls up a website and tells me to pick what I want. As I glance down, it's all kitchens and bathrooms. He starts measuring, and I look through the online brochures. The door pushes open as Tank and Dice stroll in with the others in tow. There's a ruckus of laughter and ribbing as they all congratulate us on the upcoming wedding, before sitting me in a chair in the living room area. Tank wraps me up in a blanket with Steel's phone and tells me to add what I want to the basket, and he'll sort the rest out.

I grin up at him as he leans down and kisses me. "I love you, love!" He smiles down at me.

"I love you too." I grin freely for the first time since I can remember.

"Tank, there's plenty of time for that. Let's get cracking!"

In the time, I've picked the kitchen and bathroom items, tiles and units. Everything has been ripped out and is out on the decking. The whole place is an empty shell, bar the seat I'm sitting in. "Can we salvage any of it?" I ask, as it seems a shame to throw it all out.

"The furniture will be donated, but you're having new everything. We'll go furniture shopping in a few days once we get the kitchen and bathrooms done."

I yawn and stretch in my chair. It's been a long, emotional day, and I just want my bed. That's when we hear the screeching of tyres, and everyone runs out of the lodge.

Ray

Skye asks me to speak with her in private, so we head off to her room. Once we've finished, I head back through to the living room. "Dane, I need you to grab your laptop and head out with me. Steel, I will be back before morning!"

Storming towards the door, I grab my trainers, snatch the truck keys, and head out.

Climbing into the truck as Dane piles into the passenger-side, I peel out of the gates.

"What the fuck's happening?" Dane asks as he flips the laptop open.

"I want you to find everything on a guy called Darren Staines. We're gonna pay said motherfucker a visit." I tell him the address I have for him, which is a trailer park up the coast. "I need to swing by The Tower. I need some supplies." I wink at him.

We pull up off the track on the way to the trailer park, hiding the truck in the undergrowth and walking around the back. We lay in wait for the arsehole to show his face.

"So you gonna tell me who this guy is?"

"All in good time, Daney Boy!" I grin back at him.

"Well, something has lit a fire under your arse, as I've never seen you so excited, and after the last few weeks, I thought we'd lost you."

I grimace. "Well, I've still not dealt with anything that happened on that mission. I'm fucking numb, Dane. I'm trying to pretend they aren't dead and they're just at home. So that's how things are going, but this, this will help."

As we find his trailer, it's dark. There's no one home, so we break in and lie in wait.

"What's the plan of attack?" Dane questions. We're on either side of the door, sitting on the floor in the dark.

"Grab him, gag him, tie the fucker up. Then I need to search the place and take back what we need. Once we've got everything, we'll take him back to the truck, and then I'll come back here, light the fucker ablaze and take the motherfucker back to the office."

"Well, okay then." Dane says with a smile on his face. I can't see it, but I can hear it in his voice.

"Wanna talk about you and Dice while we wait?"

"Nope!"

"Well, okay then!" I fire back at him as we sit in silence once more. About an hour or so later, the lock jiggles, and then I hear keys drop, and then there's a thud against the door where I think he's fallen over trying to find his keys, and then there's muttering and more curses. "Fuck's sake!" I stand ripping the door open and dragging the twat inside.

"Thanks!" he slurs.

"Fucking twatwaffle." I mumble as me and Dane grab him and strap him to the chair with duct tape, muffling the mumbles with a length across his mouth.

Flicking on the light, Dane grumbles, "Ah, bright light, bright light."

Making me chuckle, I say, "Come on, Gizmo!"

"What are we looking for?" Dane asks.

"Anything that mentions Alice Montgomery."

"Who the fuck's that?"

"Irrelevant."

Darren is taped to the chair so tight he can barely move or make a sound, so we set off looking for anything we can find. Honestly, there's nothing here that would have said she ever lived here, but when I find the room that would have been hers, I completely strip the place and find a shoe box full of photos of her and her mum from when she was little, and there's a loose panel on one of the walls with some cash and some paperwork stuffed in it.

"Smash the walls apart!" I shout through to Dane, and then I hear him doing as I ask. When we meet back in the central area, he has a shoebox of his own and a folder with some paperwork in it. "What's in the folder?"

"Birth certificate, social security info, bank account for Alison Montgomery and life insurance policy."

"We'll take it all." I rummage through the cupboards, find a rucksack, and dump everything into it. Cutting dickhead from the chair, we drag him out into the night. I turn the gas on and leave it. Pulling the door shut, we leave, dragging him quickly out of view. Once we get him to the truck, we throw him in the back, and I run back to light the place up. Pulling out my phone, I start filming. I push the door open and throw in my lit matchbook before taking cover. The place explodes almost immediately as I'm knocked on my arse with a chuckle. I get up, step around the side of a different trailer and film the chaos for a few minutes before making my way back to the truck.

"Home, Jeeves!" I laugh at Dane as we head back to the MC.

Flying through the gates, we head straight for the barn. With a screeching of tyres, we skid to a halt, flicking up gravel everywhere. I jump out and fling open the barn doors as Dane screeches inside. We hear a commotion from the lodges as I run inside the barn. "I need him in a cell before they get here." Dragging him out and down into the office, I say, "I want him naked!" as I grab the collar from my bag.

Attaching the collar and stripping him, I throw him in the cell and slam the door. I hop up onto the table with my legs crossed as Dane leans against the wall. We can hear voices getting closer.

"I told you to stay at the lodge!" I hear Tank whisper-shout, but seriously, dude, you're still fucking shouting. I hear a female voice, which must be Skye's, but I can't make out what she's saying.

"That's my fucking truck… Ray, is that you down there?"

"Yeah, I'm down here, baby. Skye, I've got your wedding present! Come down and see."

Dickhead starts thrashing around, but we've taped his wrists behind his back and his mouth back up, so it's just a lot of muffled grunts and banging.

Tentative steps are taken down into my office as Steel comes in first with his gun raised, lowering it when he sees me sitting relaxed on the table. Tank follows behind, gripping Skye's hand tightly. "Tell the others to stay up there!" I shout over.

Once the three of them are inside, I lock up, and Skye jumps. "What is this place, Ray?"

"It's my office, kiddo." I lift my hand, and she reaches for it. Coming to stand at the side of me, I say, "I've got you your wedding present. It's up to you what you do with it!" I grin at her and then step to the side. The thrashing starts up again, and she jumps back and gasps as he slams his body into the bars, pleading with her with his eyes.

"Is that…? " she trails off.

I nod, and she gasps, pulling her hand to her mouth and turning to slam herself into Tank. "Who the fuck's that?" he snarls.

"Darren Staines … Alice's mum's boyfriend." I grin.

"What the fuck?" Tank bellows as he drags Skye behind him to protect her. "Why the fuck would you bring him here?" Tank yells at me.

"For me!" Skye steps out from behind him. She walks over to me and hugs me. "I don't know if I can do this!"

"You don't have to do anything! He can suffer as much or as little as you want, he can die fast or slow, he can suffer at your hand or mine, but the one thing he won't do is leave my office breathing!"

"You did this for me? For the baby?" Skye asks.

I nod. "I did." This fucker could ruin everything if he found out about the baby she's carrying, and she won't be able to bring that baby into the world knowing he's still out there.

"Give me your phone!" She hands it over. I tap a few things on it, then whistle for a bit. "Waiting for the app to download!" I wink at her, and then when it does, I log in and set it up for her, waving her over. "Right here, I've logged it in, this scrolls through, this zooms in. It's a live feed 24/7."

She scans the room, smiling when she sees the cameras and glances back at the phone. "What does that do?"

"Wait!" I rush over to the cell and grab the tape from his mouth, ripping it off and making him flinch, but he rests himself back against the bars.

"Alice?" he groans out.

"Press it now!" I whisper as she does. He screams and drops to his knees, shaking and convulsing as he gasps to the floor.

Her eyes widened. "Did I do that?"

I nod, excited at the look on her face. "It will only let you shock a maximum of ten-second bursts. I don't want you to fry him before you decide what you want to do with him. But you can take as long as you like to decide. I'm not feeding the bastard, but he can have water, so I say you've got two or three months before he dies anyway. Suppose that's enough, great. If not, let me know what you want to do. This, you can keep an eye on everything, but if you want to come down here, just ask." I tap the table, and she follows my gaze and grins.

"You can strap him to that?"
I nod.
"I can do anything I want!"

"Anything, or I'll do it if you would rather!"

She starts crying and throws her arms around me. "Thank you, Ray!" She grins, and I kiss her on the forehead.

Clutching the phone to her chest, she walks back over to Tank's arms. "Can we go back to the apartment now? I'm still tired."

He nods and wraps her in his arms as he leads her up the stairs. I push the button to open the hatch.

"Skye," I say before she reaches the stairs, "Here!"

"What's this?"

I hand her the rucksack, "It's everything I could find at the trailer that you might want, also…" I tilt my phone and hit play. She watches with a gasp and a sad smile.

"Is it really gone?"

"Yeah, it's really gone!" I smile at her.

"I'll head back too," Dane says, following them out."

"Skye! Turn that app off for a couple of hours, yeah?"

"Why?" Her head pops back over the opening as I wink at her and point my thumb in Steel's direction. "Jesus!" she mumbles and shuffles off.

I press the button, closing the hatch back down. "I'm sorry, baby. I'm just…"

He stalks towards me and leans down, picking me up and placing my arse on the table. "You don't have to talk about any of it. Just don't run away, okay?"

I nod and close my eyes, resting my head on his chest as he pulls me closer. Leaning over, I click a button, and the table rises a bit higher so I'm level with him.

"Nice!" He grins at me as the dickhead starts shouting from the cell.

"Can you pass me that box over there?" I ask Steel as he goes to grab it. I turn to Darren, "You need to shut the fuck up, as if you ruin the moment between my man and me, I will make you die the slowest, most painfully horrible death imaginable! Do. You. Fucking. Understand. Me?"

Steel hands me the box, and I press it as Darren's body shudders, convulses, and slams onto the floor. "Well?"

He nods and slinks back to the cot in the corner.

I pull Steel back between my legs and pull his t-shirt over his head, licking up his body and nipping at his piercings as I go. I grab the front of his jeans and start unbuttoning them, pulling out his dick and wrapping my hand around his length.

"Fuck, I've missed you!" He grins as he leans in and devours me, kissing me like it might be our last. I groan into his mouth as I fumble to rid myself of my joggers. He yanks my hoodie over my head, leaving me naked. There's a gasp from the cell. "Look at her again, and I'll gouge your fucking eyes out!"

There's a shuffle, and I glance over to find Darren facing the wall, and with a chuckle, I say, "Fuck me like you mean it!"

I grin at him as he cups my arse and yanks me to the edge of the table. I'm at the perfect height as he slams into me, and I sprag my arm behind me, holding me up. Still slightly back so he has to lean over me, he puts one hand flat at the side of me on the table, and the other cups my arse cheek, slamming into me again, and my head lolls back. He bites down hard on my collarbone, making me scream out in pain and pleasure as he buries himself as far inside me as he can. I can almost taste him he's so deep.

He slams into me again, and my eyes roll into the back of my head as his teeth clamp down on my nipple and he tugs at my piercing, making my eyes water and my pussy clench, causing him to groan.

Slamming into me again and biting down on my other nipple, I grab the back of his hair in a death grip, pulling him onto my nipple as hard as I can. He sucks it into his mouth as he slams into me again, biting down and then sucking.

I feel myself clench on him again, and he groans, licking up from my tit to my neck before clamping down on the delicate skin there and sucking it into his mouth, causing me to buck and moan against his thrusts. He's fucking me like it's a punishment, but all I can think about is how I can be bad again. As he bottoms out inside me over and over again, my core starts to clench, and my body starts to shake as he slams into me, just hitting my clit in the right place. I drop my head back as I feel his hand grip the back of my hair and pull me to his lips, smashing his mouth into mine. His tongue plunges in and out as punishingly as his dick. My arm can't hold me any more, and I drop back as his body covers mine, never slowing his assault, smashing his hips into me at a whole new angle.

"Hades, fuck!" I roar as I plummet over the edge, my orgasm ripping through me so hard that I think I can taste colours and see smells. My eyes roll into the back of my head as my lashes flutter closed before a feeling of emptiness and weightlessness hits me.

My eyes fly open. Steel pulls out of me and takes a deep breath before spinning me over and slamming my front onto the table. His hand pushes on the back of my neck as he slams back into me, and I groan as my legs dangle, not quite reaching the floor. As he pulls back, he pushes a finger in as he pushes his dick into me, and the tightness and the burn feel so good. As he pulls back out, slamming another finger in with his dick making me gasp for breath as he removes both fingers and slams them into my arse, and fuck me, the sensation, it's so mind-blowing.

I'm full, and as the burn subsides, he slams into me again, making me bite down on my lip, and I get that coppery taste filling my mouth. I grab onto the table and lift one leg up as he slams into me again, and I slide my hand underneath me into the gap I've created. I slide my fingers in with his dick, and he groans. I push my fingers in and out with his thrusts, circling my clit with my thumb.

I start to gasp, and my core starts to clench. He grabs my hair and rips my head back, making my back arch against him and thrusts in deeper as I hear him grind his teeth and his thighs clench. I hear a groan and gasp that doesn't belong to Steel, and I know our guest is getting himself off, so I grab for the button, and as my orgasm hits, I gasp out. I squeeze it in my hand, and the piercing scream rips through the room as we both fall over the edge. Steel roars his release as I scream mine, and poor Darren screams for a whole other reason. As I look around, his hand has clamped shut around his dick, but his body has tensed and yanked his arm. He's nearly strangled and ripped his own dick off, and it caused me to break out laughing as Steel slowly pumps in and out of me, making sure I get every last drop. His body collapses on mine, and he chuckles in my ear. "You, wife, are a terrible person."

I grin over my shoulder at him as he pulls out and flips me back over. Wrapping my legs around him, I pull him closer to me and groan as his softening dick slides against my lips and my clit, causing me to wrap my legs tighter and drag him against me.

He gasps, "Ahh, it tickles."

He shudders as I grin at him, slide my hands up his chest and behind his neck. I slide myself against him again. Fuck knows why, but this always sets me off as I grind again. As he slips against me, I can feel him thickening again and I slide my hand between us as i guide him in causing a shudder from us both as he lazily starts to thrust as the sensation builds, and the feeling of his come sliding around my thighs has me panting, I grind on him, totally dick-drunk, as I can't get enough.

His breath hitches as he starts to harden even more, and his thrusts quicken as he grabs me with more intent, pulling me onto him again as he lifts me totally off the table, spinning us around till he's perched on the table. I wrap myself around him as he slides back and turns so he's lying on the table with his legs hanging off the end. Sliding my hand down to his wrist, I clamp him to the table, and I slip the other hand in and clamp him down while I seat myself properly.

"Be a good boy and hold tight, baby." I start slowly as I grind myself onto him backwards and forward, as if I'm trying to rub him through the table. My thrusting becomes more hectic and frantic as I grind into him, leaning over and biting down on his nipple, pulling the piercing into my mouth. I can feel his hand twitch as if he's trying to grab me, but he groans when he's unable to. Sliding across him, rubbing our slickness against us both, has me groaning.

I shudder, and he gasps as I grind and try to fuse our hips together. I sit up straight and slide my hands up my body, pinching and tugging at my nipple piercings as I ride Steel into oblivion, groaning and grinding. The heat between us feels at boiling point now, and the build-up of friction is causing black splotches around my eyes.

I gasp. I'm grinding onto him as I shudder, and fuck me, this one is even more intense. I thrust my head back and slam against him. He roars as I feel his red hot come fill me again while I continue to gasp and chase my end. After a few more grunts and groans as I grind my hips, I reach down and pinch my clit, and fuck me, I go off like a firework. Grabbing it again, I sit up and pull at one of my nipples again, yanking at the piercing and screwing my eyes shut while I take what I want from his body.

"Baby, look at me!"

I look down to meet his gaze, and that's it. I'm done for. I roar and shudder as I scream in pure ecstasy, and my orgasm forces his come out all over us, and I flop to his chest.

"Motherfucker," I gasp out as he chuckles. Looking up to meet his gaze, he leans up and kisses me as I reach down and release him from his binds.

"Fuck, I love this table!" He grins at me.

"Fuck, I love you more!" I pick up the black box and squeeze it again till I hear dickhead flopping around like a wet fish, and I chuckle. Sliding off Steel, I try to stand, but my legs have gone, so he grins and helps me up. Grabbing our clothes, we get dressed.

"Stay with me?" he says in the softest voice possible.

"I'm sorry I didn't come home sooner!"

"We'll talk about it when you're ready, but I want you back in our home, in our bed!"

"Come on, take me home." I smile up at him. Just as I get to the bottom of the stairs, I press the button again for good measure. Ya know, because I'm an arsehole like that, and the fucker deserves it!

Skye

As I make my way to my room, I say a quick goodnight to Tank and slip into bed. I pull out my earbuds and slide them in, connecting them to my phone. Opening up the app, I can't help it. I know she said not to, but I'm too curious. As it flicks to life, the noises that fill my ears make me jump and gasp. I flick to a different camera, and it's the money shot. I can't take my eyes off the naked bodies as they slam against each other. There's a weird warming sensation between my legs, and it's starting to feel wet. I rub my legs together to ease the sensation, but I'm so turned on. I've never felt like this before, ever. I've been close when Tank kisses me, but he always breaks off before it gets this heated.

I slide my hand down my body, and it causes electric sparks. I slide my hand between my legs and gasp at the slickness that's already coating my inner thighs. I slide across my clit and gasp as I dip my fingers into my soft, warm lips. I've never touched myself either, ever. I've never had anything good sexually happen. It's always been taken and forced, so this is a whole new experience.

I'm winging it as I slide my fingers in and out of myself, and as I rub around my clit the sparks are flying through my body. I roll onto my side as I pick up the pace. I have the phone clutched tight in my grip, and I can't stop watching. It's the sexiest thing I've ever seen, and as Ray starts to orgasm, I feel myself going over with her. *Oh my god, oh my god, oh my god.* I can't believe that just happened and how great it felt.

"SHIT!" I shout out when I feel a hand on my shoulder.

"Love? Oh… erm, sorry. I thought you were having a nightmare."

I gasp as I look at him, and I fly up so I'm sitting up, ripping my earbuds out. Then, a smile falls across his face. "Is that Ray and Steel?"

"Shit, I… er… wanna watch with me?" I shrug. I mean, it can't get any more awkward. He slides in behind me, between me and the headboard, and I gasp as he kisses my neck. "I wanna feel like that!" I whisper. "I wanna feel as good as Ray does."

"Have you ever done anything… willingly before?" he asks, and I shake my head. "Okay, so let's just take it really slow, okay? If you want me to stop, just say!" I nod. "I need to hear you say it, love."

"I promise I will say stop if I want you to!"

Steel pulls out of Ray, rolls her so she's on her front, and slams back into her. I can't take my eyes off her face. It's so beautiful and passionate, and ecstasy is written all over it. Tank slides my PJ top over my head and slides one of his hands around my front so he's cupping my breast, running his thumb across my nipple, causing it to pebble and goosebumps to shoot along my skin. He nips at my neck, kissing down it and along my shoulder, nipping at that next. Every trail of his lips, tongue, and teeth causes my skin to bump and tingle. His other hand runs along my stomach and plays with the band of my sleep shorts, causing little shudders.

"You okay, love?"

I nod, biting down on my lip. I've never been touched like this before, so gentle and tender, but the roughness of his thick fingers is causing electric sparks to follow in their wake. Sliding his hand under the elastic of the waistband and into my pants, I gasp, and he freezes.

"Don't... stop," I manage to gasp out as he slides his rough fingers straight over my clit to enter me.

My head lolls back as he pushes the first finger in, and his thumb passes over my clit, causing me to buck. After giving myself what I believe to be my first orgasm, I'm so responsive to his touch.

I'm literally trembling as he makes another pass over my clit while pushing another finger inside me, causing me to gasp out. He has really big hands, and his fingers are thick and strong.

"Jesus," he whispers into my neck. "You're so tight and so wet."

He nips down on my neck again as Ray lifts her leg and slides her hand under herself. The groans coming from them both push me to the brink against Tank's hand as he slides his other hand across my chest to pinch my other nipple, pushing a third finger in.

Ray and Steel both come, and I'm gasping and panting as my eyes are glued to the screen. Tank is nipping at my neck and pinching my nipple as his fingers thrust in harder this time, ripping an illicit moan from my lips, and he groans into my shoulder. I can feel his solid length pushing into my back through his boxers, and his bare chest is slicking against my naked back. I can feel his heat against me, and his smell, being this close, is driving me delirious. My eyes roll back in my head for a second as I hear Ray and Steel moan again, and as I open my eyes, I gasp again as she's strapping him to the table and she's on top of him. Wow, she looks so confident and sexy, and I wish I were as free as she is.

Tank rubs my clit again as my breaths come in erratic. I'm so full and overwhelmed by all the new sensations. I never believed for a second this could feel so good. I grab his wrist with my free hand as I start to frantically grind onto his fingers as Ray picks up her pace. He chuckles into my neck, causing me to shudder against him.

"You gonna come for me, love?" he asks in that deep, rumbly voice of his, and I bite down on my lip.

I mumble. "Please, Tank!" I gasp. "Don't… stop!" And he flicks his thumb over my clit again, then pushes on slightly harder and rubs in circles. I try to buck off the bed, but he holds me across my chest as he sucks and licks against my neck.

"Tank!" I gasp. "T-T-Tank!" I roar as my second-ever orgasm rips through me, and it turns out the one I gave myself was nothing compared to this. I get black dots across my vision. I thrash against his hold and feel him grin against my neck.

He holds me tight, kissing my neck through the shudders. Once my breaths return to normal, and my heart has almost stopped racing, he slides his fingers out of me, I turn in his arms, and he leans back slightly. I can't take my eyes off him as he smirks at me.

"I wanna do that again!" I say with a grin as I slide against his body, causing a moan. I slide up to reach his lips and draw him in for a kiss. Heat starts to pool again, and my hips grind into him, but he grabs them to hold me still.

"Let's take this really slow, okay? We don't wanna go too fast, and it be too much all in one go, okay, love?"

I sigh, letting out a bigger sigh as I deflate slightly in his arms and look away from him. After watching Ray, I'm sure he'd sooner have someone like her than someone so inexperienced like me.

He tilts my gaze to his. "You're the most beautiful thing in the world ever. You know that, right?" I half smile. "Hey, don't ruin this!" He tilts my chin up to look at him. "I want to so bad, believe me! I just want to give you time to ease into everything. We've got our whole lives to have sex like that!" He points at the screen. "But to get there, we need to build slow, okay?"

"Okay." I sigh again. "Will you stay the night?"

"For a little while, at least." he says as he slips under the covers, pulling me off him and against his side, taking the phone off me. "Shall I turn this off now?" He grins.

"I think they're done anyway." I smile at him.

He chuckles. "You like watching, huh?"

I shrug. "I've never seen anyone do… anything like that before. It was just so… sexy."

"You're so fucking sexy." He grins into my mouth as he kisses me. "Now come on, love, it's been a big day. You need to get some rest." I nod against his chest and slide my arm around his waist, and he grins into my hair and wraps both his arms around me tight. "I'll stay until you fall asleep, okay?" I nod as my eyes flutter shut, and I breathe him in with a smile on my face.

When I wake, I can feel his warm body still holding me, and I can't help but smile. I run my fingers across his tattooed body. There's barely any skin without a tattoo on it. This is the most undressed I've seen him, and he's solid muscle. I trace my fingers around the lines of the tattoos on his chest. "You're staring. It's creepy." He grins against the top of my head, dropping a kiss on it.

"Morning, handsome!" I kiss his chest as he tilts my chin up to meet his lips.

"Good morning, love!" He smiles into our kiss.

"I don't ever want to sleep on my own again, and I don't want to wake up alone ever again." I lean up and kiss him more. I start to get a bit heated after everything last night. I'm kind of in the mood for testing boundaries. My leg is wrapped across him, and I subconsciously grind myself into his hip, causing me to groan involuntarily.

"Sorry, love, I have to go. I've got work."

"Really?"

"Uh-huh." He kisses the top of my head. "I promise you if you wanna try something… new tonight, though, I'm all yours."

I sit up quickly, causing him to groan as I'm still topless. My breasts aren't massive, but they bounce, making him bite his lip. "Nope. Nope. I have to go." He leans as if he's going to get out of bed, but he throws me back as his mouth latches around my nipple as he gropes it with his hand. I groan and grab his head, gripping him to my breast as my eyes roll into the back of my head.

He nips my nipple with his teeth, then pops it out of his mouth, rolling me onto my front and slapping my backside.

"Naughty, distracting fiancée." He grins at me. "Tonight, I'm all yours. Choose something fun." He winks at me as he skulks out of the room, and I throw myself back into my back and let out a sigh of frustration.

I lay and stare at the ceiling for a good thirty minutes, then I throw my PJ top back on and head into the living room. Ray's sitting on the sofa reading, but no one else is around.

"Morning! Where is everyone?"

Turning, she smiles. "Hey. They're at the lodge getting started. How are you feeling?"

"Erm… good?" I shrug.

"I know it's a lot. But you don't have to rush into anything with dickhead in my office, okay?"

I nod, tugging at the bottom of my top. "Actually, can I talk to you while it's just us?"

"Sure, what's up?" She places her Kindle on the coffee table and turns to look at me.

Looking at the hem of my top as I twist it between my fingers, I say, "I did something I shouldn't have last night …"

"Okay…?" She sounds confused.

Sighing. "I came back here and logged into the app!" My cheeks flush with embarrassment, and I can't look up at her.

She barks out a laugh. "You secret little perv you!" She nudges my shoulder, and as I look over at her, she's waggling her eyebrows at me. "So what did you think?"

I gasp and flush again, twisting my fingers into my top. "I gave myself my first orgasm while I watched you! I'm so sorry. I didn't mean to. It was just… I've just never… I couldn't help… I don't know what came over me!" I huff out a frustrated breath. "Then Tank caught me thinking I was having a nightmare from all the moaning. Then he watched the rest with me and gave me another orgasm, and now I'm confused!" I rush it all out on a single breath, then huff out in relief.

"So you and my brother." She cocks a brow in my direction. "Watched me and my husband have mind-blowing sex multiple times in my office while I had a prisoner chained up and repeatedly shocked him, and you got yourself off, then Tank came in and got you off too?"

"Yep!" I look at the hem again. "That about sums it up.

"So… what's confusing?"

"How do I get from where I am with Tank to where you and Steel are, because I want that!"

"Firstly, can you go and take that Care Bears fucking PJ set off, and let's go shopping and get you some more age-appropriate clothing? We can talk on the way!"

"Seriously?"

"Yep!"

"Oh, and Tank said I can pick something new to try tonight, and I need your help. I want to suck his … you know, and I don't know how!" I bounce up off the sofa and run to my room.

I hear Ray mutter, "Fucking Hades!" under her breath as I push through the door, but all I can do is smile.

Ray

So, after the mammoth shopping trip, we get back in the truck. I hand Skye a little bag with a grin on my face. "Here!"

"What's this?"

"Open it." I chuckle.

She eyes it wearily before opening up the bag and then peering inside. She gasps, then slams it shut. "Oh my god! Is that…?" Letting out the breath she's holding as I smile back at her.

"You want some pointers." I nod to the bag. "Grab it out, and I'll talk you through it. Also, if you wanna start having sex for fun, you need to find what you like and explore yourself when no one's around." I wink at her, and her face flames.

"Ray, I don't think I can do that?"

"Sure you can! If it helps, the footage from the office is stored in the cloud. You can watch it back!" I bark out a laugh as her legs clamp together, and she shuffles in her seat. "You getting a bit uncomfortable over there?"

"Get lost." She grins at me as she pulls at her clothes. She's flushed and turned on just from thinking about the footage she saw!

"Right, grab it out of the packaging. I'll show you with your hand first and then your mouth, and then you can do a bit of both." I hear gasps and chatter through the glass as we get to the lessons. As I turn, there are faces full of horror. "What's up? You never seen anyone giving a blow job to a dildo in a car park before?" I smirk out the window.

"Can we continue this at home?" Skye blushes again.

"Sure, kiddo." I laugh at her mortified face as we pull out of the car park and head back to the MC.

As we get back to the apartment, we head inside. No one's around, so we head to Skye's room. "Right, what do you want to know?"

"Everything." she exclaims as she scooches back onto the bed and crosses her legs."

"Right, first, let's get some batteries." Piling them in, I hand her the vibrator. "Right, put it on your nose!"

"My nose? Why would I do that? I thought it was for down there!" She looks at it, confused.

"You can test them on your nose to get an idea of sensation, but when you're on your own or with Tank, you use them down there."

"I can use it with Tank?"

"Sure, if you both want to. You can do anything you like if you both want to."

"Right, so grab him like this, and move like this, okay?"

"Like this?"

"Yep, that's good." I twist her hand. "Now, like this."

Her eyes widen. "Okay… okay, I think I got it."

"Now lick." I lick up the length. "Flick." I flick my tongue around the head. "And suck." I plunge it into my throat. "When you gag, swallow!" Wiping the vibrator on my shirt—gross—I hand it over, and she tries it a few times, testing her gag reflex. "You've got skills." I wink at her, and she grins around the pink vibrator in her mouth, making me chuckle.

"How are you feeling about everything?" I ask as she pops the vibrator out of her mouth and tosses it on the bed.

"I gave Dice the bag. He's gonna look through it for the documents to change my name, and then we can get a marriage certificate. I'm hoping that won't take too long."

"When you get that stuff back, come see me, and I'll take you to the bank and get you an account set up with some money, so you won't need anything."

"Ray, I can't ask you to do that. It's too much!"

"Trust me, Skye. I've got more than I will ever need, my kids will need, or the kids of my kids. So don't panic. I will get you set up."

"Ray, I don't know how to thank you for this life of freedom you've given me. Who would've thought that getting sold was the best thing that could ever happen to me!"

"Just answer me honestly, okay?"

"Okay."

"Is this what you want, Tank? The baby? To stay here?"

She nods excitedly. "I thought I was going to get rid of the baby. I honestly thought that! Then, while you were away, when I got rushed to the clinic, I panicked that I might lose the baby and Tank really stepped in and protected me and then said he would be the baby's dad whether I wanted to be with him or not. He wants this baby so much. But he told me that if I wanted to be with him too, we could be a family. We could have it all, and I'm falling for him so hard. He's patient, kind, protective, and caring, and I couldn't ask for more, Ray."

"That's all I need to know, kiddo."

"Still with the kiddo, huh?"

"Yep, and this one"—she points to my bump—"will be lil kiddo!" We both bark out a laugh. "So, what kind of wedding do you want?"

"Just the courthouse. Nothing fancy, inner circle for snacks or something after somewhere that's not the bar, though."

"Ooh, I've got an idea. Come with me."

I grab her hand and drag her through the apartment and down the stairs, heading to the front of the garage. "Wait? I'm not having my reception in the garage."

"No, dickwad. The coffee shop!"

"Coffee shop?"

Knocking on the door, I push it open. "Demi, you here?"

"Out back, Ray."

"Come on, Skye." Dragging her inside, she gasps.

"Oh my god, this place is so sophisticated." Skye gasps. "Demi, this is amazing." There's dark, rich wood panelling halfway up the walls, a black tiled floor, and the seats are the same dark wood with dark leather upholstery. There are eight tables and two booths in front of the window. The seats are a mix of benches, small armchairs and stools. There's a counter with high bar stools against it, with a glass display case for the cakes.

There's a massive fancy coffee machine at the back with a long counter beside it, potted plants hanging from Macramé plant pot holders suspended around the place and the walls are painted a sage green.

There are sage green napkins, crockery and little vases on the tables, tying everything together with sage green cushions on the small armchairs. Some aprons are hanging up in the same green, and there are piles of towels in boxes to the side of the counter.

"So, Demi, how do you fancy having your grand opening with a wedding reception?" I just bulldoze straight in with no subtlety whatsoever. As I shrug, Skye bounces on the balls of her feet, clapping her hands.

"You're getting married?" Demi looks confused. "When? To who? How?"

"Not sure yet. Soon, though, to Tank, he asked. I said yes, it was wonderful."

"But… but… you're … what? You're nineteen, and he's… Jesus."

"Ah, yeah, you missed the big reveal. Skye's twenty-four, she lied, and it's new, but they're head over heels, and he's thirty." I laugh

"Really? He's only thirty? You sure?"

"Kinda getting off track, ladies." Skye butts in.

"Damn, sorry, Skye, I would love to."

"Sit down with Demi and go through what you want. I'm paying, so whatever it takes, Demi, let me know what help you need. If you need a catering company or waitresses, whatever, I'll drop you my card off tomorrow so you can start getting what you need. We will have a date by then for you, okay?"

"Oh my god, this is so exciting. I need to call Tank." Skye grabs her phone out of her pocket, and as soon as Tank answers, she starts animatedly telling him everything, throwing her arms around, describing every detail in this place, then asks him if she can have the reception here. Then she pauses and bites her lip, pulling it between her teeth as she nods while she walks back and forth across the floor. Me and Demi just stare, grinning at her. "Uh-huh, K, love you." She hangs up, turns to face us and screams. "He says I can have anything I want, whatever makes me happy. And he says two weeks at the latest, so however quick you can make it happen." She jumps up and down, then screams, "This is gonna be the best day ever."

After Demi and Skye review all their options, we leave together. Demi's heading up to the lodge she and Bran have moved into. Bran's doing it up at the minute, but I think he's avoiding everyone.

"Hey, Demi, before you go, how is he?"

She shakes her head. "I don't know, Ray, he's so on edge and grumpy all the time, he won't talk to me, and when we do, we just fight. I'm hoping it's just stress from the renovations."

"Hey, it'll be fine. How about me and Dane pop up later to see if we can't help out a bit?"

"Ray, will you? That would be amazing, thanks."

I nod, give her a hug and head back up to the apartment with Skye. "So you all set for tonight?"

"Yeah, I'm really nervous but excited!"

"You got this. Just remember to lay him down on the bed, don't kneel in front of him. You'll feel less dominated that way. Just take your time and breathe, okay?" She nods as I head inside.

Steel heads over to the bar, and me and Dane take a few bottles of tequila to Bran's lodge. Well, four. We take four bottles.

As we get towards the lodge, we can hear yelling from Bran and pleading from Demi. I take off running and shove my way through the door as Bran is towering over Demi, screaming in her face about god knows what.

"Back the fuck up, dickhead!" I slam the bottles down on the kitchen worktops and step in between them both, putting my hands on Bran's chest and pushing him back a few steps. "Take a fucking walk, Bran. Dane!" I bark at them and nod towards the patio doors.

"Demi…" he gasps as Dane pushes him through the doors.

Fair play to her. She waits till he leaves before she breaks down into tears. "What's happening, Ray? It's like he's a totally different person. I don't think I can do this anymore."

"Hey, don't say that. Don't give up on him. He needs you more than ever. We went through some stuff while we were away that's just gonna take some time, okay? But leave it with me for a couple of days. Why don't you go stay at ours? You can have Dane's room, and we'll stay here and try and figure this shitshow out, okay?"

I fire a quick text off to Steel to tell him Demi's coming to the bar to him and to take her back to ours later. That should give Tank and Skye some time before they end up with the house full again. Fuck's sake, it's like a juggling act around here. I might need to have that revolving door fitted after all.

"Grab a few bits for a few days and meet Steel at the bar. Go get shit-faced with your brother and let me deal with mine, okay?"

She grabs a bag and loads it up just as Bran and Dane walk back in the door.

"I'm sorry, beautiful. I'm just… wait, you're leaving me? Demi, please."

"I'm just gonna stay with Steel for a few days while Ray and Dane stay with you. I'm only down the road. Remember I love you, okay? Please come back to me!" She sniffles as she wipes her eyes, and he pulls her in for a hug

"I'm sorry, I'm so sorry, beautiful."

He kisses the top of her head, and she turns and leaves.

"Text me when you get to the bar." he shouts out as she scurries through the door."

He turns and punches the wall. "Well, this is a right royal fucking shitshow if ever I've seen one. What the fuck am I doing? I wanted to come home to be with her so I didn't lose anyone else, and I'm pushing her away and making her hate me."

"Come on, let's stoke up the fire pit get our tequila on, and sort through these fucking… feelings." I nod to the door.

"Can I sit this one out? I'm fine." Dane hangs back near the front door."

"Are you fuck fine. You're fucking things up with Dice. You won't even speak to the poor guy. You're both being dicks. Outside, now! Don't make me make you!"

"Fucking hell!" Dane grimaces but heads out anyway. Grabbing the tequila and blankets, we all head out back, lighting the fire and sitting back with a bottle of tequila each.

Bran

We take a seat and demolish half a bottle of tequila each before anyone talks. "Why am I even here? I've got better things to do." Dane grumbles.

"Family therapy! Suck it up, arsehole!" Ray spits out.

"Look, shit went sideways. We all fucked up; we just need to move on." Dane chugs more drink.

"No, I fucked up! That's why they're dead. Because of me!"

"Don't be so fucking stupid, Bran. You did not fuck up!" Ray slaps me round the back of the head before chugging another drink herself. "Mistakes were made! But 'we' did not fucking make them!"

"They should never have been there," Dane agrees. "They'd been out of the game too long. Their last mission was what, four, maybe five years ago? They were fucking retired, for fuck's sake!"

"Who gave them fucking clearance to be there?" I ask, glancing at both my brother and sister.

"Who do you think? They're fucking Alpha 1. They don't need anyone else's permission," Ray spits. She's fucking fuming.

"What do we do now?" I ask as Dane keeps fidgeting. We're all starting to slur our words, but we're still making sense, so that's a good thing.

"I'm retiring from the Mercs. I'll still help with the dealing and distribution, even the security, but the Mercs can fuck right off. I've got too much to lose now!" Ray spits again, her words coming out like venom now.

"If you're out, I am too. I can't lose Demi. I need to step up and stop being an arsehole before I ruin everything. I need to get my head on straight."

"I'm staying in. I've literally got fucking nothing to lose." Dane shrugs and slurs more than before, swaying a little. Our bottles are nearly empty now.

"Are you fucking kidding me?" Ray stands up, getting right in Dane's face. She must have got up too quickly, as she rests a hand on his face to steady herself. "Nothing to fucking lose. Are you shitting me right now?"

Dane launches himself off his chair, knocking her hand away, and throws himself at her. They both stumble to the ground. "Yeah, that's right, Mrs. I'm married to the hot, sexy, wonderful, fucking Steel." He punches her in the ribs. She grins at him and punches him back.

"That's right, Mr Wounded Pride, because the hot, sexy, wonderful fucking Dice turned you down. Ya big fucking baby. He's working through some stuff. You need to be patient. Instead, you threw it in his face, and now you're whining like a lil bitch about it!" They're rolling around on the floor, laying punches to each other's ribs.

"Well, it's not my fault your fucking husband's smoking hot, and I've got no one!" Dane sniffs and slurs his words, blinking rapidly.

"You're such a fucking dick-wadding arse-wiping fart box!" She punches him in the jaw, and his head whips around. She jumps to her feet, bouncing on the balls of her feet. I sit and chug the last of my bottle and glance around. Their bottles are virtually empty, but there's another one, so I open it and grab a swig.

"You're such a fucking dildo, you wet bender!" Dane screeches at Ray as he lunges for her, missing and staggering forward. She kicks him in the arse, and he goes down, rolling onto his back. She straddles him and tucks his hands by her side under her legs.

"You're such a fucking cockwombling bellend, you sliding patio fucking door, you absolute fucking douche-canoeing twatwaffle." She starts jabbing at his chest. "Tut tu tu tu tut," and then shouts, "Ding!" She slaps him around the face, then does it again. "Tut tu tu tu tut." Then slap. "Ding"

"What the fuck's she doing?" I flinch at the deep, gravelly voice of Steel, who is sitting in the chair next to me, and as I lean forward, Dice is in the other one.

"Typewriter!" I mutter, shrugging. It's all I have to give in reply.

"You think you're so much better than everyone cos you're stupidly freakishly fucking strong for an early arse!" Dane insults Ray again.

"Tut tu tu tu tut." Slap. "Ding." She laughs. "If you were that bothered, you could have followed your boyfriend into Narnia instead of standing outside the closet bitching about it."

"Fuck you, bitch tits. He's not my boyfriend. He didn't fucking want me!" He roars at her. "Wait… Did you just insinuate that he's that far in the closet he's in Narnia? Actually, that's a good one, but you're still a cunt muffin."

Dice turns to Steel. "Should I be offended?"

"Yeah, Dice, I would be if I were you!" Steel shakes his head as Dice leans forward, licking his lips at the carnage that's going on in front of him.

"Is he pissed?" I ask, and Steel nods. *Ah, that explains it!*

Dane manages to wriggle his hand out while Ray's on the next round of the typewriter, and he swings up to slap her round the face, but she grabs his hand and leans down and licks all the way up his face.

"What the fuck is wrong with them? I thought you guys didn't fight among yourselves?" Dice asks, leaning forward again like he can't look away.

"Family therapy!" I shrug again.

"That literally explains nothing." Steel shakes his head. "How long will this go on for?"

"Until one wins."

"What the fuck are they trying to win?" Steel asks.

Dice leans forward again, mesmerised by the twats rolling around on the floor. "They're making no fucking sense whatsoever."

"Firstly, I can punch like a freight train for anyone, not just an early arse, and secondly, fucking bite me." She slaps him around the face again, and he screams.

"One day, Steel's gonna realise what a fucking cunting bitch face you are, and when that time comes, I'm gonna tell you I was right!"

"You take that fucking back." She punches him in the jaw, and he manages to shove her off till he's straddling her.

"No, I'm gonna wait till he realises, then I'm gonna turn him bi and make you watch me fuck him, and then you and Dice can be lonely little lepers together!"

"How the fuck will we be lonely together, you fucking muppet? And you don't have a big enough dick for Steel. He will laugh at your fucking chipolata!"

"What's a chipolata?" Dice looks confused as all hell.

"You take that back. I have a monster dick, and you know it!" Dane retorts.

Dice leans forward. "He's right!" He nods.

"Oh, please, I've got a bigger dick than you!"

"Bitch!"

"Twat!"

"How much longer?" Steel drops back into his chair.

"Not much now. Once they reach single words, it's almost over." I slur as my head drops back on the chair. "It's too much like hard work keeping my head up to watch those two fuckwits."

They back and forward another few shots each, and Ray punches Dane in the chin and knocks him off her. He rolls onto his back, both panting and cursing. He slaps the back of his hand against her stomach. At the same time, she does him, winding each other as they both sit bolt upright, gasping for air.

"Steel?" Ray gasps out in shock.

Dane gasps, "Dice?"

"How long have you been here?"

"Long enough." They both grin at the two twats, who are covered in grass and leaves and look completely ridiculous.

"So… family therapy, huh?" Dice smiles.

"How's that working out for ya both?" Steel asks.

Ray gets up and leans a hand down to help Dane, who grabs it, but when she's got him halfway up, she lets go, so he falls on his arse and sticks her tongue out at him.

"Yep, we're good." She smiles at Steel.

I just shake my head as I'm too old for their shit.

Mine, Ray's and Dane's phones bling all at the same time. We all pale, and we look at each other. Shit is about to get worse.

MEETING AT THE TOWER 07.00 TOMORROW

"Fuck," I spit out, and Dane and Ray cast glances at each other.

"So, little brother, are you in or out?" Ray turns to face him.

He slowly turns his head to look at Dice, and they make eye contact. It's the most Dane has given Dice since we got back, and Dice gives him a shallow grin. Dane lets out a shaky breath before replying, "I'm out!"

"We end this tomorrow!" Ray informs us, and we all nod. "K.F.D!" She grins. "K.F.D," we repeat, and all hug.

"Yeah, that's great and all, but what the fuck just happened!" Steel sounds pissed.

"We need to head out first thing. We've got some shit to clean up, and then we're done!" Ray explains without explaining anything. "I need to stay with my brothers tonight."

Steel nods and stands, pulling her in tight. "Remember what I asked?"

Ray nods. "I promise!" She kisses him like she's not kissed him in forever, and they both groan. Dane and Dice look really fucking awkward as I turn and leave. Dane is right on my heels, though.

"I thought you might wanna talk to Dice,"

"I just can't right now. I'm too drunk, and I will say something stupid again!" he slurs, and I nod as we head into the lodge, followed by Ray.

White Knight

I'm pacing backwards and forwards. My mind is racing. I'm chewing at my thumb as the last few weeks' events swirl around in my brain.

"I need to tell them!"

"Brother. This will not end well!" White King tells me as he sits at the desk while I wear the carpet out in front of it! Don't you think there's enough shit going on at the minute without throwing a Molotov cocktail at the situation too?"

"We've lost too much. I can't not tell them! I'm retiring!" I blurt out, and he just glares back at me.

"I think that's for the best. I'm retiring, too. I'm too old for this shit, and we have enough teams active to not notice the loss."

"I can't believe it's come to this! I mean, what the fuck were they thinking? It was fucking reckless." I sigh as I flop into the chair opposite. "They should never have been there in the first place."

"At least we agree on that!"

The alarm goes off in the office, telling us they're here. I take my place beside White King and stand at ease. They walk in, nod, and assume the position before flopping into the chairs. My eyes go wide, and White King jumps to his feet.

Ray lifts her finger as if to say wait a minute before talking. "I'm here to speak to my dads!"

"This is not the time or the place. This is an official meeting. You will remain respectful and behave appropriately," White King barks.

Ray takes a long, slow blink as Reaper steps into the driver's seat. Bran and Dane fold their arms across their chests in unison. She slowly rises from her chair, glaring daggers at him. "Bull-fucking-shit!" She places both her hands on the table and leans towards him. "This is exactly the fucking time and exactly the fucking place. Firstly, we lost two more of our fucking dads this month on a job they should never have been on.

"Secondly, not seventy-two hours later, the police inform us that there's been a fire! A motherfucking fire tore through the whole Adventure Centre, leaving nothing but ash while we were all apparently on a family fucking holiday in the States.

"Thirdly, you took off and left us when we needed you the most. If Steel hadn't found us, we would be in our room dead from the amount of fucking tequila we were drowning ourselves in.

"So fourthly, you can both go fucking fuck yourselves and fuck right off, and officially cut the bullshit because we're done. We're out! Game over! The motherfucking end!"

She flops back down in her seat. "Oh, and these are yours!" Then she proceeds to flip us both off.

We both just stand there gob-smacked, and Bran and Dane grin like the stupid motherfuckers that they are. "You fucking bookends got anything to add?" I ask smarmily.

They both lean past Ray to look at each other, then flop back. "What she said!" Bran adds.

"What they said!" Dane replies.

The look of hurt on all their faces fucking cripples me. We handled this all wrong, and it's only gonna get worse from here. I step around the table and pull Ray to her feet, grabbing her into my chest. "I'm sorry, Squirt!" And I hug her like it might be the last time. Once I hug her enough, I step in front of Bran and pull him to me, too. "I'm sorry." And then I grab Dane. "I'm sorry. I love you all. You know that, right?"

"Fuck's sake, this is supposed to be official!"

"Bernie, shut the fuck up and stop acting like an asshole." I shoot over my shoulder at him.

He climbs out of the chair and heads round the table, too. "I'm sorry." He opens his arms wide, and they all step in! "We do need to have a serious discussion, though, okay?"

We all take a seat around the desk again.

"When we left here, we went straight to the Adventure Centre. We emptied everything we thought you would like to keep. It's all in the storage rooms downstairs. Then we torched everything. None of us wants to go back there. We wouldn't have kept the place going. This way, we get the insurance money." Bernie speaks coldly and almost robotic as he glosses over the information.

"Like we need the fucking money!" Dane spits.

"It would have been nice to be asked what we wanted to do with our childhood home," Ray mutters.

"Anyway… the official ruling will be arson, but seeing as we all have an alibi, we will be fine. Steven and JJ used the private jet to come on the mission, but the logs say they came here instead for a vacation. They died in a car accident this morning, and the funeral will be next week."

"Are you fucking shitting me? You passed off their deaths from last month on a fucked up mission as a car accident this fucking morning?"

"Yes! That way, we can cremate them here. We brought everyone else home with us, too."

"That was our fucking home! We have more fucking family members in urns than we do breathing right now!" Bran rolls his eyes and rubs his jaw."

"Look, we're doing our best in a shit situation, okay?" I try to placate everyone. "We just need to regroup and re-game plan."

"So, what now?" Ray looks us both over, trying to figure out what's gonna go down from here.

"Alpha 1 is retiring!" Bernie adds

"Delta 1 is retiring too!"

"Wait, what the hell?" Bernie spits out.

"We're done! We've been at this since we were twelve. Training since we were five. It's fucking draining. We will help with the rest, but the Mercs, we're done!" Ray insists, and the others nod.

"One last mission? The five of us together!"

"Why the fuck should we?"

"One last mission. Together, to end this. We're going after Dante. Then Cade and I will take over the day-to-day running of the Mercs and security, and you three are the new faces of dealing and distributing. We've kept everything far too hush-hush, and now

Dante is convincing everyone he's a bigger fish than he is by passing himself off as The Armoury. We'll take him out!"

Ray looks between her brothers, and they both nod. "Fine. But if I die on this mission, my husband will skin you all alive."

"It won't come to that." I smile. "We have an inside man!"

Ray flies up out of her chair. "Don't say it. Do. Not. Fucking. Say. It!"

"We made Liam an offer he couldn't refuse. We sent him back to Dante, and he's been filling us in on him. We still don't have a visual or a description, but Liam's getting closer, so it's just a matter of time, and we have Kent working on some stuff."

"Kent?" Dane barks. "Are you serious." He shakes his head. "Kent is an imbecile."

"Kent is good at what he does." I say firmly.

"No! Kent tells you he's good at what he does, but the guy's a fuckwit."

"Look, we need to keep everything close to our chests on this one," I tell Dane to placate him further.

"That's exactly why I need to be the one on this."

"He's right. Kent's a twat knuckle if ever there was one! Dane should handle this. He's more than an upgrade on fucking Kent!" Ray's input is always so "professional". I've no idea how we thought this meeting would go through the correct channels.

"You know I agree with them." Bran adds. I don't know why they get three votes. They vote the same way they always have. They have each other's back regardless. They're an immovable force once they lock their answers in.

"Fine!" Bernie mumbles. It's been a long, long, long few weeks, and I think we're ready to be done.

Ring Ring Ring

Glancing at the phone it's the encrypted line. I nod to Ray, "You're up, you're in charge now."

She scoops the phone up barking down the line. "What?"

"Where's Daniel?"

"Dead! …Dean? …Is that you?" She spits down the phone.

"Fuck. Yeah Ray, It's me. I need your help."

"Where the fucks Rocco?"

"Dead."

"Motherfucker!"

"I need to triple our order."

"Is this gonna blow up in my face Dean? I swear to Hades I will skin you alive!"

"No. Always a pleasure Ray, say hi to the chuckle brothers for me."

"Motherfucker hung up!" Ray tosses the phone down.

"What the fuck do The Rippers want triple the guns for?" I ask her.

"How the fuck should I know, you heard as much as I did!"

"Right if we're done here I need to have a word in private with you, Ray, before you head downstairs to sort out your stuff."

"You're doing this now?" Bernie winces.

"I'm doing this now."

"Come on, boys, we will head down and get started." Ray nods to them, and they head off after Bernie. They don't have secrets, and I know she'll tell them straight away, but we need to have this conversation alone.

"Here." I pull a chair around for her to sit in and pull the other one so it's facing hers, and we both sit. I lean forward on my elbows and chew on my thumb. She slaps my hand away.

"Spit it out, Pa! Whatever it is, I can't deal with it till you spill."

"Okay, so… I think I'm your dad."

"Excuse me?" She leans forward, mirroring my posture.

Sighing, I repeat, "I think I'm your dad!"

"Oh… I fucking heard you, alright! I mean, what the fuck are you talking about?"

Sighing, I say, "When your mum and dad were trying for you, something wasn't working. Your dad decided a quieter life may help, so we set up the Adventure Centre. By that time, they were already under our private clinic, and whatever the medical reason, they couldn't have kids together, so your dad asked us to help."

"You fucked my mum?" She gasps and sits back in her chair.

"No! …Hades!" I sit back, too. Hades, we even react to shit alike. "No, I didn't fuck your mum!"

"Well, what then?"

"We all made a 'donation', and they took eggs from your mum, and well, you get the gist!"

"Is that even fucking legal? Ethical? What the fuck, Pa?"

"It's a grey area, but with our connections …"

"So what makes you think I'm yours?"

"I've always thought you were mine. I mean, fucking look at us. It's not like it's not feasible. You're too much like me not to be mine!"

"But Bas was nothing like you. We're twins. That doesn't mean anything."

"You're fraternal twins, which means two separate eggs, which could also mean two separate fathers. We never checked because it didn't matter; you were ours, but now they're all dead. I just don't want to live any longer without knowing if you're my actual daughter… I want you to be. It's all I can think about."

"I keep hearing a lot of what you want! But what about what the fuck I want? You're telling me my dad died. I murdered him, and he might not be my dad, then two of my pas die, and they could be my dads, so I could have lost my dad all over again?" She stands as she rises. "You're a selfish arsehole, CADE!" As I rise from the chair to meet her, she punches me straight in the temple, and my eyes roll, and I fall back on the chair.

There's a slap on my face, and I try to open my eyes. Bernie's face is over me, and the boys are behind him, arms crossed, shaking their heads at me. "Well, that went well!" Bernie grins as he pulls me to my feet.

Shaking my head and trying to get the fog to clear. "It could have gone worse!" They all chuckle and shake their heads.

Dane jabs a thumb over his shoulder. "We're gonna go after her. Erm… you're not our dad, too, are you?" Dane eyes me suspiciously, but I shake my head. "Could you be her dad, though?" He eyes Bernie, and Bernie just shrugs.

"Let me know when you find her, won't you." I plead, but they will do what she says like they always do. They nod as they walk away.

Bran

Dane grabs a laptop and starts scrolling for Cade's truck, the truck she took when she hightailed it out of there, screaming at the top of her lungs as she squealed out of the parking structure.

"She's heading back to the apartment! She's either gonna fuck Steel or fuck someone up! Either way, someone's getting fucked!"

Pulling up at the apartment, the truck is nowhere to be seen. Steel's just walking across the parking lot and waves us over. "Shit, he's gonna flip if we've lost her… again." Dane points out the obvious.

"Hey… where's Ray?"

"There was a… 'disagreement' between her and Cade. She took off in his truck. She headed this way, so she must be here somewhere!"

"Wait, Cade's alive?" Steel grips the door and rips it open in shock!

"Of course he's alive. What are you talking about?"

"We tracked the footage and the two body bags, and they didn't get off the plane."

"Fuck, it was Steven and JJ. We lost them on that mission, Steel."

"Fucking hell. No wonder you are all fucked up!"

"That's an understatement."

"Right, one shit show at a time. How bad a disagreement?" Steel cocks a brow as he leans on the door of the truck.

"She punched him," I tell him.

Dane laughs. "Under-fucking-statement!" He shakes his head. "She punched him that hard, she knocked the motherfucker out! Then stole his truck."

Steel lets out a breath. "Then either the barn or the gym."

We head to the gym first, but there is no sign of her, so we head to the barn. The truck's parked inside.

Then we look at each other. "Can anyone actually get in?" Steel asks.

"Yeah, I can." Dane steps forward.

"Wait, how come you can get in and no one else can?"

"I built the system. I wasn't gonna leave her with the only access." He steps up to the scanner.

"Does she know?" I ask him.

"She's about to!" He shrugs as the bale moves, and we can't hear anything. It's deadly silent!

As we enter, it's empty. Well, apart from the guy she's got locked in there. Where else would she be?

"Baby? Where are you?"

Steel's clearly the brains as he just grabs his phone and calls, and she answers. That seems a bit too easy, but hey. "Okay… they're here… No, he's not… okay, love ya, baby." Then he hangs up.

"She's at the apartment wedding planning with Skye and Demi."

"Say what?" I can't fathom it, "She's gone from full-blown Reaper to a wedding planner. Okay, let's go see what's going on."

As we walk through the door, she's pacing, chewing her thumb, just like he does.

"Hey!" I say calmly, and she walks straight into my arms. I don't wanna spook her. "Big night, huh?"

"You know?" she asks, hurt flashing across her face.

"Dad told us as you left." She sighs out a breath as Steel pulls her from my arms, and she welds herself to him.

"What's wrong, baby?" he asks her in the quietest voice I've ever heard him use.

She huffs and shakes her head. "Cade thinks he's my dad."

"I thought they were all your dads?"

"No, my dad was my dad, the others are my pas, same but different, now my dad is not my dad and my pa might be my dad, or their dad could be my dad, not my pa, and fuck…" She drops onto the sofa while Demi and Skye sit there with open mouths like a pair of goldfish.

"Well, baby, I know it's a mind-fuck, but I'm really proud of you." Steel kisses her on the top of the head, and her eyebrows shoot to her hairline.

"Proud of me?" She sounds so small and so surprised.

Leaning down and pulling her into his chest, he rumbles, "So fucking proud, baby. You didn't run away. You came home."

She physically sags in his arms and buries her face in his chest.

"Ray?" Dane sheepishly breaks the moment. "What do you wanna do?"

"Fuck knows. This changes nothing between us. You're my brothers, no matter who our dads are, but Cade? I want to hug him and kick his arse all at the same time. I'm so confused."

"Is it really that much of a surprise? I mean, come on, you're his mini-me and always have been, maybe we all suspected. Maybe sleep on it and get a test to find out before you hug or hit." I shrug, and she laughs, pulling away from Steel and heading towards me.

"I love you." She pulls me in for a hug and then kisses my cheek. As she ends the embrace, she walks over to Dane and does the same to him.

I drop onto the sofa beside Demi. "I'm sorry, beautiful. I'm so sorry." I don't touch her. I just sit at the side of her, but she climbs over my lap and straddles me, cupping my face.

"Are you gonna tell me what's going on?"

I look over her shoulder, and Ray and Dane both nod. "They're gone. They're both dead." I rest my face into the crook of her neck and breathe her in.

She pulls back from me and stares straight into my eyes as I feel them well up. "Bran? Who's dead?"

It's barely a whisper, and admitting it feels… too real… too raw. "Steven and JJ!" And the tears flow from us all, but none of us make a sound. Demi grabs me and pulls me in as Steel grabs Ray in one arm and Dane in the other and pulls them to him. Once I see he's got them both, I break. The sob tears out of me as tears stream down my face. No one says anything, but

I hear the door click, and I assume that Skye has left the room, but the door clicks again, and something is placed on the coffee table. Then there's movement towards the kitchen, and as I look over, Skye has placed a box of tissues on the table, grabbing the alcohol from the cupboard and lining up glasses on the worktop.

I stand, and Demi wraps her legs around me as I walk over to the worktop and rest her arse on it while grabbing us a glass each.

"To Steven and JJ!" I say, raising my glass. "To the men that helped raise us."

"To Steven and JJ!" they all repeat.

"They were too good for this life!" Ray murmurs.

"We were so lucky to have them," Dane nods, still cradled against Steel's side.

Slamming our drinks back, I say, "Beautiful, I wanna go home."

"Take me home then!" She kisses me as I lift her up and stride for the door. Her legs wrap around me, and she nestles into me. I realise I am home.

Dane

As Bran leaves, I feel so alone, even nestled against Steel. "I'm going to the bar if you don't need me!" I say as I take a step back from Steel, but Ray grabs me.

"I will always need you, little brother! Always." She smiles at me and pulls me into her embrace.

I give her a tight-lipped smile, but at this moment in time, I know it, but I don't feel it. I just feel alone, so I nod and leave, heading over to the bar.

As I walk in, the rest of the Psycho Six are gathered around their table, and Ares and Scar are over in a booth, so I give the others a cursory wave as I pass, making sure not to look at Dice and all his annoying beautifulness and make a beeline for Ares.

"Shit, you okay?" Scar pulls me in to sit beside her, and I shake my head. I'm unaware that Ares moves until a bottle of tequila is placed on the table with some glasses, and he pats me on the shoulder and sits beside me.

"Wanna talk?" he asks, and I shake my head. I've no idea where to start, so I just take the lid off the bottle and take a big drink. Scar rubs circles against my back, and Ares's leg is right next to mine. I can feel the heat radiating off him along my arm and down my thigh. "Do I need to kill anyone?" I shake my head, and he relaxes slightly, nudging me a glass.

I look at it but then chug from the bottle again. "Hey, Dane, can I talk to you for a minute?" I look up into those beautiful, rich, warm brown eyes, and those dark lashes that flutter around them, and I almost break that he's not mine, and he doesn't want me, and I know he's just trying to smooth things over and make sure I don't out him, but I would never do that.

"Not right now, Dice, I'm… I'm… busy." I chug another mouthful from the bottle.

I hear him mutter, "Clearly!" under his breath as Ares shakes his head and Dice leaves.

"What's going on with you two?" Scar asks, cocking her head to the side, but I don't answer. I just take another swig. As I swallow, she grabs my face and turns it to her, raising her brow like she knows I'm full of shit!

"Nothing! Absolutely nothing." I blow out a breath and take another swig.

"Dane, what's wrong?" Scar asks as her phone rings. "It's Ray!" I nod to her to answer it. *Maybe I won't have to say anything.* "Ray… yeah, he's with me and Ares… okay… what's going on? …Shit." A stray tear runs down her cheek, and her hand that's rubbing circles wraps around me. She pulls me closer and rests her head on my shoulder. "You okay…? There's more…?" Her mouth just opens and closes like a fish, but nothing comes out, and another tear rolls down her cheek. "Okay… you okay? Yeah, love you, too. K.F.D!"

Scar slides the phone down on the table and snatches the tequila from me, necking a massive mouthful. She then looks down at the bottle to see it's three-quarters empty and looks over at Ares. "We're gonna need another bottle."

As he stands to leave, Scar wraps her arms around me, and I break. I sob into her and pull her against me, holding her so tight I might break her. I feel him then, in that instant. I feel him near, his gaze on me, and I feel Scar shake her head, and then he's gone. That empty, alone feeling comes back, and I cling to Scar like she's my life raft and, at the moment, she's all I've got.

After a few minutes, my sobs break, the tears dry, and she's just holding me. I hear the clunk of the next bottle hitting the table, and I break from Scar, looking up at Ares. "Sorry, man… I didn't mean… I shouldn't have…"

As I go to stand, he pulls me into him and just holds me, too. I stand awkwardly for a minute before I relax into the hug. Fuck, these guys are gonna have me balling again. "Stay!" he whispers in my ear.

Looking at him, he gives me a sad smile and claps me on the shoulder. I sit back down and take the bottle again. We pass it between us, but none of us speak. We're halfway down the second bottle when the door swings open, and Scar gasps. I glance up to see who's there.

He swaggers over to me. "You good, kiddo?" Cade asks.

"Yeah, Pa! I'm good," I slur in his general direction, but he must be pissed as he's blurry as hell.

"How's your sister?"

I shrug, as I've no idea. "She bolted, went home and then I came here, so your guess is as good as mine."

"Where's Bran?"

I shrug again. I mean, I could answer, but I'm too drunk to care and not drunk enough not to care.

"Can I join you?"

I look over at Scar and Ares, and they shrug, so I shrug. That's the most he's getting, so he slides into the chair, picks up the bottle and takes the last dregs. The scowl on Scar's face is a pretty picture.

"Ah, come on, princess, don't look at me like that!"

"I'm not looking at you like anything, Uncle Cade." she spits at him.

"Watch your mouth, Scar! You don't know what's going on." he mutters to her without looking away.

Ares is just about to say something, and Scar raises her finger to him. "Firstly, I know exactly what's going on. Secondly, you're a fucking idiot, and thirdly, drink on your fucking own!" She stands up, and he has to look up to meet her gaze as she scowls down at him. "I will forgive you when she does, and not before!"

"Princess!" He grabs her wrist as she walks past him, and she just glares at his hand as it engulfs her. Ares is itching to do something but also trying to give Scar the space to sort this herself. "You don't understand!"

"No, it's you that doesn't understand! She didn't need this on top of everything else! You're a selfish prick!" She snatches her hand away and stalks through the bar.

"I have actually no idea what's going on, man, but if you've fucked with Ray, you're on your own!" Ares rises too and follows after Scar.

"You gonna fuck off too?" I roll my eyes, or they roll on their own; I can't decide. I'm too drunk to know either way. I feel like I'm in a washing machine as I try to stand and do a shit job of it. Falling forward, I catch myself on the table. "Fucking hell." Cade stands up to grab me as I try to step around the table. That's when the smell hits me, engulfs me as arms go around me, pulling me to him.

"Fucking hell, Dane." Dice tosses my arms around his neck so we're face to face, and I smile as he turns to face Cade. "What the fuck did you do? I've never seen him like this before."

"You've just not been around long enough. Give it fucking time." Cade tosses at Dice. "Give me a hand to get him to my room. I think it's best if I don't show my face at Ray's tonight."

"Did she do that to you?" Dice asks Cade as I sway in his arms.

"Yeah, just a misunderstanding."

I laugh to myself out loud, and Cade tosses me a glare.

"Maybe he should sleep it off in my room?" Dice insists.

Next thing I know, I'm being tossed over Cade's shoulder. As I flip down his back, my face slams into his arse, and that's about all I get.

Waking up the next morning, I feel a hot body beside me and freeze. Shit, shit, shit. What did I do? Who the hell is this?

"Fuck's sake, you still take up far too much room for a little 'un!"

A sigh of relief as I turn to face him.

"Why am I here?" I groan.

"Because I thought if I carried you back to her place, she might stab me instead of punching me. This seemed the best option.

"Perfect." I shove myself out of bed and head towards the door, still clothed with my trainers on. I don't even know what fucking time it is. As I storm through the bar, there's a screech of a chair being pushed back.

"Hey? How ya feeling?"

I wince as I turn to face Dice, fucking perfect. He's there, all sexy as hell, his hair glistening and those eyes just devouring every sad inch of me. He's in faded jeans and a tight pale blue t-shirt with his cut on, and I'm in last night's clothes, stinking of tequila and regret. I close my eyes, give him a two-finger salute, and head out the door.

"Dane, wait." He grabs my wrist, and I glare down at it and back at him. "I just wanna talk! What's going on?"

I just shake my head. If I talk, I might vomit, which might make this morning suck more than it already does, so I just snatch my hand back and walk out the door and back to my bed

Steel

There's a knock at the door, which is fucking weird as I can't remember anyone ever knocking. I shove Hades off my knee, drag my arse off the sofa, and open the door.

"What are you knocking for?" I grumble at Cade as he's stood there looking shifty as fuck.

"I thought it was the safest option."

"She's not here." I say, stepping back to allow him in.

"Did Dane make it back this morning?"

"Yeah, he went straight to bed. He looked like fucking shit, to be honest."

"Yep, I literally had to throw him over my shoulder and put him to bed in my room… erm, your room!" He shrugs.

"Your room. I don't plan on needing it back like ever!"

"You're happy then? I mean, the two of you? She's doing good?"

"Yeah, we're good, and I couldn't be happier. You'll have to ask her directly how she is."

"What do you need, Cade? While I'm enjoying the scintillating conversation, I don't think you're here to ask about my marriage."

"Did she tell you what happened?"

"Kind of," I reply. I got the gist, and there really didn't need to be anything else said while she was processing everything.

"I fucked up!"

"Ya think?" I cock a brow, because seriously, dude!

He sighs long, and I get up and make us coffee.

"Do you think it would be ok for me to wait for her to get back?"

"I'll text her. You know damn well if she doesn't know you're here and she walks in, she'll feel railroaded and split!"

He nods and sits back on the sofa. Fuck, this is gonna be a long morning. It's my first day off in weeks with the coffee shop and the lodge for Tank and Skye.

"How's the lodge coming on?"

"I haven't even been up there since I got here. I really should make a start, but ya know." He just shrugs.

"I can get the boys to help after the wedding if you like. The coffee shop will be open by then."

"Wedding? Coffee shop?"

"Ah, you've missed out." So I fill him in, and we chat about all the work that we've done, and actually, it's not so bad. It is freaky how alike he and Ray are. Their attitude and mannerisms are very similar, but Bran and Dane are so similar to her, too, so it could just be learned behaviour. I get a text back from Ray saying it's okay for him to wait. Well, that's what I tell him anyway.

Husband: Hey, baby. Cade's here. He wants to wait for you to come back. Is that okay?
Wife: I don't give a flying fuck what he wants. He'll have a fucking long wait. I'll be back when I'm back.
Wife: Maybe tell him to hold his breath and await my fucking return.
Wife: Better still tell him to fuck off onto the balcony and come back in when he sees a fucking pig flying.
Wife: Love you. xx
Husband: Love you too. x

Skye

We're sitting on the sofa, getting ready to leave, when the door opens, and Dane walks in.

"What the fuck happened to you?" Ray tosses over her shoulder at him.

"Life!" he huffs as he stalks towards the bathroom.

"Where are we going, anyway?" I ask Ray, as she just said to get ready, and when I went to grab breakfast, she said we were getting it while we were out.

"Secret."

"Why?"

"Because I can."

"That makes no sense."

Her phone chimes, and she looks down at it. "Come on. We're ready."

As we descend the stairs, Demi, Scar, and Beauty are waiting by Steel's truck.

"Let's do this." Ray cups her hands around her mouth and bellows.

"Wait. Skye." I turn towards the clubhouse as Dice comes jogging along with a large manila envelope.

"What's this?"

"You might need it." He winks. But as I go to open it, he drops his hand onto mine. "Later, you can open it at breakfast." I nod and climb into the passenger seat of the truck.

"Right. Do I get to know where we're going now?"

"Girls' day!" They squeal like teenagers, and I've never had a girls' day even though I don't know what one is and I don't know what that means, but I find myself squealing too.

We pull up outside this nice bistro in Ravenswood and head inside. Once we've ordered, Ray taps the envelope.

I pull it open. There are five envelopes in there, so I tip them on the table. They're all numbered between one and five.

"Go on, open the first one." Scar claps.

I open it; it's an invite.

You are invited to celebrate
the wedding of
Thomas Pershing
&
Skye Pershing
Tomorrow at The Courthouse
12 p.m.

"Shit," I whisper out.
"Shit good? Shit bad? Skye?"

I turn it over, and they all squeal again. Ray just grins.

"You all knew. I can't get married. I've nothing to wear. What the hell am I going to do?"

"You're gonna eat your breakfast, and then you're gonna open envelope number two." Ray just grins again.

"You all know what's happening, don't you?"

"I'm in charge today. Tank's orders. So breakfast, then more excitement!"

As our breakfasts arrive, I slide the envelopes back into the larger one.

Ray leans over and places her hand on my arm. "Don't panic. We've thought of everything. Your only job today is to have fun, okay?"

My eyes well a little, and I nod. "Thank you!"

After we eat breakfast, I get out envelope number two. There's a card inside. I open it up. "It's an address." I turn the card over. "Just an address, nothing else."

"So tap it into your phone, and let's go." Ray jumps up from the table and goes to pay.

"Ray, I can't let you keep paying for everything. I need to start looking for a job or something."

"Nonsense, you keep cooking that little one! That's the only thing you need to worry about." She pulls me in for a hug. "Now come on, kiddo, let's find this address."

As we follow the map, we end up outside the bank. I look down at my phone, the address, and then back again. "The bank? Did I type it in wrong?"

"Come on, let's go inside and take a look." Ray coos.

I grin as she pulls me through the door, as we walk into the foyer. An older gentleman greets me. "Ms Pershing, I'm Mr Greene, the manager here. If you want to follow me, the rest of your party can sit over there. Ladies, someone will bring you some refreshments while you wait."

I look at Ray as I'm so confused, and she nods, giving me the green light to follow Mr Greene. No pun intended. As I follow Mr Greene, we head upstairs and through a set of doors. Tank is in the chair in front of the desk.

He stands as I walk through the door and steps towards me, extending his hand. "Morning, love." He grins, pulling me into him and giving me a chaste kiss. Pulling me to the seat next to him.

"Ms Pershing, would you open envelope number three, please?" Mr Greene asks.

"Sorry?" I'm so confused as to what's happening right now.

"Envelope number three, Ms Pershing," Mr Greene replies.

I open up envelope number three. It has in it my birth certificate. Attached to that is my legal name change certificate and my social security card with my new name on it. My mouth drops open. Everything is legally changed to my new name. "Tank?" I gasp.

"Ms Pershing, if I could take your documents, we can set up your accounts." I lift my hand and pass him the envelope with everything in it. As I lift it, my hand is shaking.

Tank rests his hand on my leg. "Love?"

I smile at him as I immediately calm down and rest my head on his shoulder. His arm slides around me as Mr Greene leaves, and he strokes circles around my back.

"I missed you this morning!"

"You did?" I smile up at him. He just makes me feel safe and loved, and I'm not sure I've ever felt like this in my life.

"Open envelope number four, love."

I slide the envelope out and open it. There are two keys on a key ring with a heart on it. I turn them over and look up at him, confused. "What are these for?"

"Our lodge is ready, love. Tomorrow after the wedding, will you come home with me?"

"Really?" I throw myself into his lap, throw my arms around him, and pinch myself again.

"What are you doing, woman?" he growls at me.

"I just don't see how you can be real. I don't know what I've done to deserve you. I hope I'm… enough."

"Love. You're my universe!"

My eyes well, and a few tears stream down my face. "Don't cry, love. This is supposed to be a happy day."

"Tank… I've never been this happy."

The door opens, and Mr Greene walks back in. That's everything sorted. We just need a few signatures, and your new cards will be delivered to your new address in a few days.

We sign the paperwork, and I get to write the new signature I've been practising. We thank Mr Greene and head back downstairs.

The girls are sitting waiting, and Tank pulls me into his arms and kisses me like he's never gonna let me go, but after a while, he pulls away. "I will see you at the courthouse, my love!" He kisses me again and heads out as he reaches the door.

"Tank!" I run towards him and throw myself into his arms. "I love you!" And I kiss him like I'm trying to convince him I can't live without him.

As Tank leaves, I hear a snigger behind me. "Damn, girl! That was way hot!" Ray's fanning herself with a brochure about savings accounts, which just makes me laugh. "Open the last envelope."

Pulling open the envelope. "It's another address." Typing it into the phone, we follow the map and end up at a dress store.

"This is my present to you. Let's go. You can have whatever you want. Money is no object!" Ray pulls me into her and whispers into my ear. "I want you to have the best life can offer you. You deserve the world."

I pull her down towards me. "I don't know how to ever repay you for all you've done for me, but tonight, I need to end this. I want my wedding day to be a fresh start. A new life, a new me. Nothing left of the old one."

Ray nods and winks. "Whatever it takes!" She pulls my pinkie into hers.

"Whatever it takes!" I repeat. She pulls me into another hug before we head into the shop.

It's a whirlwind of trying on a million dresses, and when I try on the last one, I cry. "This is it." I've followed my feelings, and I've never had feelings before of any nature, and this place, these people have woken something in me, and now everything is bursting out of me. I need to make sure my old life dies tonight so I can start my new life tomorrow. "This one! I want this one! It's perfect."

"You heard the lady. Ring us up." Ray barks at the sales lady.

We make it back to the apartment, which is empty when we get there. Ray thought Cade was still here, but he clearly had enough of waiting. We have been out all day. I don't know what's going on, but Ray is not a big talker when it comes to things like that. We have something to eat, and the girls leave. It's just me and Ray. The boys are at the lodges.

"So talk to me. What's the plan?" Ray asks but then just sits back on the sofa.

"I want it to hurt! I want him to wish he was dead, and I want to cause that!"

"Kiddo, I'm not gonna lie. It takes a piece of you to inflict pain and then kill another person!"

"Ray, he took everything from me. There's nothing left for him to take! But he needs to die tonight, and I need to be the one to do it!"

"Okay, come on, then." She walks into the kitchen, rummages in the fridge and pulls out a chicken. "It's the best I've got! We don't want you going in there as a complete novice. He needs to know you mean business, and you need to fake it till you make it! Also, we need a word you can say where if you need me to take over, we can pass it off as a power play, not a cop-out, okay?" She hands me the knife. "Now kill the fucking chicken. Remember, though, a human will bleed like a motherfucker."

After giving me a few pointers, Ray leads me to her office. She leaves me to wait in the barn while she gets "him" ready. I can't even say his name. She sets him up and fastens him to the table.

Ray told me whatever happens, I need to be confident in there, even if I can't do anything myself. I need to blag that I can't be arsed and for her to just end him, but I want to be strong. I want to do this for me, my life, my family, and my husband so we can have a fresh start. Tomorrow is a new day. Tomorrow is the start of the rest of my life.

Heading into the office, I walk down the stairs, slowly contemplating my actions, wondering if I'm making a mistake, if this will change who I am, and if this will make my life difficult. Can I live with this if I do it? Will it make me a worse person? Will it make me a terrible person? I honestly don't know, but I have to try. He took everything from me. I will not allow him to take my future. I will not allow him to affect my family. This ends tonight.

"Ray." I nod as I walk into the room. "I see you two have been getting acquainted. Make yourself at home. What was it you made me call you? …Daddy? Yeah, that's it. Make yourself at home, 'Daddy'. Get comfy, because you're not leaving this room alive."

"Alice?" His voice rasps as I look over him. Ray has him naked on the table. He's strapped down at his ankles, thighs, waist, chest, neck, head and wrists. "You're my special little girl. You know that, you know I love you."

"Special little girl? Are you kidding me right now? You started fucking me when you killed my mother! I was ten!" I graze my hands across all of Ray's knives, and she nods.

When I asked her what advice she could give me, she said not to hesitate to stab him with the pointy end. As long as it's not the main artery or it will be over too soon. It's funny that as I look at him, she has crosses drawn all over his main arteries, so I don't hit them by mistake. Ray tried to teach me where they were, but I was panicking too much. I guess this is the option she came up with, and I have to admit it's extremely effective.

I slide the knife I choose over his shin, and it strips all the hair. "Damn, that's sharp!" I mutter as he tries to flinch. I drag the knife up his body and stick it right in under his chin, pushing it into his jaw. There's a trickle of blood that runs down his neck, and it causes a twitch at the side of my mouth.

"Can you remember what I used to say to you?"

"Alice, please, this is just a misunderstanding."

"Misunderstanding?" I shake my head and pull the knife to his eye, watching as he tries to move his head and get away from the blade. "I used to beg!" I hold the knife steady, and an eerie calm washes over me. "Do you remember what you used to do? You used to laugh and push me down and fuck me harder." I push the knife steadily into his eye while he screams. I'm lost in the moment, but I feel Ray's hand gently graze the back of mine, and she shakes her head once, clearly letting me know if I stab too far, it's game over.

Taking a breath, I step back, wiping the knife on his own skin. "Do you know what he sold me for?" I look over at Ray. "Tell her!" I slide the knife into the fleshy part of his stomach. "Tell her how much I was worth after you destroyed me for nearly fourteen years."

"A-a-a c-c-carton of c-cigarettes, and a c-c-crate of b-beer!"

"Ray, what happens if I stab him here?"

"Let's see, shall we?" Ray holds my hand and pushes it steadily into his gut. Once it's in, up to the hilt, I let go. She grins at me before knocking the handle, making him scream out even more.

I leave the knife in, step back around the table, and go to Ray's toolbox. "What do all these do?"

"Wanna have some fun?" Ray grins across at me. I know she's using these specific words to insight terror into our captive, and the specific tone of voice to sound deranged, and that creepy smile to add to the illusion, but honestly, I couldn't love her more than I do in this instant. At this moment, I know that Ray saved me; she could have left me there to rot, but she gave me hope. The life she's offering is more than I thought I ever deserved, and this baby is an absolute blessing.

Tank is everything I never knew existed, and tomorrow, I will be Skye Pershing, wife of Thomas 'Tank' Pershing, mother-to-be, and I will live happily ever after. I will make sure I never have a nightmare about this piece of shit again tonight. Tonight, I want to try every one of Ray's devices, knives, gadgets, spikes and, worst of all, her way of mentally torturing, because I want it for him. I want it all.

I want my baby never to know fear, to never know abuse, never to know hunger. I want my baby to know love, and I will wipe this stain from this earth so he can't ruin anything or anyone ever again. I couldn't save myself. I tried over the years. He killed my mum, raped me daily, tortured me, starved me, beat me, sold me and tried to destroy me, but Ray, Ray gave me something to live for, so I have five hours before the start of a new day, before the start of my new life. I intend to make it count.

I'm panting, leaning on the table. It's been four and a half hours of stabbing, cutting, yanking, twisting, breaking, burning, peeling, ripping, poking, electrocuting, scratching, sawing, crunching, and everything else Ray's twisted little mind could come up with.

I've removed nails, fingers, toes and ears, his dick and a leg. I gave up on removing limbs. It was really hard work, and the smell after cauterising them made me gag. I don't know if I'll ever be able to go to a BBQ again! I'm exhausted, and my demons don't look so scary now. He's a shell now, nothing more. He's pissed and shit himself. He's puked, and the stench is horrific down here.

"You're ready!" Ray smiles over at me. "How do you want to end it?"

He's not coherent anymore. His tongue was ripped out a while ago. There's a bag of bits on the floor. "All the king's horses and all the king's men couldn't put Humpty together again." I smile as I think that, and Ray barks out a maniacal laugh, jolting me out of my thoughts.

"You're right there, kiddo!" She laughs again.

I look at her, puzzled, before realising, "Did I say that out loud?" And she laughs again, nodding her head.

Taking the knife and the hammer, I ask, "If he had a heart, where would it be?"

Ray runs her fingers over the damage I've left across his chest and along his rib, counting down. Then, before finding the point I need, she takes my hand, rests the tip of the knife into position and takes a step back, nodding.

"You are nothing. You didn't break me. I will never think of you again after you're gone, and this child will only ever know his father, Tank. No one will remember you or mourn you, but me and my family will flourish."

I pull my arm back with the hammer and smack it down onto the hilt of the knife. There's a pained sound, but he's practically dead anyway, and as the last spark of life leaves him, my breaths become clearer, my heart beats steadily, my body feels lighter, and I feel the old me die with him.

"Goodbye, Alice!" I whisper as I hold my heart, and a tear rolls down my face. Then, strong arms band around me and hold me while I sob. When I look up at her, I'm drained. I'm covered in every bodily fluid imaginable. But all I can do is smile.

"I'm so fucking proud of you right now. You are a warrior. When someone tells you you can't do something, I want you to remember this moment, not him, but this. You are a phoenix reborn from the ashes. Tomorrow is the beginning of the rest of your life. I love you, but you fucking stink, so let's go shower and go to bed."

I laugh and hug her again. "I love you. Thank you for everything!" As we head out the door, I ask. "What about all that?" I gesture at the mess I've left.

"It's already gone!" She winks at me, and that makes me smile as I walk out of that room and into the barn. The air smells fresher, the night sharper, the stars brighter and my future full of possibilities. As we step out of the barn, I stand staring at the sky. A deep rumble of a voice barks out across the night.

"What the fuck happened to you?" Then there's heavy pounding as someone runs towards me as I look over at the love of my life, my husband-to-be. I smile.

"I've vanquished all my demons. I'm free!"

Ray

There's hammering on my bedroom door, and I so want to stay in my warm bed, cocooned by the smell of my husband even though he's not here, but then the door flings open, and a frantic Skye comes bolting through it and dives up onto my bed jumping and starts shouting, "I'm getting fucking married today!" over and over again. She's followed in by an extremely excited Rottie, who also dives up, licking at my face while bouncing around like a looney.

I'm the motherfucking Reaper, and this is what my life has become. I try to shove the slobbering dog off me as I push up to my feet and start bouncing, too. You know what they say, if you can't kill 'em, join 'em, or something like that. The dog starts jumping up and down, and there's slobber flying everywhere as the front door opens, and Skye squeals and runs into the living room. Demi, Scar and Beauty are there with boxes of shit.

I step into the room. "What the fuck's all this?" I scrub at my sleep-deprived eyes.

"Hair and makeup." Demi shrugs like I'm an idiot. Ah, yep, that makes sense.

I walk over and slap Skye on the arse. "Shower now!" She runs off as I step into the kitchen and start making breakfast.

Steel and I are going to the courthouse as witnesses, and the rest are going to finish setting up the coffee shop. Most of it's done as they went there last night while we were playing in the fires of hell, and Skye was being reborn.

When we emerged from the bowels of Hell, Tank swept her into his arms and told her she was the most beautiful creature he had ever seen.

What is it about our fucked up men that love us covered in someone else's blood? I shrug to myself as fuck, I missed my man last night. All I wanted to do was crawl into his soul and light us both on fire.

Once Skye emerges from the bathroom, we all sit and have breakfast, and the girls go to town on Skye while I shower.

We pull up at the courthouse, and I reach into the back and grab the bouquet of flowers we got for Skye. We also hired a photographer to take pictures of everything, and she took Skye and us up to the woods and back fields for some pictures before we left.

She pulls up behind us and gets out, taking pictures as Skye climbs down from the truck. She straightens her dress and walks around to me. I take her arm.

"Are you ready? It's not too late to back out."

She gasps in horror. "What the fuck, Ray?" It makes me chuckle. She doesn't swear much, but it makes an impact when she does. "I'm marrying your brother!" It's a strong statement, and I smile. They really do love each other. "I don't see their bikes. Do you think he has cold feet after last night, you know, the whole…" she trails off as if she doesn't know what to say to describe the fucked up state he found us in.

"Ares dropped them off so we can all drive back together." I grin, and she relaxes. "Come on, let's get you married. We have a party to get to."

Tank

I'm pacing back and forth in the waiting area as Steel chuckles to himself. "Calm down, Brother! She'll be here!"

"She's late!" I grumble.

"Tank, the clock hit twelve like three seconds ago! She will be… wow!" Steel stops mid-way through what he's saying as Ray steps to the top of the stairs. She's got her hair down in soft flowing curls and a little makeup, which she doesn't normally wear. She's wearing a flowery dress, which obviously isn't hers, and she has her badass biker boots on, too, which makes me think someone made her wear the dress, and this is her rebellion.

I smile at her, but that soon drops away from my face. As Skye steps up behind her, there's a big window behind them, and the sun beams onto them. Skye is a vision of beauty. Another woman rushes past them and starts taking photos, but I can't take my eyes off her.

She's wearing an off-white, fifties-style tea-length dress. It's got a poofy underskirt which flows out from just under her boobs, hiding our bump. It has a sweetheart neckline, a lace-over dress, and three-quarter-length sleeves. I feel like a fish out of water. She's taken my breath away. Her brown hair cascades in soft waves like Ray's and is pinned to one side with some small white flowers! She's perfect.

As she steps forward, her hand comes up and rests over my heart. I'm sure she can feel it pounding out of my chest as she holds it there for a few seconds before sliding it up over my chest up my neck to cup my face.

She looks up at me, and she smiles. "Fancy getting married?"

"Fuck yeah!" I whisper out as she presses a chaste kiss to my cheek, but my eyes flutter shut, and just the feel of her so close has my mind spinning. I'm addicted to her touch, to her scent, to her perfect smile, and to those eyes. I could dream my life away lost in those eyes.

And just like that, we're married! I feel like I'm floating in a dream. As Steel drives us back to the coffee shop, I can't believe I'm married. I can't believe I'm the luckiest man alive. My wife will want for nothing, my son will want for nothing, and I will spend every day trying to make her as happy as she makes me.

As we pull up outside the coffee shop, it looks stunning from the outside. There are four little bistro tables and pairs of chairs along the front outside of the large window. Beside the door, two large topiary hearts are standing in large planters on either side, with fairy lights trailing through them. A white ribbon is tied across them with 'Mr and Mrs' printed in gold. Everyone is standing in two rows on either side of the door at the side of the red carpet that's laid out for us to walk down.

Demi stands at the end opposite Bran with some large scissors. We make our way past everyone. Viking, Carmen, Roach, Catalina, Dice, Dozer, Beauty, Scar, Ares, Blade, Dane, Priest. Ray and Steel are behind us, and as we reach Demi and Bran, she hands us the scissors, giving us both a hug. "Congratulations, I'm so happy for you both."

As she pulls back, she gestures towards the ribbon, and Skye takes the scissors, turning to face everyone, and I step to her side. "I want to thank you all for accepting me into your family. It's something I've never had before, and when I arrived, you all welcomed me without even knowing me. I've found more love here in these months since I arrived than I've ever had in the rest of my twenty-four years. I'm sorry I lied to you all about my age…" I take her hand as she trails off.

I kiss the back of her hand and hold it against my heart. "I want to introduce you all to my wife … Skye Pershing!" Everyone whoops and hollers, and confetti rains down all over us. "I would also like to introduce you to my son!" I reach across with my hand and place it on her stomach, and she blushes. "Well, he will be a few months yet, but I'm gonna be a dad!" I scream out, and all my brothers rush us and hug us. I've never felt more content. When the ruckus dies down, Skye shakes her head at me, smiling. She knew I couldn't keep it in any longer. I've been dying to tell them all since the second I decided this little bundle and the woman carrying him would be mine. Mine to love, mine to protect, and mine to cherish.

Skye steps forward and cuts the ribbon. Demi ushers us to step in first. There are two young girls inside. One has a tray with two champagne glasses that say Mr on one and Mrs on the other. Demi leans over Skye's shoulder. "Yours is non-alcoholic," and Skye breathes a sigh of relief as we take the glasses and step through the door.

"Wow, Demi, this place is beautiful." Skye's voice comes out as a whisper of awe, and she beams at all the details Demi has added for the wedding.

The photographer came through the back while we were in the scrimmage outside and has been taking photos of us as we enter. Our faces must be a picture, as this place is stunning!

A banquet table is lined along the left wall with sage green accents on the white linens. In the centre of the table are three cakes on stands with flowers entwined around them. There's a spread of finger food laid out around them.

Each table has a mini topiary heart in a pot with small fairy lights wrapped around it. Pendant lights are hanging from the ceiling all the way around the space, but they're dimmed, and there are fairy lights all the way around the banquet table, the booths and the counter.

Everything feels so romantic. As everyone filters in, they all take a glass, and the celebrations begin. There's background music, and people eat and drink, and even a few of us manage to have a dance. This place is gonna hold a special place in my heart, and I can't believe our family has pulled this out of the bag for us.

The day has been perfect. After seeing Skye last night covered in god knows what and blood, I honestly wondered if she would be okay today. But the more I look at her, there's a softness to her that wasn't there before. She's breathing a little deeper, a little freer, with a little more purpose. Those beautiful big brown eyes with the gold flecks that normally glisten are sparkling. It's like the gold has been regilded. It's brighter and more iridescent. Her smile is more relaxed and wider than I've ever seen it.

"You're staring!" she whispers into my ear, kissing my neck and making me shudder.

"I can't believe you're mine!" I say honestly because at this moment, as I look into those eyes, I've found my home and purpose, and I can't wait to start this adventure of our new life together as a family!

Dane

It's the morning of the funeral. I'm unsure how we're gonna get through this. We just seem to be losing more and more people. I honestly know I have more people now than before, but I've felt alone for the longest time. I don't know if it's because, at one time, we only had each other, the four of us, me, Ray, Bran and then Scar, but now Ray has Steel, Bran has Demi, and Scar has Ares.

I have a hot guy I can't get out of my head who I love but hate. I want, but I don't. I can't bear to be near, but can't bear to not be with him. It's a total mind-fuck, but honestly, I'm just hurt that he didn't want me, and I can't seem to get over him. Maybe I should try getting under someone else. Isn't that what they say?

As we head out to the cars that have been sent for us, Ray and Steel are waiting for me. Bran and Demi are going with Scar, and Ares is hugging Scar like he might not see her again. These things are family only. This is gonna be fun, as Ray and Cade have managed to avoid each other until now. He's going with my mum and dad, so at least there's a bit of separation for now.

Pulling up to the military base and checking in, the whole place has a sombre mood. This base isn't just any base. This is our headquarters. Although we work out of The Tower, this is our base of operations.

As we head through the gates, we're surrounded by our organisation. We pass ourselves off as a military base. It's run as such: uniforms, vehicles, everything. It looks like an official base, but looks can be deceiving.

Once the funeral is over and we have two more urns ready to collect in a few days to add to our collection of ash family members, we head to the bar on base!

Ray and Cade sit on opposite sides of the room but face each other, neither one wanting to back down from the fury they're reigning down on each other through their glares alone. Steel, Bran, me and Dad are standing at the bar in the centre at the end of the room.

"Do you think they realise how much this actually makes sense?" I ask as we cast our gazes from one side to the other.

"I mean, it seems kind of obvious standing here watching them." Bran adds.

"They're both as fucking stubborn as each other. We know from experience how long their feuds can last!" Dad reminds us. Fuck, yep, I mean, that whole Jeremy thing blew over quicker than we expected, but I think we just felt more detached because we were over here, but fuck, this could be the worst yet!

"It really is scary looking at them like this! I mean, what if it's not even true? We really should push them to do something about getting some answers."

I think I'm making a smart observation till Dad chimes in, "This isn't even about the results. They're irrelevant at this point!"

"What do you mean?"

"He's always wanted kids, and then what happened happened, and she was born. That first time he held her, she was his. DNA never came into it. He always tried to be impartial, but when it came to her, he never was. He sure made to look like he was, but she was his little girl. That's why he never met anyone. No one was gonna replace her. When Daniel died, it left a gap, and he wanted to fill it. He couldn't bear to be away from her, and that's why he moved back. Why do you think he's at the club?

"But now Steven and JJ are gone; he wants to be her dad so bad, he couldn't see it wasn't the time. And for her, he's always been her dad. We all have. She loves us all the same. She's just hurt we didn't tell her and then how he went about telling her. In truth, it's that she didn't know, not that it's a possibility. She just feels deceived. She won't love him any more or any less."

"So, basically, she's her father's daughter?"

"Yep. That about sums it up!"

Once we're all adequately shit-faced and the Mexican standoff has gone on long enough, we decide to head home. As we get dropped off, I head to the bar. I'm still in my clothes from the funeral, but I rip my tie off and my jacket off and open the top few buttons on my shirt, rolling up the sleeves. I'm three sheets to the wind as I push through the doors.

Before I make it to the bar, I hear someone shout my name, and as I turn round, Johnny storms through the doors and throws his arms around me. Johnny must have been driving the car that brought Scar, Bran and Demi back, as Scar's just walking in behind him with Ray and Steel.

I've known Johnny for years from the base; he's always nice, and we often have a chat. I've spent a lot of time there learning security systems and computers, and he would often drive me home if I spent a little too long in the bar. He's generally a really nice guy.

Wrapping his arm around me, he pulls me into a hug and whispers into my ear. "Fuck Dane, I'm so sorry to hear about JJ and Steven. If you need anything, you have my number, okay?"

I pull back and look at him and smile. "Thanks, man, I really appreciate that, it's been a while. We should have a catch-up at some point."

"Yeah, I'd like that." He puts his hand against my cheek and smiles, then pulls me in for another hug.

"Are you fucking shitting me right now?" there's a roar from the corridor, and a stool comes hurtling by me. I mean, I'm drunk, so it feels like it nearly takes my head off, but in reality, fuck knows where it's thrown from or where it ends up.

Johnny pulls back, then steps back, looking towards a pissed-off Dice stomping across the bar. "I'll erm... see you soon, Dane." He scurries past Dice. Dice doesn't even spare a second glance at him. He takes a one-way ticket to chew me out, and he's almost arrived at his destination.

"What the fuck do you think your fucking doing?" He spits at me as he shoves me in the shoulder, making me stumble back a few steps.

"What the fuck is wrong with you?" I push him back.

"Are you fucking kidding me? I walk into my club to find you all over someone, rubbing my fucking face in it!" He shoves me again.

"What the hell are you on about!"

"You!" He jabs me in the chest, and I rock back again. "Fucking showing off your new boyfriend! No one gives a fuck, Dane!"

"Fuck you!" I punch him in the jaw, and his head spins to the side. When his gaze flicks back to me, he rubs his jaw.

"You motherfucking piece of shit!" he roars at me, slamming both his hands into my chest and knocking me back even further. I'm at the far end of the bar right now, and everyone is just staring. "I should fucking kill you!" he spits, and the venom in his voice makes it ring out hoarser.

"Fuck you, Dice!" I go to storm past him with a shoulder barge, but I'm still reeling and still pissed, so my movements are a little more sluggish than normal. That's when he grabs me around the throat and shoves me back a few steps, slamming my back into the wall between the back door and the fireplace.

"I'm still fucking talking to you!" he screams in my face, and the rage just hits me. As the rage washes over me, I feel a steady sense of calm flood my senses, and I raise up slightly and push my neck into his hand.

"Don't fucking start something you can't finish! I will fucking end you!" I push against his hand with my neck, forcing him back a step.

His gaze widens a fraction before he tenses up and takes in my face. I've felt my muscles tighten, and my grimace turns to a full-on snarl, and the venom I spit at him clearly brings with it a second of realisation. He glances down at my lips as I snarl at him, and in that split second, he grabs my hip with his other hand and steps forward with all his weight, forcing me back into the wall. When I gasp at the impact, that's when it happens. He slams his body against me and his lips against mine, and it takes a second for me to realise he's kissing me. My chest is pounding from the altercation, and my breaths are coming in ragged.

I reach one hand up to the back of his neck and the other to his waist and drag him as close as I can get. There's a battle going on, but I'm not totally sure if we're on separate sides or the same one.

There's a metallic tang as the collision has split one of our lips, but I don't know whose. I don't care. I kiss him back like my life depends on it. His grip on my throat tightens and rips a feral growl out of me as I pull him against me, grinding our bodies together.

"Wait? Dane's gay too?" I hear the voice cut through our moment, and Dice freezes against me, pulling back slightly and then taking a step back. He relaxes his grip slightly before slamming me back against the wall. The hard edge to his features that has just dissipated returns with a vengeance, and he snarls as he storms out of the back door without looking back. I slide down the wall panting till I'm on my arse with one knee up and one leg stretched out. I drop my head onto my forearm, resting on my knee while trying to regain my breath. He fucking does this every time, pulls me in, then rips my heart out again.

"Dane?" Ray's in front of me, reaching down and pulling me up. I take in the look on her face and shake my head as I push past her. I push past them all, walk straight out of the front door, and head home. What the fuck is wrong with him?

Dice

"Wait? Dane's gay too?" I hear the voice cut through our moment. Fuck, they know, and I freeze. I'm so lost in him being here, being so close and with him, whoever the fuck that guy was, I just lost it. Pulling back slightly, then taking a step back, I relax my grip slightly before slamming him back against the wall. I feel the tension ready to erupt. I'm about to snap. I snarl as I turn and storm out of the back door without looking back.

"What the fuck was that?" I spin around, and Ray's standing there with what looks like rage spilling from her.

"Ray, don't please… I can't deal right now, and I don't need you taking sides. I know he's your brother, but he pushes my fucking buttons!"

"Is this what you think this is? Me taking sides?" She shakes her head. "Dice, I love you, but what you just did in there was so fucked up! Do you know where we were today?" she huffs out and turns to walk away.

"What does it matter where you were? He comes in here. This is my home, Ray, flaunting his new fucking boyfriend in my—"

WHACK! My head whips to the side from the punch to my face, and I stagger back. And when I whip my gaze back and shake my head to rid the blurring as she's really rung my bell, she's storming away around the back of the building toward the apartment.

I bend over, rest my hands on my knees, and breathe. As I shake my head again, the door swings open, and as I stand, I stagger again. Fuck, she punches like a Mac truck. Once I clear my vision, Steel is standing there, arms folded, pissed as fuck at me!

"Steel, don't man. I can't deal right now!"

"Seriously, you pull that shit? Firstly, that guy! That guy you flipped out about was the driver. He's known Dane for years and just driven us back from Steven and JJ's funeral. He was offering his condolences! And you act like a fucking child, as if someone's touched your train set. The same train set that you tossed aside and didn't even want! I suggest you stay away from both of them for a while! Whatever you said to Ray, she actually came to see if you were okay! You're a fucking idiot!"

"Steel… wait… I'm sorry, okay?"

It's not me you need to apologise to, Dice!" He turns and stalks away after Ray. I drop to my ass where I am and then flop onto my back. Shit, I've right royally fucked up, and now everyone's gonna hate me!

I don't know how long I lay out there, but when the noise from the bars drifts to silence, the stars in the sky are brighter than ever, and as I lay there contemplating how seriously I've fucked it. I realise I can't make this any worse, so I dust myself off and head to the apartment.

As I sneak up the stairs and through the door, Hades looks at me but goes back to sleep. I'm glad they always leave the door unlocked. I'm also glad at least the dog likes me right now, and I know there's only Ray, Steel and Dane here, so I sneak through the living room and into Dane's bedroom. He's face down on the bed, laid diagonally across it. The sheet covers his ass and one leg, but the rest of him is bare. I start to strip out of my clothes as I stand there in my boxers. I'm trying to decide, naked or not?

Will he be more or less likely to kick me out if I am naked or not? Fuck, I'm overthinking this. I strip out of my boxers and slide onto the bed beside him. Fuck, he smells so good. I slide my hand across the bottom of his back so gently I can barely feel it myself. What the fuck am I doing? I don't know why I can't think straight when I'm around him, but I can't. It's like all reasonable thoughts go from my head, and I'm rendered insane!

I freeze. I can't keep doing this. I gently move my hand and sit up to get off the bed when he turns his head over to face me. "What are you doing?" he rasps out in his sleepy voice.

"Nothing… I'm just… leaving!"

As I go to stand, his hand grasps around my wrist. "Why?"

"Why, what?" I stand there, aware that I'm naked and standing by the side of the guy I've just attacked, and then I proceed to break into his home, get naked, and climb into bed with him.

"Why, everything?" He rolls onto his side to face me, still holding my wrist. "Why don't you want me?" He sounds so… quiet, so small, and I feel shame, I did that. I made him think I didn't want him. I made him feel like shit; all he ever wanted to be was mine!

I scrub a hand down my face. "I'm sorry! I should go!"

He lets out a sigh and releases my wrist. "Don't bother, don't come back. I'll move out next week!" He turns to face the other way and pulls the covers up over his shoulder, and it feels like he's shutting the door, closing me off for good, and I can't let that happen.

"Dane… please… I just… fuck!" I sit on the edge of the bed, but he doesn't move. "Dane, please just talk to me. I'm going out of my mind. I don't know what the hell I'm doing?"

"Do you think any of us do?" He sighs again like this is the most pointless conversation ever.

"What do you want from me, Dane?"

"Nothing, Dice. You've made it clear you're not interested in anything other than making my life miserable. So just do what you do best and walk away!"

"That's not fair!"

"No, Dice! What's not fair is you letting me wank you off, then deciding you don't want me, then letting me give you a blow job, then deciding you don't want me, then kissing me in front of everyone after trying to beat the shit out of me, to only decide you don't want me!"

I rest my hand on his shoulder, and he snatches it back, so I place it on there firmer and turn him onto his back! "I'm sorry, I do want you! I just don't know how to make that a reality."

"Have you thought about trying not to be such a dick?"

"Fuck off." I shake my head. "I should have seen that coming."

"You're off the hook!"

"What do you mean?"

"I mean, you're off the hook; just go. I won't chase you any more. I'm heading back to my dad's next week, then I'm heading out to finish uni. I'm transferring out of state. Like I say. Off. The. Hook! Can you close the doors quietly when you leave? I don't want Ray asking a shit ton of questions I don't have the energy to answer."

He goes to roll back on his side, but I throw myself on top of him and slam my lips onto his. His arms are wedged under the covers, so I cover him with my weight. I grip his face in my hands. "Don't go!" I rasp out my voice raw from the emotions and my mind spinning from the thought of him leaving. "Please? Don't leave?"

I look into his eyes, the lights from the parking lot lighting through his window so his face is tinted by the glow from the lamps. "Don't …"

"Dice." He sighs like he's already packed and out the door.

"Please?" I almost sob as I kiss him again. This time, I grind myself into him a little and nip his lip. "Stay… help me?" I kiss him again. "Please? Dane?" I kiss him again, and he actually parts his lips slightly with a groan, and I take my shot.

I slide my tongue along his lip and thrust it into his mouth, tangling it with his. I rock my hips against his. I can feel his hard dick pushing into my leg while I'm sure mine is trying to force its way through his.

I can't break away for a second, so I continue kissing him as I might never get this chance again. His arms find their way out of the covers, and he slides one into my hair and the other to my waist and pulls me into him. His grip on me is starting to become punishing. I slide my hand under the covers and cup his dick sliding my hand around it, "Fuck, he's huge". He grins into the kiss, and I pull back slightly while his grin widens.

"You said that out loud?"

"What?"

He pulls me back to him, and I groan as I start to slide my hand up and down his shaft, causing him to groan into my mouth.

I'm so fed up with being alone and not feeling and not being, and I just give myself over to this feeling. I forget everything, and just this once, I let myself go. I grind again, and he bites down on my lip. I groan at the sensory overload. I've fucked guys before, but this is already so different. My usual encounters are brief, a quick release and done, but Dane lights me up like the fourth of July, making me want to take my time to see what this is between us. I just need to get out of my head and say. "Fuck it."

"Fuck what?"

I pull back again. I slide my hand up and cup his face. "Fuck me! You're so fucking beautiful." I stop pumping his dick and grab the covers and rip them off, I lay at the side of him, and he turns to face me as I pull the covers over both of us. I pull back and look down every inch of his body. The guy is fucking perfection, and I wonder in that second what the fuck I'm dicking about at.

"I want you so much. It's driving me insane." I sigh. I'm panting and staring straight into his eyes. The lust is still there, but my mind is so loud right now I'm overwhelmed.

"What's stopping you from having me?"

"Me… I'm not sure I know how to do this!" I gesture back and forth between us.

"Do you want to be with me?" He cups my face and tilts my gaze to his. "Seriously?"

I close my eyes and sigh. Why can't I just say it? Why can't I just be free to be me? Surely, my brothers will love me no matter what, right?

"You're thinking of them, aren't you, and what they'll say?" I snap my eyes open, and his hazel eyes glint in the pale light from outside. "I can't do this with you if you're just gonna keep dipping a toe in, trying it out and backing off. If you want me, I want you! All or nothing, Dice. I don't wanna keep us a secret. Maybe I should go give you some time."

I start to panic, shit, shit, shit. I can't let him go. I rip the cover off and jump off the bed. I start grabbing my clothes and start yanking them on. Sighing, he rolls over like he's done, and I walk around the bed and kneel down beside him. "I'm gonna tell them! I'm gonna tell them all now!" I lean in, cup his cheek and kiss him.

When I pull back, we're both slightly breathless. He says, "Dice, it's 4 a.m.!"

I glance at the clock. "I don't give a fuck. I need to tell them I can't do anything with you until I'm honest with them and myself." I let out a frustrated breath. I rise to my full height and storm out of the apartment while I still have the balls to do something about this.

Pulling out my phone, I message the guys.

Dice: Meet me in the bar! Now!
Priest: What the fuck, man? It's 4 a.m.!
Dice: I know what fucking time it is. Meet me In the bar! Bring the others.
Viking: Dude, seriously?
Dice: Now!
Blade: Be there in 5.

I call Tank, as he will be up at the lodge. "Brother, you okay?"

"No, Tank, I'm not. I need to talk to you. Can you come to the bar?

"Sure, when?"

"Now! Can you knock on Dozer?"

"Give me five, okay?"

"Thanks, man!"

Dice: Ares you up, brother? Can you meet me in the bar?
Ares: Fuck, Dude. It's 4 a.m.
Dice: I know.

I call Steel, and he answers straight away. "What's up? Did you leave the door open when you snuck out? If the dogs fucked off, you can help fucking find him!"

I ignore his question. Of course he fucking heard me, fuck's sake! "Can you meet me in the bar now?"

"Sure." He sighs. "If you're gonna do this, Dice, do it properly, Brother, all in. They've been through a lot. Make sure this is what you really want. Then grab it by the balls and make it your little bitch!"

"Seriously, that's the worst piece of advice ever!" I hear Ray groan beside him. "Remind me not to ask you for a pep talk!"

I hang up, laughing to myself, as she's not wrong.

As I reach the bar, I grab the tequila and take a sip. Well, actually, a quarter of the bottle, but fuck it, I need it. I'm sitting at the bar, my leg bouncing up and down as Steel walks in. "How come you're here first?"

He shrugs as he sits beside me. "Heard you break in! Got dressed in case I needed to come in and break you guys up!" He shrugs again.

Blade and Priest are next. They just take one look at my face and plop themselves down. Ares comes through in his boxers and boots. "You couldn't have gotten dressed?" Steel shakes his head at him.

"Why do I need to be dressed?" He pulls the tequila out of my hand and tosses it back as Tank comes in the back door. Out of breath, he's clearly jogged down, and I appreciate that.

Viking stalks through next in a robe, a fucking robe. "Right, let's get this over with. I was half buried in Carmen, and if this takes too long, she will rip your dick off!" He snatches the tequila from Ares and takes a swig.

"What, no Dozer?" Steel asks, just as the back door flings open, and he walks in.

"Thanks for coming. I need to talk to you all, and this isn't gonna be easy. I just need you to know this changes nothing for me. I'm still me, and I hope you can all see that. I don't want things to change between us, and I don't want you to look at me differently. I want you to still be my brothers! I don't care about anyone else; you guys are my ride or dies, and I need you to remember that when I tell you what I'm about to tell you."

"Dice!" His hand rests on my shoulder, and I swing my face to meet Steel's. "You're rambling, Brother. Just breathe and say those two words. It's only two. You can do it, okay?"

I let out a shaky breath and sigh. "I'm gay!"

And nothing. I glance around the faces. Nothing, no reaction, no what the fucks. Just nothing.

"What the hell, guys! I hit you with this massive revelation, and you've got nothing to say?"

"Dice… oh no, I can't believe you're gay… I never would have thought it… I love you… I'm going back to bed!" Viking gets up, kisses my head, and stalks back out of the room.

"So … you're gay, huh?" Steel says with a smirk on his face.

"You already knew, shithead!" I bark at him. This is kind of anticlimactic. I thought there would be a massive row, a punch to the face, maybe a holy shit. I walked around naked in front of you, you bastard, but nope, not a fucking thing!

"Did you all know?" I sigh, well this sucks.

"I mean, I think we thought you were bi, but does it really matter? I'm glad you've admitted it to yourself, man, but it's 4:30 a.m., and I'm knackered! I love you, though," Blade says as he heads out.

They all give me a hug or kiss my head as they leave, and I'm left there shell-shocked by the lack of explosion or life-shattering fucking epic fight scene. I kind of expected some fallout.

"So, you gonna stop fucking around with Dane now and actually be together?" Steel turns to face me with a look of concern on his face.

"Yeah, I'm right royally fucking that up. What the fuck do I do to make it right? I've no idea what I'm doing. I've never been in a relationship."

"What are you gonna say to Ray?"

"Fuck, I'm gonna beg and plead, and I might have to install her that tech she's been after in the office and take her for ice cream, but I will suck it up and hug her till she's not mad at me anymore!"

"Then do that with Dane, dude. They're basically the same fucking person. Ray just doesn't have a dick, and Dane does! She's your best friend. How can you not have noticed?"

I scrub a hand down my face. He's fucking right. How can I not have realised? When I said I wanted her with a dick, I didn't think it would be so literal.

"Come on, dickhead. You've got some grovelling to do!"

"Won't Ray be asleep now?"

"Fuck's sake, Dice, not Ray, Dane!" He shakes his head as we head out of the door.

When we get to the apartment, I head into Dane's room, and he's sleeping where I left him, a little more central than before, so I just strip down and get in beside him. I don't wake him up. I just get as close as I can without disturbing him, and I go to sleep myself.

I'm drained. It has been an emotional rollercoaster, and I'm beat.

Dane

I wake up and try to move, but there's an arm pinning me down, and as I try to turn, a grumpy, raspy voice says, "It's too early, shhh, sleep," and tugs me tighter against his naked body. *Shit, naked body.* I can feel his dick stirring against the side of my leg, and now I can feel mine.

"What are you doing here?"

"Babe, it's so early. Please, go back to sleep!" Dice grumbles.

"Babe?" I question.

Where the hell did that come from? But he just replies with, "Yeah?" like I'm the one calling him babe. Have I woken up in a different dimension or some weird shit like that?

I pull out of his arms and go to leave the room. "Why?"

I turn to face him. "Why what?"

"Why are you leaving?"

Barking out a laugh, I say, "I'm going for a piss." I pull on some boxers. "I'll be back in like two minutes, okay?"

"Fine." he grumbles and looks at his wrist like he's timing me, but the guy doesn't even wear a watch,

As I walk back into my room, the door clicks softly shut, and I stalk back to bed. I strip off again.

As I climb in, he reaches out and pulls me to him. I'm half laid on him, half on the bed, and he crashes his lips to mine, dragging my body against his. He reaches down and cups my arse, pulling me closer, grinding into me, and I pull back slightly.

"Dice," my voice comes out as a gravelly moan. "Are you sure about this? If we go any further, I don't think I can come back from that."

"Dane, don't stop."

"Dice, I need to know what you want."

He drags me in for a bruising kiss, and I give in. I let him take it, and I grind myself shamelessly against his thigh. I reach down and cup his balls. He grabs my wrist, staring me straight in the eyes. I think he's having second thoughts till he says, "Dane, I need you inside me right now! Babe, I need you to fuck me."

And I don't need telling twice. As I move off him, he groans till I pull the lube from the bedside drawer and lather it over my dick. Putting some on my hand, I climb in between his legs, sliding my hand down between us and massaging the lube between his cheeks. He groans and grinds against me. I push a finger in, causing him to shudder. He drags me back in for a kiss as I go to push a second finger in.

"Dane, just fuck me, please," he pants, pulling away from the kiss before slamming his mouth against mine again, so I line my tip up and gently push forward.

"Fuck," he gasps out as I pull back slightly. Before I'm in anymore, he tenses up, and I relax, kissing him less frantic this time. He grinds into me. "Dane, now!" I stare down at him at the sheer desperation etched across his face.

I take a breath and slam into him. "Fucking Jesus," he gasps out as I pull back and slam into him again. There's nothing romantic or gentle about our first time together. It's desperate, dirty, and all-consuming as I lose myself to the feeling I've craved for so long. I slam into him repeatedly, lean on one arm, slide my hand between us, and wrap it around his length. I squeeze before driving into him again. He bucks underneath me as I slide my hand over his shaft, and I can't stop. I can't slow. I just keep driving into him as his eyes roll into the back of his head, his breaths coming in jagged and ragged. He's panting, and he's hanging on to the bed. His knuckles are white from the tight grip, and as I slam into him again, he bites down on his lip. I watch him let go as streams of come cover his abdomen while I can't contain myself any more and slam into him again and again, following him into oblivion.

I collapse against him, panting and trying to breathe, when his gaze catches mine. "Shit," he gasps. "That was... fuck, I'm screwed." He slams his lips against mine as I start to move slowly, this time sliding my body up and down his. "Shit," he gasps out.

"You didn't think we were done, did you?" My voice drops, and the raspy gravel comes back from the over-exhaustion. I grin down savagely at him. "I'm only just getting started." I bite down on his shoulder, causing him to buck into me and groan. Leaning down, I bite his nipple. "I hope you like it rough." I slide my hand around his throat and lean as the lust flashes across his eyes. I can feel my dick hardening again, and his eyes go wide as he does, too. I grind down on him as I grip tighter and slam into him, causing a roar to tear from his lips, and I brutally pound into him relentlessly. I bite down on his nipples, his shoulder, and his neck and mark him as mine.

My eyes flutter open, and he's wrapped in my arms. I fucked him till we both passed out. He stirs in my arms, and my dick starts to twitch. I knew if we crossed that line, there'd be no going back for me. I know I can't now, even if he wanted to. As his eyes flutter open, those warm brown pools of his soul stare at me like he can't quite believe he's still here, and honestly, neither can I.

"Hey." I smile over at him as I pull him in closer and give him a kiss. It's supposed to be gentle, but as I start to kiss him, he groans, and my dick twitches, and he groans again.

"Seriously?" He winces.

"How are you feeling?"

"Honestly? Like I've been fucked six ways to Sunday by a fucking racehorse!"

I bark out a laugh, and he groans again. "Can you fuck off and stop being so sexy while I'm struggling here. You're such a dick!"

I grin down at him and kiss him again. Then there's a knock at the door. "Yeah?"

"Can I come in?" It's Ray, and Dice is shaking his head so hard it might fall off.

"Sure!" I laugh, and Dice digs me in the ribs and pulls the covers up to cover him a little.

Ray walks in with a tray of pancakes, fruit, and some juice.

"You know you're my favourite sister, right!" I say smugly.

"Yeah, yeah, you say that to us all."

As she turns to walk away, Dice calls out, "Ray! I'm sorry!"

She waves her hand at him. "Don't worry about it. Just call it one in the bank."

"One in the bank?" he grumbles. "What's that supposed to mean?"

She winks and walks out, and I laugh. "That's not a good thing. It means she now has a free pass next time she fucks up, she can literally do anything, and you can't even get mad about it!"

He scrubs a hand down his face. "Is it too late to put a stop to this?" He gestures between us. "I think I might wanna stop the ride and get off. I feel it might not be as much fun as I thought it would be."

I bark out a laugh while he looks a little sheepish and winces as he drags himself to a sitting position.

"That bad, huh?"

"Totally worth it!" He grins back at me before twisting and wincing again.

Skye

I knock on the door and stand and wait outside. The door swings open. "The fuck you knocking for?" Ray walks off, leaving the door open behind her, and drops onto the sofa beside Dice and Dane.

I lift my hand in a little wave. "Hi, guys!"

"Hey, Skye," they both say back, and I just stand there like a right weirdo.

"Well, you just gonna stand there, or are you coming in?" Ray's acting like I haven't moved out.

"I was just wondering…" I trail off, unsure of how to ask.

"Can you wonder further inside with the door closed, maybe?"

"You're such a dick," I mutter. "I've missed you."

She laughs. "I bet you have, kiddo!" she winks at me, and I flush slightly.

"Can I talk to you a sec… in private? If you don't mind?"

"Sure, kiddo. Shall we go to your room?"

I nod and follow her through the door as we walk into my room. She stops and turns, and I throw my arms around her and hug the life out of her as close as I can, with my growing bump crushed between us. I truly have missed her.

"Hey, you okay?"

I head and sit on the bed, "I… I…. was just wondering…?"

"Yeah, we established that bit! Whaddya need Skye?"

"I wondered if I could grab a few bits of clothes to tide me over."

"Skye, it's all yours! You take what you want, okay?"

"Really?"

"Yeah! Is that all you came for?" I look down and shake my head.

"Hey, what's wrong? You know you can tell me anything, yeah? Has my brother done something stupid?"

"No, its nothing like that, it's just we're married now, and we share a bed, and we've fooled around a little, but it's like I'm this porcelain doll that he doesn't want to dint or mark, and I'm really struggling with hormones, and I just want him to fuck me. I didn't think I would ever want that, but it feels like my skin is itching when he's not touching me."

"Yep, you need a good fucking, alright!" She grins at me. "So, what do you need from me?"

"I need you to show me how to get what I want without him fobbing me off!"

"Are you sure you're ready for that?"

"I'm so far beyond ready. It's ridiculous!"

An hour or two later, I'm armed to the back teeth with everything knowledge-wise I could need, and Ray helps me pack up all my stuff. Dane and Dice are bringing it to the lodge for me any minute in the truck. I want to walk to clear my head, but my mind is racing.

After Dice and Dane leave, I head to the kitchen and prepare dinner. While that's cooking, I head to the bathroom. I do everything Ray suggested. I shave, I pluck, I primp, I curl, I pamper, I put on my sexiest underwear, well, some of Ray's underwear. She assures me it's new, and I slide on one of the new dresses Ray got me. And I wait, and I wait a little longer, and the door opens, my mouth dries, and my heart races. I have to get through dinner first, but to hell with that. I switch everything off. I can't wait a minute longer. Tank's just taking his boots off by the door. "Hey, love, I'm home!" He shouts this every day, even though I'm standing there waiting, and it's cute.

"Hey, husband!" I grab his hand and drag him through the house, straight to the bedroom.

"Everything okay, love?"

"Uh-huh!"

I spin him around so his back is to the bed, and I rip his t-shirt up over his head. "Skye?"

I put my finger to his lips, then lean up and kiss him. My hands slide down his ripped body and to the waistband of his jeans. Unbuttoning the jeans, I slide them down his legs to his calves, his dick springs free, and I'm relieved to see it's hard. If it isn't, this will not go to plan, so I lean forward and push him back hard on the bed.

He falls onto his back, and I don't wait for a second. I climb up on him and reach between us. I grab hold of his dick, and he groans, and I slide my pants to the side and run him through my wet lips.

"Skye?" he gasps, but I don't give him a chance. I slide myself on him. "Fuck... Shit, Skye, the baby!" he gasps around a choked breath, his hands come up to my waist, and his eyes are filled with concern.

"He's safe, handsome!" I rock forward and gasp. Fuck, is this what it should have felt like all along? Every time I rock forward, I undo one of the buttons on my dress. His eyes burn a trail along every button. My skin is on fire where we touch, and as I unbutton the last one and open up my dress, my underwear is on show. He mutters, "Holy shit," and bites down on his lip. I start to pick up my pace grinding against him, and damn, that hits the spot.

I groan as I start to heat from the centre of my soul, and I clench. He groans, and it spurs his hand to slide up my body till he's cupping my breasts through my bra. With a flick of his fingers, the bra is tucked under my breast, and he's pinching my nipple between his thumb and finger. My hands slide up his chest till they are resting on his pecs, and I slide him in and out of me as I feel like I'm burning up. I'm gasping for breath and rolling my hips like my life depends on it. One last slide as my clit rubs against him again, and I explode. "Shit. Shit. Shit," I gasp out as I scream my release, and Tank roars under me as I feel his come firing out inside me. I'm over-sensitised, and everything's tingling; electric pulses are running over every inch of my skin as I flop forward onto his chest, crushing my bump between us, and we're both panting, trying to gather our breath.

I try to push up on his chest, but he grabs me and pulls me in for a dirty kiss. I don't know how long we stay like that, kissing and nipping at each other's tongue and lips, but I groan as my hips move of their own accord, causing him to groan against my mouth. I chuckle as I do it again. "You're playing with fire, Mrs Pershing!" He nips my lip again.

"Oh really, Mr Pershing? How so?"

"You've started something now, and I don't think I will ever get enough! I was trying to be a gentleman and give you a little time."

"Clearly, I wasn't looking for a gentleman when I chose you!" I clench around him again, and he groans, gripping my hips and grinding me into him. I can feel his come coating my thighs, and I slide against it as he gasps out.

"I don't think I'm ever gonna get enough of you now."

Grinning down at him, I say, "Let's test that theory, shall we?" I rock myself against him again as his fingers grip my hips with bruising intensity, and I slam my head back and cling on for dear life as I don't think I will ever get enough of this man either.

Ares

"Dice?" I shout as I storm into the bar. "Where the fuck is Dice?"

He's been at Dane's all week, Priest states from his usual spot. "Shit, I need you all at Ray's now! Blade, Priest, Viking and Tank follow me. We walk around to the garage to grab Dozer and Ray,

"Where the fuck's Ray?" I bark at Dozer as I storm into the garage with the others on my heels. "Fuck, it smells good here. How do you get anything done?" Dozer shrugs as he brings his takeaway coffee cup to his lips. "She does fucking takeaway?" Everyone chuckles.

"Where is Ray?"

"She left early, needed to stop by Bernie's. He needed a hand with something."

"Shit, everyone up to Ray's, then we can grab Steel, Dice and Dane while we're there." As we storm out of the garage while Dozer locks the doors down, I slip into the coffee shop for a fix.

Shoving through the door of the apartment, Dozer says, "It's so nice of you to join us!"

"Dick!" I mutter as I clutch my hazelnut latte to my chest. This is so good!

"Where's Dane?" I ask as I look around the room.

"Needed to drop by uni to drop off an assignment." Dice shrugs.

"Why is no one around when I need them?" I shake my head and take another swig of my coffee. So good! "Dice, I need you to crack this message. It's encrypted."

"Who's sending you encrypted messages?" Dice asks.

"If I knew that, dipshit, I wouldn't need you to crack it now, would I?"

He gets up, storms out of the room, and comes back a few minutes later with his laptop, plugging it into my phone. He gets to work. "Shit, it's an invitation... it's from The Armoury." Dice turns the computer around to show us.

"Show me that!" I bark at it. "It's just a date, time, and location, is it? That's today, in two hours."

"Wait, that's a good hour and forty-five ride from here. That doesn't give us much time to decide what to do or even whether to go after all the shit they pulled with the kidnapping or whoever was behind it!" Steel shakes his head. "What we gonna do?"

I start pacing, scrubbing my hand down my face. "Tool up. We leave in five, we're all going. I wanna get there early so we can scope it out, then I'm taking these motherfuckers down if they try anything. I don't give a shit how fucking scary their reputation is!"

Everyone starts moving, and in five minutes, we're on the bikes, pulling out of the parking lot.

An hour and a half later, and we're here. We all broke the land speed record to get here as quickly as possible. We scan the area, but there's nothing. It's an empty warehouse that's been disused for years. We've spanned out and checked out the surrounding area inside and outside, and there's no one here, no cameras, no sign anyone but us has even been here in the last ten years.

"What do you wanna do, boss?" Priest asks. We're all on edge, total sitting ducks,

"It's two minutes till the meet. We wait, stay vigilant, eyes on a swivel. Leave the bikes idling incase we need to get out of here, fast. I wanna know as soon as anyone approaches. We leave in five minutes if no one shows. We're not waiting any longer."

As the clock ticks down, there's a rumbling noise. "What the fuck's that?" I glance around but see nothing. "Sounds like a… it can't be… A fucking helicopter. Everyone out, heads down, take cover to stay safe. If this is an ambush. I want them all dead!"

The helicopter hovers over the land out the back; dense trees surround the area, but there's a massive clearing all the way around the warehouse. As the helicopter lands, three figures get out, and a voice echoes around the open space. "Welcome, gentleman."

As the figures step forward, they're all dressed in black tactical gear. The dust from the ground is flying everywhere, and as they stride across the open field, it's difficult to see anything other than three blurry black figures. They stop about twenty feet away, and the helicopter shuts down.

As the dust settles, we take in the three figures. "Are you fucking taking the proverbial piss right now?" I bark across the space between us.

"Is this a joke? Steel spits out.

"Will someone tell me what the fuck's going on?" Dice shakes his head, rubbing his eyes to see if they deceive him, but they don't. It's fucking them dicking around.

"Welcome, gentleman," she says with a massive grin on her face. "You've been accepted into the fold. You are The Armoury's newest recruits."

"Ray!" I bark. "You best have a good reason for whatever the fuck you're trying to pull."

She walks forward, and Bran and Dane flank her with smug ass grins on their faces. Once they reach us, Ray says, "I'm sure you have a lot of questions, All of you."

"Where the fuck do we start?"

"You're with The Armoury? That's how you knew the guys who kidnapped us weren't!" Steel takes a step towards his wife and then stops. She just nods in reply.

"How long have you been in The Armoury?" Priest asks.

"We're not in The Armoury," Dane replies. "We are The Armoury."

"What the fuck does that even mean?" Dice spits clearly as blindsided as the rest of us.

Bran takes a step forward. "It means we aren't part of the organisation. We run it. Our dads started it twenty years ago. We run this side of it now!"

"Why didn't anyone tell me?" Steel asks.

"Baby." Ray steps forward, but you can see the hurt on Steel's face, so she stays a few feet away.

"When our dads took you and Demi to the bank to sort out everything, you kinda freaked at the stuff they told you, so remember they said they would leave the rest for a bit till things sunk in? This is one of the many things we waited to tell you. You and Demi are financially part of The Armoury. There are other bank accounts in your name, as it all started from the initial buy-in your dad was a part of!"

"So what does this mean for us all?" Blade takes a step forward, eyeing Ray cautiously.

"It means now you get the good stuff, the best guns, ammo, knives, fucking armoured trucks, whatever you want, you can buy-in and distribute as you wish. Obviously, there are certain rules and certain people we won't allow you to deal with, but you will buy directly from us, just now your clientele will have a better range, shall we say. Higher quality and untraceable, which also means they'll pay more. So what do you say, gentlemen, wanna see behind the curtain?"

We all shift uncomfortably as we glance around at each other. I mean, we trust Ray, we know Ray, but this is a big fucking deal. "Tell you what, guys, if you wanna come, load your bikes into the warehouse and lock it up." She tosses us some keys. "If not, jump on them and hightail it outta here, no harm, no foul." They turn around and head to the chopper.

"What the fuck is going on, Ares?" Dice asks.

"Man, I don't know how I feel about this. I mean, would it feel safer if it was someone we didn't know?" Blade asks, just as confused as the rest of us.

"They haven't become the organisation they have by inviting every Tom, Dick, and Harry in. It makes sense for them to have been this cautious," Steel reminds us.

"It's Ray! I'm in!" Tank says. "I trust her with my life, and you lot do too, so what the fuck are we bitching about?" Tank turns and strides towards the bikes, riding his into the warehouse and coming out, heading over to Ray.

"Well, I'm in, obviously!" Steel shrugs. He definitely wouldn't be getting laid for a while if he didn't follow her!

"Fuck it." Dice throws his hands up and takes his bike inside.

"Come on. We're in this together," I say to the rest of us. "All or nothing, I suppose!"

As we all climb aboard the chopper, I glare at Ray. "You're a slippery motherfucker!"

She winks at me. "You don't know the half of it, Brother!" A shiver passes through me. I pass it off as the chopper having an effect on me, but I'm beginning to wonder if we actually know Ray. And can we truly trust her? I'm withholding passing judgement right now, but I'm not taking my eyes off her. She's so embedded into all our lives that if she betrays us, there will be no coming back for any of us.

We're all handed blindfolds. "You are taking the piss right now," I spit in her face.

"If you didn't know me at all and I was just someone for The Armoury, you wouldn't be so on edge or unwilling to trust me. I'm still me, Brother! I would still give my life for yours. Nothing has changed." She hands me the blindfold, and I snatch it from her grasp. "You're getting the VIP treatment, Ares. I've been fighting for a long time to bring you all into the fold, so trust me when I say you're getting closer than anyone else ever has!"

"Is that supposed to comfort me in some way?" I snipe at her.

"No, Boyband. It's just a reminder!"

"Sounds more like a threat to me!"

Grinning like the motherfucker she is, she leans forward, "If I wanted you dead, 'brother', you would be!" she spits at me, then sags back into the chair and looks out the window folding her arms over her chest clearly done with this conversation!

We all don our blindfolds and fly off in silence for what feels like about forty minutes until we land. There's noise and rustling around us and a door opening and slamming.

"You can take them off now." Bran or Dane says, and when we open our eyes, Ray is gone.

"Where the fuck is she?" I bark out.

"She thought you might feel more relaxed without her here!" Dane tells me with a soft smile.

"I feel more on fucking edge not having her in my line of sight." I mutter.

"No one's ever been here. This is top secret. Ray fought tooth and nail to be able to bring you in, and she's vouched for you! If this goes to shit, it's all on her. No one else who we deal with knows who we are. You're the first!" Bran tells us all.

"Is that supposed to make me feel better?" I look around, as I don't think it does.

"She's got as much riding on this as you guys have. If you don't trust her, say now. We can end this and take you back. Once you see behind the curtain, there's no going back." Dane barks out as his hand grips the door to stop us from getting out.

"I want her here where I can always see her!"

"That doesn't sound much like trust!" Bran sounds dejected as he sits back down. "Blindfolds back on, guys. We'll have you back home in no time."

"Pres?" Tank spits out. "Are you seriously questioning Ray's loyalty right now? After everything she's done for us? Don't you think she's proved herself time and time again, and she told you there were things she couldn't tell you. You don't get to decide whether we trust her or not for the rest of us. I will follow her to the bowels of hell. I'm going with or without you!"

"And how do the rest of you feel about all this?"

They all look at each other and nod. Steel speaks for them all. "We're all with Ray. Always have been!"

"Of course you fucking are. But what about the rest of you?"

"Pres. I say this with the utmost respect. You're acting like a butthurt lil bitch! Get over yourself and go talk to her!" Blade tries to reason. "But we're with her. She's one of us!"

"Fine," I snipe as I cross my arms over my chest and sulk like a fucking toddler. I'm fucking hurt and upset, and I feel deceived, but I also feel so stupid that I didn't see this, stupid that I feel hurt and betrayed by it, as deep down I know she would die for me, and I would her. "I wanna talk to her alone."

"Come on then, we'll start the tour, and when we get to her, you can… chat." Dane shakes his head as we step out of the chopper. We're surrounded by massive aircraft hangars. We can't see anything other than those. As we head off to the first one, we reach the door. Bran places his hand on the scanner, and we walk through what looks like a tiny room. There's a desk with paperwork in piles on it. "NDAs read them, sign them. We can't go any further till you all sign them. We will take you back if you don't want to sign! Last chance to get out, gentlemen."

After a few grumbles from me, I do the same after the others pick up the pens and sign, no questions asked. "This way, gentlemen!" Dane leads us through the door. At the end, it's a massive hangar of armoured trucks lining each side, probably sixteen in total.

"Just how big is this operation?" I grumble at no one in particular.

"This is our main base. We have five others, slightly smaller ones, around the country," Bran informs us like he's just told us what he had for breakfast.

Stepping out of the doors at the end, there's just open space, nothing! In the distance, we can see the perimeter fence, but it's just open grassland.

"Well, that was a short tour," I grumble.

Dane shakes his head at me.

"You really are a miserable bastard, aren't you?" Bran laughs, and everyone joins in once the noise dies from them all laughing at my expense. I can hear a vehicle approaching. When I look over to my left, there's a big enclosed back truck. Bran and Dane climb in the back, and we all follow like the fucking sheep we're obviously turning into. There's a bench seat along either side, and as we all sit, Bran bangs on the back of the cab, and we set off.

"Where are we going?" It seems everyone else is happy to go along for the ride. I'm kinda freaking out inside, which is manifesting itself as a major dickhead on the outside.

We stop and get out. As we round the truck, we're in front of what looks like an office building of sorts. As we head through the doors, there's a reception area, and we must sign in. Visitor badges are waiting for us with our pictures on. All the guys have nice pics, and when it comes to mine, it's awful. I mean, it looks like I'm trying to multiply the square root of pi with a rhinoceros while smelling an eggy fart!

"What the fuck is this?" They all look, then bark out laughing. "Who's in charge of sorting this shit out?" They all laugh again. "It's her, isn't it? Fucking bitch!"

"Hey, watch it!" Steel barks, so I pull the lanyard around my neck and shut my mouth before we end up scrapping.

We head up to the third floor as we push through the doors. There are offices on either side of the room. There's one large room at the end, and there's a row of cubicles, two cubicles wide down the middle.

When we get halfway up the room, Steel stalks off ahead, throwing open a door marked "Delta 1". When I reach it, Ray's in there, and Steel throws his arms around her, pulling her in for a filthy kiss. There's nothing PG about it as he grabs her ass and pulls her to him. There's a slight cough, someone clearing their throat from behind the door as we all swing and look at the bloke in a suit with a clipboard.

"DA, this is my husband."

"Ah, Mr Black Queen, it's a pleasure. Shall we finish this later, BQ?"

"Yeah, thanks, DA."

Steel leans forward and shakes the guy's hand, still keeping Ray's ass in a vice-like grip in the other one while still pinning her to his body.

"Pleasure." Steel says as he's practically crushing the guy's hand while he shakes it.

DA nods and removes himself from the room, going to the cubicle outside.

"What the fuck did you do to this photo?" I don't know why I can't help myself when it comes to Ray; she just pokes, and I flip. It's kind of our thing.

She just barks a laugh at me. "They were taken while you walked through the armoured truck garage. That was the look on your face." She shrugs.

I scowl at her. "Ahh, come on, Boyband! What can I do to sweeten you up and make you love me again?"

"I don't know that you can, Ray! I'm just not so easily brought or bribed."

She steps away from Steel and walks up to me, sliding her hands around my waist. "What about a pen or a keyring with The Armoury on?"

"They have those?" I gasp out. "Yeah, that would help a little." I realise I'm making this easy on her. "But it's not enough."

Hmm." She pulls me in and taps her lips. "What about… a baseball cap?"

"Do you have those jackets like the F.B.I., with 'The Armoury.' on the back? That would be cool! Just saying!"

"I think they all went at the last promo roadshow. I can get DA to check, though."

"Seriously?" I grin at her.

"No, dipshit! We're a top-secret fucking illegal organisation. We do not have pens, key rings, baseball caps or jackets with our name plastered all over them. I mean, who even does that?"

"The F.B.I!" I mutter.

She rolls her eyes at me. "How about some new bulletproof vests and a go-on a rocket launcher? Final offer!"

"Are you taking the piss again?"

"Nope."

"Deal. I would have just accepted the go on the rocket launcher!"

"I would have offered an armoured truck!"

"Fuck!" I mentally kick myself as everyone bursts out laughing. "Fuck off, she's not funny!"

"Come on, let's head over to stores." She grins as she takes my hand and leads me back downstairs. Steel is grinning like a motherfucker like he always does when she makes one of us look stupid.

We walk out of the building and across the street into a hangar. There's a long counter just through the doors and then a wall with a door in the centre. The hangar is massive, but the wall is about ten feet from the entrance. Ray rings the bell on the counter, and a guy walks through the door.

"Hey, Mike!"

"Hi, BQ, who are your friends?"

"My husband and my brothers."

"Nice to meet you, gentlemen. What do you need?"

"A nosy!" She winks at him.

"Do you even have clearance for that?"

"Mike, don't ask stupid questions. You know I have unlimited access to whatever the hell I want!"

He laughs. "I'll need to see your identification then."

"You motherfucker, you know I never carry that thing with me!"

"Well, I can't really just let anyone in. It'll cost you!"

"Fuck, you're gonna fleece me?" She shakes her head. "Wanker! Should have waited for Tango to be on. At least he's nice to me!"

"Liar, Tango is not nice to anyone!"

"Fair point, damn it!" She rests her hands on the counter. "What's it gonna cost?"

"You know that thing you do that I really love!"

"Really?"

"Yep!"

"In front of my husband and my brothers…? Fuck's sake, Mike! I'm trying to be cool here!"

He's nodding the whole time. "Do it!"

"Give it to me!"

He hands her a Rubik's cube and a blindfold, and she turns it over and over in her hands before turning to us, "Can one of you put that on me, please?" she asks, shaking her head. Steel steps up and ties the blindfold on before stepping back. We all move so we can see, and she says to Mike. "You got the timer?" He just nods.

"If you're nodding right now, Mike, I can't fucking see you, you twat!"

To which he laughs, "Yeah, I've got it, three, two, one, go!"

She starts turning and twisting, and the only sound that can be heard is the turning of the cube. It's like we're all holding our breaths. She slams it down on the counter and rips the blindfold off, "How long?"

"12.98 seconds." he laughs out. "So, so close! That's the fastest yet."

"Fuck! I'm fucking coming for you, Tommy!"

She laughs out, and we all just look at each other what the fuck's going on? "Who the fuck is Tommy?" I shake my head as I've no idea what just happened.

"Never mind! Do we get in now?"

She grins at Mike and waves the completed Rubik's cube at him. He snatches it up and starts messing it up again. "Sure, but I'm gonna mess it up real good for next time!"

"Yeah, you do that, Mike!"

She lifts the flap in the counter, and we all walk through. As she opens the door, she grins and walks through. "Holy shit! This place is huge!

"Bulletproof vests are this way." She turns and heads to the left.

They're top-of-the-range military-grade Kevlar reinforced, but so light and thinner than any other I've seen. "No way this shit works!"

She's just grinning. "Try one at the gun range if you like!"

We all grab one, and she goes to walk off. Steel turns and winks at us. "Hey, baby." He walks up to her and grabs her for a steamy kiss. He has her back against the shelving in seconds, and we all separate and disappear. I mean, when are we gonna get a chance to do this again?

I hear her laugh. "Devious man!" And then she jumps on him, and we run, fuck this place is huge.

"So what else are you fancying?" Bran says from behind me, and shit, I forgot about him and Dane.

"Where's Dane?"

"Probably trying to convince Dice to give him a blow job!" He shrugs, and I bark out a laugh.

"What can I get away with taking? I waggle my eyebrows at him?"

"Well, while Steel is keeping Ray occupied, I would say anything you like!"

"You're not gonna stop me?"

He shakes his head. I whoop as I jog down the aisles. I grab all sorts: a rucksack, a pair of boots, some ammo tins, a cargo net, a sleeping bag, a camping stove, a gas mask, some matching combats, a jacket and some socks, amongst anything else I can carry.

When we get back to the door, Ray and Steel are nowhere to be seen, and neither are Dice and Dane, but we've all got a shit tonne of stuff. Tank's even got a tent stuffed under his arms and some camping gear.

"You guys got everything you want?" Mike asks as we push through the door.

"Yup!" I grin as I shrug the rucksack up higher.

Mike presses a button and a Tannoy bings. "BQ, come and get your reprobates. They've emptied the place!" He laughs down the mic.

After about five minutes, Dane and Dice come through the doors, empty-handed and flushed-faced.

"Ah, no fair!" Dice mumbles when he sees us all standing there armed with our haul!

"You got a blow job. Quit whining!" Dane tosses in his direction, and Dice gives him a face of thunder as we all laugh.

"Fuck's sake, come on, be quick!" Dane snipes at Dice, dragging him back inside.

Ray and Steel push through the doors next, and we all burst out laughing as Ray looks down at herself.

"Fucking hell!" She mutters as she takes her top off, turning it the right way around, and throws it back on, elbowing Steel in the ribs. "Blade catch, Everyone got what they want?" She grins, tosses a jar of something at Blade, his eyes go wide and he grins, and we all nod like kids at Christmas. "Where the fuck's Dane and Dice?"

She glances at Mike, and he grabs the Tannoy again. "They're going without you!" he shouts down it, and then we hear a thundering of boots as they're clearly making their way back to us. As they burst through the door, Dice has his arms full of crap too, and a massive grin on his face.

"His smile's definitely bigger this time. You're clearly not doing it right, Dane!" Blade laughs.

"Fuck you!" Dane blobs his tongue in Blade's direction, and we all laugh.

"Right, come on then, dickheads, let's hit the firing range and then head over to the rocket launcher before we head back! Thanks, Mike," she tosses over her shoulder as we all walk out the door crowing about all the shit we got.

"What did you get, Blade?"

"Fishing stuff and this!" He grins shaking the jar Ray gave him. "It's an upgrade for Blade Darts, now we can have Flaming Blade Darts, and I'm gonna ask

Bernie and Cade to take me fishing sometime." He grins over at Dane, who smiles back at him.

"Ooh, can I come?" Tank asks. "I've never been proper fishing."

"I'm sure they'll take you all if you want to." Dane laughs, and we all grin.

After a few hours at the firing range playing with every gun we can name, we head over to the rocket launcher. Apparently, there's a row of barrels filled with sand and a firing platform about two hundred metres away. As I climb up on the platform, Ray takes the launcher from the guy who met us there and shows me how to kneel and hold it. She moves the guys to the side and out of the way because of something called back blast and loads me up. "I'll count you down from five, okay?"

I nod. We're all wearing ear defenders, and Ray stands at the side but slightly to the front and shows me her hand counting down with her fingers. When she makes a fist, I release, and the power of that thing is amazing. I think I just came in my pants, and there was barely any recoil.

"Holy shit, who do I have to suck off to get one of those?" I ask as the guy takes it off me and boxes it back up!"

"My pas!" Ray grins at me, and I smile back

"It would be so worth it!" I say with the biggest grin on my face. "So now you're my favourite club sister again; what now?"

"I'm your only fucking club sister, dick!" and she punches me in the ribs, and I laugh out. I really do fucking love her. Well, I love her rocket launcher anyway. I think to myself as we head back to the chopper with our bags of swag and a grin on my face.

Ray

After a few weeks of quiet normality, coffee shop for breakfast, Barbie bringing me lunch at work and making the most of the quiet house, it appears Dice has moved in while he and Dane are doing up their lodge. It seems all the guys have them, and now Bran and Cade, too. It's the quietest it's been in a long while. We head over to the bar to catch up with everyone. I've been keeping my distance from Cade, because, well, shit hit the fan, and now I'm feeling guilty because when I think back on growing up, he was my person, my closest confidant, and I feel like maybe we should just get the test and be done with it.

Cade's the first person I see walking into the bar, and I groan. I turn and hug Steel. "I'm gonna try and fix this or kill him trying."

"It's die trying, baby, but ya know what, I like your version better."

"Cade!" I bark as I sit at the bar next to him.

"Cade, huh? Not even Pa anymore, then?"

"I'm not calling you anything else till we have the test. I've booked it for two days time, at 10 a.m. I will meet you out front at 9 a.m., and we can discuss our options on the way. Sound fair?"

"Sounds fair." he grumbles as I rise from the stool. He stops me with his hand on my arm. "I really am sorry, Squirt. You're my world, and I don't know how to not have you love me back."

"Cade, I don't love you any less than before just because I'm mad at you. I still fucking love you, you knobhead!"

"Turning and hugging me, I can't lose you too, Squirt. I just can't."

"Then you won't." I give him a kiss on the cheek and head back over to my brother's table.

My phone rings, and it's Pa Bernie, so I answer it. "Hey Pa, what's up?"

"Hey, Squirt, I need a favour. We booked a security job for next weekend, and I need a woman, and we have no others free. How are you fixed?"

I groan down the phone. "Details?"

"Ball, the guy's wife can't make it, but he needs a date, and he thought rather than an escort, which his wife wouldn't like, he would go with security instead. His family has money but nothing to make him a target. There's no background of any issues, so it does appear he's just trying to keep the wife sweet. He's already got the outfit, so we will send it over. I've arranged the limo so it will pick you up first, then grab him on the way."

"Fine." I hang up, flop in my chair, and groan again.

"What's up, gorgeous?" Steel asks as he sits next to me and starts kissing my neck.

"I've gotta do a job for Pa next weekend, security, a fucking ball of all things."

"Doesn't sound totally terrible."

"Yeah, neither did the last one." I grumble as I rise from my chair and head to the bar. Grabbing the tequila, I head over to talk to Scar. It's been a minute since we had time together alone.

"Hey, Sis." She smiles up at me from Ares's lap.

"Hey, you. You got a minute?"

"For you? Always!"

"Do me a favour, Boyband, and fuck off for a bit, yeah?"

He kisses Scar like he might never see her again and slides out from under her, shoulder barging me out of the way with a feral grin on his face.

"You're such a lil bitch." I laugh after him, and he turns, blobs his tongue out and flips me the bird, to which I respond with a bark of laughter. "Knobhead!" I shout after him.

"Where's your head at?" she says softly as she rests her head on my shoulder.

"Can you ask me an easy one, ya know, maybe the meaning of life, or some quadratic equation, something that I can actually stand a chance of answering."

I feel her chuckle against me, and then she lifts her head to face me, "It's been a tough time, huh?"

"Understatement." I shake my head. "So, how's the office going? When's Pops moving here?"

"He'll be back in a few weeks for good. He's winding down with the firm back in the UK and handing it over in two weeks, then they're gonna run it. The firm here is ready to go. Just a few finishing touches to the apartment upstairs where he's gonna live. He wants to be close but not too close." She laughs at that. They love each other; they were all each other had till I showed up with my crazy lot. But if they're working together, they will definitely need some separation.

"That's good news. How's things with Boyband?"

"Perfect." She grins at me.

"Wow! Bold statement." I laugh. "I know what you mean, though. Who would have thought our perfect men were in the States?" I shrug.

"I know I can't quite believe I'm in love with the president of a biker gang. I mean, who even am I?"

"Wanna get shit-faced and celebrate our awesomeness."

"Hell yeah?" She laughs. This girl would follow me off a cliff if I asked it, but in fairness, I would do the same for her.

We drink, laugh, and rip the piss out of the guys, and then I'm vaguely aware of his presence. I turn too fast, but the room spins, and I hear Scar chuckle. Steel slides in beside me, and I slide onto his lap so I'm straddling him.

"Hey, wife."

I grind onto him and moan. "Hey, husband," my voice comes out breathy as I grind into him again.

"Have I told you that I love that you're a horny drunk?" The gravel in his voice rubs against all my nerve endings and down to my clit, and fuck, I could just fuck him here, and I wouldn't care.

"Once or twice." I slur into his neck as I nip my way down it and along his collarbone. "It should be illegal how fucking hot you are," I whisper against his ear as I nip down on it, and he groans, his head falling back as I grind my body into him. The next thing I know, he's standing, and my legs wrap around him as I'm carried to the door! I wave at Scar as she laughs, and as I'm carried past the boys, they shake their heads at me as I'm fully aware that even though I'm being carried, I'm still grinding onto Steel and biting his neck.

As he kicks the door open and we make it outside, I'm slammed against the side of the building. "Fuck, baby!" He grunts against me as he tries to force me back inside through the side of the building, and my head slams back against it as he grinds into me, hitting that sweet spot.

He pushes against me again, grinding his hips, and the friction between him and my jeans has me panting, and I'm soaked. He slams against me, and I groan, trying to pull him closer as I gasp and pant into his neck. I bite down hard as an orgasm threatens to rip through me, and he thrusts against me again. I would say I'm dry-humping him at this stage; but there's nothing dry about it. I'm drenched, and I rub myself against him, chasing that orgasm as he pins me against the wall with his hips. My lips have moulded around him through my jeans, and I'm about to explode as every rub lights me on fire. "Fuck!"

I bite down on his neck, and I get a coppery tang, and I'm sure it's his blood I can taste, and as the orgasm hits, I can't help but lick and suck at that spot. Fuck, this is so hot. I grind again, the lights explode behind my eyes, and I release him as my head flies back, and I scream into the night sky. I feel him shudder as a few curses of his own ring out into the night.

"Couldn't even make it home, huh?" I hear the smug voice of one of my brothers.

"Ah," I pant. "Do you need to see how it's done? Get some pointers?"

Steel laughs against my throat as he nips it and kisses along my neck. Rubbing against me, he growls in my ear, "I wanna do that again with fewer clothes this time."

He backs away from the wall as I sag against him, and he tosses me over his shoulder, smacking my arse and inhaling. "Fuck, I love the smell of you!" he growls, and my thighs clench together, trying to find a release again, but I'm gonna have to wait till we get home. In fairness, we're only about a thirty-second walk away, but he still carries me, and then I'm weightless as I'm dropped on the bed.

My back bounces off it, and as I land again, he's ripping my jeans and my pants down and dragging them off with my boots all in one go. "Fuck you're so sexy!" He grins down at me as I lean in my elbows while he rips his t-shirt off over his head and shoves his jeans and boxers down, shucking them off with his boots and kicking them to the side. "Shit, I need a shower. I'm all sticky and gross."

"I plan on making you more sticky and gross than that, so get your arse down here. Now!" I reach forward and grab his dick and tug him forward.

"Oh fuck!" He grunts as he falls forward.

As he ends up at the side of me, I throw myself over his body, rolling him onto his back, waggling my eyebrows at him. I slide my hands up his arms to his wrists, lifting his arms above his head. I lean forward, distracting him with my tits in his face, and while he nips and bites and sucks them, I snag his hands in the rope I have attached to the bed for a special occasion.

As I lean back, removing my nipple bar from his teeth with a gasp, he says, "What the fuck?" He tries to move, but his hands are locked down tight!

I grin back at him. "Ah, baby! Looks like you're a little tied up." I lay my body against his and rest my hands on his chest and my chin on the backs of my hands. I move up and down ever so slightly, back and forward, trapping his dick between me and him.

"Baby, please?" he growls. "I need to touch you!"

Winking at him, I smile. "Don't worry, handsome. I will touch enough for both of us."

Sliding myself down his body between his legs, I lick up the length of his dick, tasting the leftover come from earlier. It sends an illicit shiver through his body as he tugs at the binds. I grin against him as I lick around his shaft, running my hand up and down his length. I cup his balls with my other hand, and he shudders against me.

"Baby!" he says in warning, but it only makes me smile as I slide my mouth around him, taking him right down my throat. "Fuck!" he gasps out as he struggles some more.

I suck him in and out of my mouth while he bucks against me, gritting his teeth from the sensitive feeling from all the chafing against his jeans mere moments ago. His breaths are coming heavy now as he screws his eyes shut while I grope at him while swallowing him whole. He bucks again, and while I'm cupping his balls, I slip my finger into my mouth, then slide it between his cheeks as he gasps at the intrusion, forcing my way in and massaging his P-spot. He bucks again as I swallow him deeper.

His eyes shoot open at the sensation, and I feel his legs tense excessively more than normal, and I can feel him curling his toes. He's gasping and bucking as I continue sliding my finger around in his arse as I take in his whole shaft, swirling my tongue before taking it back into my throat.

"Shit," he gasps, and I grin around his dick, sliding my finger in and out as I massage that special little area. "Fuck, it feels like I'm on fire!" he gasps.

I continue to stroke and suck and nip at his tip before filling my mouth again, he's bucking wildly now, and his chest and face are tinged with pink. His thighs and legs have stiffened, his toes are clenched, and he's gripping the slats in the headboard so tight I think he might snap them.

Popping his dick out of my mouth but continuing with my hand, I whisper up to him, "Relax, baby, trust me, go with it!"

I slide my mouth around him again as I feel him relax slightly, and when I up my pace, his whole body thrashes against me while his eyes literally roll back in his head till all I can see are the whites. He's biting his lip so hard I can see the blood pooling. Every single muscle in his body has solidified, and his breaths are mere pants. When I hit that spot again, he goes off with a force I've never known before, and the amount of come I swallow down has me gasping for breath, too. It seems to go on for an eternity as I continue to stimulate and swallow over and over before he finally sags slightly, and once the come recedes, I slowly remove him from my mouth and gently remove my finger from his arse.

He's staring up at the ceiling and trying to catch his breath. I can almost see his heart trying to pound out of his chest. As his breathing becomes less erratic and his pounding chest subsides slightly, he whispers out on a shaky breath, "What the fucking hell was that?"

"Is that a... what the fucking hell was that, good or what the fucking hell was that, bad?"

"It felt like I was burning up from my toes, and it took over my whole body. It felt like someone had shoved a firework up my ass... in a weird fucking hot way, fuck, I thought my head was gonna fall off!"

"I'm still not sure whether you think it was good or bad?" I laugh. I slide up his body, and he squirms at my touch. I reach his wrists and untie him, and he's still just lying there, panting.

"You okay, baby?" I'm concerned now.

"Y-y-eah!" He sighs out. "Yeah, I'm good."

"Maybe a no to that again, then?" I grimace.

"No! No, not a no." He shakes his head. "That was... I don't think I can describe it, fuck, babe!"

After about twenty minutes, just laying panting with me on my knees between his legs, he pushes himself up to sit and pulls me forward. "Shit, that was amazing!" He pulls me to his body, then flips us and throws me on my back.

"My turn." He grins against my mouth as he kisses me like I just rocked his world, and I think he's about to return the favour as he devours me and slides inside me with one thrust, making me gasp out, rocking my world in return.

He pulls me into his chest as we collapse into a sweaty heap. "Fuck, I wanna put a baby in you so bad!"

"What?" I gasp. Clearly, I heard him wrong.

"I wanna have a kid." He turns on his side to face me, cupping my face with his hand. "I wanna be a dad. I'm ready!"

"Wait. Steel, fuck, we've only just got married. I thought we were gonna wait a couple of years or so!"

"I did… we were… I just… You don't wanna have kids?"

"Not right now, no! With everything with The Armoury, Dante, and Cade, my head is all over the place as it is!" I climb off the bed, pacing and biting my thumb's side. "Then there's Skye, and we've just lost JJ and Steven. Now is not a good time, Steel. Not even remotely a good fucking time!"

I need a shower, so I push into the bathroom, turn the shower on cold, and step under the freezing water. I brace myself against the wall, letting it beat down on me.

"Baby!" There's a warm hand pressed to my back "Fuck," he gasps when he feels the cold as he reaches past me and shuts off the water, shuddering as he grabs a towel and wraps it around me, pulling me back into the bedroom, rubbing me to warm me up. I'm just numb, though. *A baby, what the fuck is he thinking?*

He takes the towel off, wraps me in my dressing gown, slides me between the covers, and then heads to the dressing room, coming back out with a winter quilt and draping it over me. He climbs in at the side of me and wraps his arms around me, rubbing me while he entwines his legs with mine to warm them up, causing him to shudder as he pulls me closer. "Sleep, okay?" He pulls me tighter and just holds me. I don't know how long he holds me till I fall asleep, but when I wake, he's gone.

Pa Cade

It's the day of the test. As I walk out of the clubhouse, she's pacing by the side of the truck, chewing the side of her thumb. It makes me laugh as I do this all the time. People mistake it for a nervous reaction, but for me, it happens when I'm thinking, planning, or plotting. It's a concentration thing, like some people sticking their tongue out when they write or draw.

"Hey Squirt, you ready?" I shout over to her so she's aware I'm approaching. I don't wanna freak her out any more than I have.

"Yeah, let's get this over with, Pa."

I don't say anything. I just give her the biggest smile. It's the first time she's called me Pa in weeks. As we drive to the clinic, she asks me about the lodge. I ask her about Dane and Dice. She asks me about the job at the weekend. I ask about Skye and Tank trying to stay away from us as a topic, and as we pull up at the clinic and park, she turns to face me.

"Promise me something?" She looks down at her hands and then back at my face. She looks almost… nervous."

"Anything, Squirt." I place my hand on hers.

"Even if you're not my dad, promise me it won't change anything. I've lost too many dads this year… I can't bear to lose another one!"

"Oh, Squirt!" I pull her to my chest and hug her tight. "The first moment I held you in my arms, I knew you were my daughter… biological or not, you've always been mine."

"Is that why you chose me over Bas?"

It's the first time she's ever mentioned what happened with Bas. I know she protected me. I know she knows what really happened, even though she never told anyone what I did.

"Yeah, sweetheart, that moment I held you, I knew I would choose you over anyone else ever."

She gives me a sad smile before pulling back. "Come on, then let's see if you're the one to blame for my fucking attitude!"

I laugh out loud as I slide out of the truck, and she meets me around the other side. I stick my hand out, "Together?"

"Together!" She grins as she takes my hand in hers. I look at her hand in mine, and it's small, but it takes me back to that first time I held her, and she gripped my finger. She was tiny, this precious little bundle that completely changed the course of my life. She made me a better man in that instant.

We walk in, check-in, and take a seat, picking up a magazine, flipping our legs up, and crossing our ankles over our knees.

"Mr King, Mrs Steel, lovely to see you both again. Please, come through." The doctor says as he pokes his head around the door. As we take a seat in the office, he explains the two tests they can do to test paternity: a blood test and a cheek swab.

We both glance at each other and then turn to the doctor. "Both!" we reply before looking back at each other and laughing. After the tests, the doctor informs us the results will be back after the weekend, so they'll call us both to let us know.

As we climb back in the truck, she says, "Fancy coming to Demi's with me?"

"Are you buying?"

"Yeah, sure! Can I ask you something?"

"Yeah, if there's cake and coffee, you can ask me anything."

She barks out a laugh, but then her face drops. "Steel told me last night he wants kids."

"O.M.G, I'm gonna be a granddaddy!"

"Agh! No, I told him no! Now is not a good time. When I woke up, though, he'd gone."

"Maybe he just needs some time to sort his head out."

"Maybe?" She huffs out, "It's just with The Armoury and Dante, and this with us, it's just not ideal."

"Yeah, fair point. You've just taken over The Armoury officially, so it's gonna take a bit of settling in, and although we're throwing everything at the Dante situation, there's just no information anywhere. The guy didn't even exist till two years ago. Dane's been at it flat out. I think Dice is taking him away for the weekend so he doesn't burn himself out. And us? I'm sorry that's one of the reasons not to."

"It's just a lot, ya know? I just was thinking it would be a couple of years, but now? I… we…" she trails off.

"Hey, it'll be fine. Steel's probably just got over-excited, and you burst his bubble, is all. He probably just needs some time. Maybe ask him to give you six months and reevaluate the situation then?"

"Six months? Yeah, things might have straightened out a bit by then. We need to bury Dante before I even think about kids. But six months would be a good compromise, providing issues one and two are dealt with."

"That's my girl." I grin over at her.

Pulling up at Demi's, it's busy. I'm surprised by how busy. "Yo, Ray," Dozer shouts over. "You doing any fucking work today?"

"Go on, you go. I'll see you in the bar later?"

"You're still going for coffee and cake, aren't you?"

"Fuck yeah, Squirt!" I wave over my shoulder as I'm already walking away from her. "Catch ya later!" She doesn't say anything, just flips me the bird as she heads towards the garage, chuntering to herself. "There's no way she isn't mine!" I chuckle to myself as I push through the coffee shop door.

Ray

It's the night of the ball, and Steel has been avoiding me, well, avoiding being alone with me, making sure I'm asleep before he comes to bed and waking up before I do. I mean, is he even sleeping at all? We've had conversations but only general chat with other people around, and I can see he's hurt, and I want to explain. I just don't think he's ready to listen yet.

"Baby? Can we talk before I get ready for work?"

"Sorry, baby," he says with a cold lint to his voice. Anyone else might not have noticed, but I do. "I have to head out. I'll be back before you leave, okay? The dress and shoes were delivered. They're hanging in the dressing room. Oh, you're gonna hate it, by the way!" He laughs humourlessly over his shoulder as he strides to the door, clicking his fingers, and Hades gets up and follows him.

Sighing, I head to the shower. *Fuck my life right now.* I scrub as hard as I can to try and wash the last few months of fucking shite off myself, but it's still there, haunting me. Dante, Cade, JJ, Steven and now Steel.

They say there's no rest for the wicked. Hades, I must have been an awful fucker! I mentally berate myself, trying to look for some positives in my life right now, and all I can come up with is Demi's apple pie, so I abandon getting ready, and, in my dressing gown, I head downstairs to grab a piece.

"Holy hell! Why are you dressed like you belong in a mental institution?" Demi giggles as I walk in. She's just getting ready to close, so I slide on the stool by the counter.

"I'm waiting for them to pick me up. I just came to get some pie and say goodbye." I huff under my breath.

"Hey, what's up? Trouble in paradise?"

"Yeah, it went up in flames a few days ago, and now we're just tiptoeing around in the ash!"

"Damn, Ray, that's… " she trails off. "What do you need?"

"Apple pie!" I point to the quarter of the pie that's left. "All of it!"

"Damn. That bad huh?"

"Steel wants kids. I said no!" I shrug. "Now he's not talking to me."

"You don't want kids?" she gasps like it's the worst thing in the world.

"I don't want kids right *now*." I shake my head. "There's a difference. It's just with everything going on, it's just not a good time, but he won't even listen to me. I just wanna wait six months or so and see if I can't get shit sorted before then." I shrug again. What else am I gonna do?

"Just give him some time. He's stubborn." She winks as she shoves the pie at me. She laughs when I slide the money out of my dressing gown pocket. "Now go get ready for work. Brans picking me up in ten, and we're going away for the weekend."

"I love you. You know that, right?"

"I love you too, Ray. Don't be too hard on him. He's just a man." She winks.

"Yeah, I know."

I head back upstairs and get ready. I straighten my hair in a centre parting and slick the sides down behind my ears. I put all my black jewellery on as this fucking dress is an abomination, and I need to feel like myself. I wear my black chain choker and bracket with my studded bracelet and my black feather and skull earrings. I change my nose ring out for my black one, and I smoke my eye makeup and put on lip gloss. I look like a goth bride. The dress is a huge ball gown with a corset bodice, which pushes my tits up to my chin.

It's a million layers of fucking tulle with a shimmer overlay. The corset back only covers half my tattoos, so I strategically lay my hair to cover the rest. Fuck, I look like I'm marrying Dracula. Well, fuck it. I step out of the room, and Steel's waiting. "Fuck!" He grins. "You look… Fuck!"

"Fucking stupid is what I look like!"

"I was gonna say fucking hot." He walks over and kisses me, smearing my gloss all over both of us and grinning as I roll my eyes. "Can we talk when you get back?"

"No!"

He frowns at my answer.

"We can fuck, because you've been nowhere near me in days, then we can talk!"

"Deal, but I'm still gonna fuck you now."

He spins me in his arms and roughly bends me over the sofa, diving under the millions of layers of dress past my thigh holsters. One side holds my gun, and the other leg my knives. He groans as he runs his fingers over them, then reaches up, ripping my boy shorts down. I mean, who wears thongs? They're fucking stupid. As I think that, his face is buried in me as he bites down on my clit, making me scream out before he forces two fingers inside me and jams his thumb straight in my arse. My knees threaten to buckle, but he's got my whole body wedged over the back of the sofa. This feels like some kind of punishment, but the way I'm feeling right now, this is just what I need.

He bites and tugs at my clit and thrusts his fingers and thumb inside me; it's not long before I'm spiralling. The heat rising up through me is excruciating. The pain mixed with the pleasure is divine as he slams his fingers in and out of me as roughly as humanly possible as I start clenching and panting around him.

"Fuck, you're such a dirty, slutty wife!" He pulls back from my clit to bite down on my arse cheek, then my inner thigh, before diving his face back into my pussy, feasting on me like he'll never have it again. I crash over the edge, he bites down on my clit, and I scream out. He then rips his hand out of me, and I sag against the back of the sofa, feeling empty and spent. He then roughly grabs my hips as he slams into me from behind. "While you're out on your fucking date," he spits at me, "I want you to remember who fucking owns you!"

This isn't like Steel. He's not jealous or mean, but something has him fired up tonight. It's calling to my inner Reaper, and she loves it. "I want you to feel me everywhere!" he spits again as he pounds into me relentlessly. "You are fucking mine!" he spits again.

"Steel?" I gasp out, but he takes my breath away, slamming into me so hard the sofa is screeching across the floor with every thrust. My eyes are watering, and my makeup is gonna be fucked, and I bite down on my lip as he's hitting everything with such intensity that I can't speak. I can barely breathe!

"You are mine, and when you get into that limo for your 'date', I want him to smell me on you, taste us in the air, and I'll kill him if he touches you! Do you fucking understand?"

"Yes!" I gasp out. He's angry. I can feel it in the way he's fucking me. He's never done this before, but I'm already thinking how I can make him this angry again, as fuck, this is so hot. My toes curl in my shoes, the ones Steel bought me. Like fuck I'd wear the ones the guy I'm going out with sent. I scream as he slams into me again, and another orgasm is brutally ripped from me.

My knees shake, and my eyes roll as I fight for breath as he continues slamming into me till he roars his release, smashing his hips against me. He rips out of me, sliding his fingers up the inside of my thighs and forcing his come back in before pulling my pants up, yanking me up by my hair and turning me in his arms.

"Fucking perfect!" he snarls at me as he slams himself into my mouth again, and I wrap my arms around him and drag him against me. "I love you!" he breathes into my mouth.

"I love you too!" As I pull back, he smooths my hair down, wipes under my eyes with his thumb and wipes around my bottom lip with his other thumb!

"I'll see you when you get home. I'll wait up!" He turns and walks into the bedroom, slamming the door behind him.

Well fuck, that was aggressive and intense, and fuck, if my insides aren't clenching at me to storm back in there and ride him like a rodeo bull while he's like this. Fuck, I'm so turned on right now, and I have to go to this stupid ball, and I bet I look a fucking state.

As the limo pulls up and honks the horn, I grimace. It looks like I'm going as is. I stomp down the stairs in my stupid dress and my gorgeous shoes, and my husband's come threatening to slide down my legs. As I get there, the arsehole driver doesn't even get out or spare me a second glance. I climb into the back, and the privacy screen is already in place. I've barely closed the door as he peels out the gates.

As we pull up outside the client's fancy gaff, I'm fully aware that it smells like I've just been fucked in the back of the limo, and that's not a good first impression. I haven't even had time to sort my makeup out.

As he slides in, he inhales, and then his pupils dilate as a hungry, lustful gaze appears on his face before he shakes it off. "I'm Mr Lewis Carlisle. It's a… pleasure. I wasn't expecting you to be so… so… beautiful."

I shake his hand. "Mr Carlisle, I'm Ray. I will be your security for the evening."

I settle back into the chair as we make our way to the event. I don't speak because I'm fully aware that he's resting his head back and is inhaling my scent deeply, and the tent in his dress trousers tells me all I need to know! Fuck my life right now.

Reaching the function, we step into the ballroom. We're handed champagne, but I just pretend to sip at mine, occasionally tipping some in a pot plant. As I pass, I'm suddenly aware of Steel's come making an appearance while I'm walking around. "Mr Carlisle, I need to use the ladies. Would you mind waiting by the bar?" He nods, and once he's seated, I head off.

Battling with all the fucking ridiculousness this dress is, I manage to get underneath it, and as I pull my pants down, I feel his come running out. I don't know why, but I reach down and try to push it back in, and as I do, I graze my clit and fuck the feel of him sliding around, and my fingers make me gasp, so I push them back inside me, rubbing the palm of my hand over my clit, I'm pumping in and out, and my breaths are coming harsh my chest and face are flushed, and as I grunt out my release there's a gasp from the bathroom.

I clean myself up, and as I walk out of the cubicle, an older woman is grasping at her pearls with one hand and white-knuckling the countertop with the other. She's slightly flushed in the face. I wink at her as I slide my fingers into my mouth before walking to the sink beside her and washing my hands.

"Such a fabulous event, don't you think?" I smile at her and leave the bathroom. The rest of the night is boring as fuck. I just want to get home to my husband and our bed and throw him around it.

Once the event has finished, we head out to the limo, and as it pulls up, Mr Carlisle opens the door for me. I step in, and he softly closes the door behind me. It's really hot in the back, and as he walks around, he removes his jacket and gets in.

The driver pulls off from the kerb, and Mr Carlisle pulls at his collar. "Can I get you a drink?" He pulls out a bottle of water, and I nod, opening the sealed lid. I take a big swig. It's so fucking hot in here, and this bloody dress, it's stifling. He keeps talking and rabbiting on about his wife, blah, blah, blah. I feel my head start to loll with the constant drone of his voice. "It's nothing personal!" he says in a softer tone.

I glance over at him, but his face distorts and fades in and out of focus. "Fuck!"

Steel

I shouldn't have fucked her like I did before she left. I was mad at her, and although I did enjoy it, and she seemed to as well, I regret treating her like that. That wasn't me. I don't know what came over me. When we talked about kids, it was in a couple of years, and I went all caveman and demanded them now.

I had a shower after she left, then tried to sleep, but I just couldn't. I read, then tried again, and now it won't be long before she's home, and I don't really want to be here when she gets back, even though I said I would wait up, so I throw my clothes on and head to the bar.

Walking through the door, my phone chimes.

Wife: Can you pick me up at the security firm's office in one hour?
Husband: Thought you were getting dropped off here?
Husband: Is everything okay?
Husband: Ray?

"Fuck's sake!" I slam my phone down on the bar.

Ares is standing there. "What the fuck is up with you?"

"Wife trouble." I spit at him.

"You picked the wrong wife if you're stressing about 'wife trouble'. Your wife is nothing but trouble!"

I sigh. I know I should defend her, but I'm running on empty, and I'm so fucking drained with everything, and now I realise why the fuck she wanted to wait for kids. "I'm such a fucking idiot!"

"Ya think? Should have picked a nice, quiet girl, one who doesn't talk back or fight back—" I punch him in the arm. "Oww!" He rubs at it like a fucking baby.

"My wife's fucking awesome, it's me that's the idiot. I'm gonna go fetch her. She's getting dropped off at the security offices?"

"Why the fuck is she getting dropped off there?" Ares questions, so I show him the messages.

"God knows, but she's not replying, so I don't wanna leave her stranded at this time of night, you know, in case something happens."

"What if someone decides to try and kidnap her?" He laughs. "They'd soon bring her back."

"Fuck you, dickhead!" I punch him harder this time, and he stumbles off the stool.

"Owww!" He rubs his arm again, and I slide off the stool and head out to my truck.

Pulling up in the car park beside the security office, I can see the limo, so I hang on a bit, but there's no driver, and no one moves, so I get out and head on over. The door on my side is shut, but as I get closer, I can see the passenger-side back door is open. I walk around and… "Shit."

There's a guy on his back, a gunshot wound between his eyes. I've no idea who he is, so I lean in the back, and on the seat are Ray's shoes, phone and her wedding rings on top. I reach over to pick them up, but my fingers come away sticky. *What the fuck is that?* I pull my hand closer. I can see in the light from the office. It's blood!

I wipe my hands on my jeans, slide the phone and rings into my pocket, and pick up her shoes. As I step back out to start shouting, there's a screech of tyres all around me, then blue and red flashing lights.

"Police! Colby Steel, place your hands behind your head and step away from the vehicle." As I raise my hands and step back, I'm surrounded by four cop cars.

"Where's my wife?" I ask as I hold my arms in the air and step away from the vehicle.

"Mr Steel, you're under arrest. Anything you say can and will be used against you in a court of law. You have the right to an attorney. If you cannot afford an attorney, one will be provided for you. Do you understand the rights I have just read to you?" One of the officers recites.

"Why?" That's all I say as I look at the on-edge faces surrounding me.

"For the murder of Mr Lewis Carlisle and the suspected murder of Mrs Sunshine Steel."

"I want to see my lawyer!" They're the last words I mutter before I'm handcuffed and forced into the back seat of the cop car and driven away. *Who the fuck is Lewis Carlisle, and where the fuck is my wife?*

To be continued…

Acknowledgements

For those of you who have made it this far in the series, thank you for taking a chance on an unknown author releasing this, the third book in my debut series. I've poured my swinging brick and little black soul into this series, and my swinging brick thanks you from the bottom of it for your support. I couldn't have done it without you all,

My mum and son,
My boozy book club Bestie,
My queen.
My besties,
The girls at United.

My new author/bookish besties for being there through my rants and the chaos. I LOVE YOU ALL!!

To anyone who's read my books, liked/shared a post/video, no matter how small you think the gesture, I appreciate you all!

There are four books in this series, so if you loved this as much as I loved writing it and can't wait to see what happens to Ray and Steel? Stand by and get ready to ride this rollercoaster with me. I promise it's only getting crazier!

Buckle up, buttercup, it's about to get even bumpier!

Books by Harley Raige

The Reapers MC, Ravenswood Series

Reaper Restrained 1 Aug 23
Reaper Released 1 Oct 23
Reaper Razed 1 Dec 23
Reaper's Revenge TBA

Printed in Great Britain
by Amazon